Also by Mia Sheridan

FINDING EDEN

MIA SHERIDAN

Bloom *books*

Published by Bloom Books, an imprint of Sourcebooks
P.O. Box 4410, Naperville, Illinois 60567-4410
(630) 961-3900
sourcebooks.com

Originally self-published in 2014 by Mia Sheridan.

Printed and bound in Canada.
MBP 10 9 8 7 6 5 4 3 2 1

This book is dedicated to Joanna, who first taught me about mercy and compassion.

THE AQUARIUS LEGEND

Greek legend tells of Ganymede, an exceptionally beautiful, young boy of Troy. He was spotted by Zeus, who immediately decided he would make a perfect cupbearer. Zeus, disguised as an eagle, swept up the youth and carried him to the home of the gods to serve as his slave.

Eventually, Ganymede had enough, and in an act of defiance, he poured out all of the wine, ambrosia, and water of the gods, refusing to stay Zeus's cupbearer any longer. The water all fell to Earth, causing inundating rains for days upon days, which created a massive flood that put the entire world underwater.

In time, Ganymede was glorified as Aquarius, God of Rain, and placed among the stars.

PROLOGUE
Eden

"I promise you I will do everything just as you
ask. But come closer. Let us give in to grief,
however briefly, in each other's arms."
—Homer, *The Iliad*

I woke under heavy blankets, my eyes popping open so I
could take in the room around me. I didn't move, just listened
and looked, trying to understand where I was. It was then I
heard footsteps moving toward me and the older man, the
jeweler, came into view. It all came back…breaking the vase,
paying for it with the locket, the homeless shelter, fainting.
I blinked up at him, my fight-or-flight instinct kicking in as
my eyes darted around the room, seeking an exit.

"It's okay. You fainted. My driver helped me put you in
my car. You're at my town house."

I sat up, pulling the covers up against my chest. I still had
all my clothes on, but someone had removed my shoes.

I opened my mouth to say something, I wasn't sure

exactly what, when the door opened again and a woman walked in with a tray in her hands.

Food. My stomach lurched and my mouth immediately started to water at the smell wafting off whatever was coming toward me.

The woman set the tray over my lap, and my gaze roamed it greedily—some kind of soup and several rolls with neat little pats of butter melting on top. My body took over and I grabbed for the spoon with shaky hands and started shoveling it into my mouth. I'd get out of here after I ate. I had to eat. In that moment, the hunger ruled me and it was too much to resist. I didn't care where I was or why or with whom. The food was the only thing that mattered. When I glanced up at the jeweler and the woman in a housekeeping uniform who stood just to his side, I saw that both of them were watching me with sad, curious eyes.

The woman took a step toward me. "Slow down, little one. You haven't eaten for a while. You'll make yourself sick if you eat it too fast. Force yourself to slow down." Then she put one hand on my back and moved it in slow circles while I slowed the movement of the spoon from the soup to my mouth. For several minutes, the only sound in the room was my unladylike slurping and then my chewing sounds as I picked up each roll and ate them in three bites apiece. The woman's gentle circles on my back never stopped, calming me, reminding me to eat as slowly as I could. A few times it felt like the food would come back up, but it didn't, and when I was finished, I picked up the napkin and wiped my hands and my face and then set it down, embarrassed to look at them. My dignity trickled back in now that my hunger had been satisfied.

"Well then, that's better," the woman said, and I raised

my gaze to her sympathetic face. It felt like so long since someone had been kind to me. Tears filled my eyes, but I looked away before they could spill down my face. She took her hand off my back, picked the tray up, leaned into the man and said something softly, and then left the room.

I swung my legs over the side of the bed, but the man put his hand on my shoulder and said, "Please, you're welcome to stay here tonight. There's a bathroom over there." He inclined his head to the left, and I glanced at the closed door he was indicating. "And this room isn't used by anyone anymore. Please stay. It's the least I can do after…today."

I licked my parched lips, trying to decide what to do. I desperately wanted to stay here in this warm place, where I could sleep in an actual bed, but I didn't understand why this man had taken me in.

"I broke your property today," I finally said.

He pursed his lips. "Yes, and you paid for it. And it could have been handled differently. I'm sorry I didn't step in."

I wasn't sure what to say to that and so I remained silent.

"Please. Let me put you up for the night. We can make other…arrangements tomorrow. Yes?"

I fidgeted with my hands in my lap. It was either say yes or go back out into the cold street. But I didn't know what his "arrangements" might be and that worried me. Still… I nodded tentatively, deciding I'd stay at least a little longer, and when I looked up at him, he seemed pleased.

"Good. Take a shower. Get some sleep. I'll see you in the morning." And with that, he turned on his heel and walked quickly out of the room.

Once he had left, I scurried over to the door and turned the lock and then stood there taking in the details of the room for the first time. It was beautiful. There was a sort of floral fabric on the walls, and I walked over to one and ran my hand over the slightly textured surface. I tried to muster up some gratitude for the lovely surroundings, but there was only numb observance. I turned toward the bed, my gaze moving over the luxurious silk and rich velvet bedding in various shades of cream and lilac. Inviting. I walked back over to it, the call to sleep too great to resist now that my belly was full. I'd shower in the morning.

I climbed back in between the crisp sheets, still fully clothed. Sleep took me under her dark wing, sweeping me away into blessed oblivion.

I dreamed of morning glories, *I dreamed of him, my love*, wispy images that twisted and turned and washed away under a wave of water so massive I was crushed beneath it. There was no breath in my lungs left to call his name, to whisper the words I needed him to know in the end—that I loved him, that I'd always love him, that he was my strength and my weakness, my endless joy and my greatest sorrow.

I woke up crying, breathless but silent.

In the bathroom, I stripped my clothes somberly and stood in front of the mirror for a moment, running my hand over my flat belly and sucking back a sob before moving quickly to the shower stall. The gentle drumming of warm water was soothing and I tilted my head back, wetting my hair. But that wave came again, rising, crushing, and I hung my head forward and let go of that which I had held so tightly inside for the past week. I sunk down to the marble floor, pulled myself back against the wall tiles, and finally allowed myself to sob as the sound of the running water masked my cries.

After I'd showered and dressed and relieved a small portion of the burden of my grief, at least for the moment, I stepped out into the quiet hallway.

The distant sound of dishes clattering drew me and I peeked into a large kitchen where the jeweler was seated in front of a plate of food, an open magazine on the table next to it.

"Good morning," he said as he stood. "You look refreshed. Did you sleep well?"

"Yes, thank you." I eyed the food sitting on the table—a plate of bacon and eggs, and a dish of fruit.

The jeweler waved me over to him. "Please, sit. Eat. We can discuss the arrangements I mentioned last night."

I nodded and took a seat at the table as he dished up food and set it before me. I took a few bites as I gathered my resolve. I wanted to stay here. The man was nice, or so it seemed. But I was pretty sure what his "arrangements" would include, and I didn't think it was possible for me—I couldn't fathom it. Not after what I'd been through. I would return to the street—I might die there, but death didn't scare me, not anymore.

There's a spring somewhere in Elysium. I'll be waiting for you, Eden. Come find me. I'll be there.

I cleared my throat. "I can't accept the arrangement you propose," I said, lowering my gaze.

Through my lashes, I saw his coffee cup halt midway to his mouth. "I haven't proposed anything yet."

Heat moved up my neck. "I understand what you want," I said softly.

The jeweler watched me for a minute and then set his coffee cup down, causing it to clatter against the saucer. His expression was...angry? Sad? I couldn't be sure. "That's not what I want."

5

I stared at him in confusion. "You said you had an arrangement we could discuss."

He took a deep breath. "First of all, I don't think we've met properly. My name is Felix Grant. Please call me Felix. Yes?"

I nodded, waiting for him to continue.

"Good. And your name is…?"

"Eden," I said softly.

"Surname?"

I looked down and cleared my throat. "I don't know."

"You don't know your surname?"

"No, I know I had one once, but after my family died, I went to live with someone else, and…I can't remember it."

He was silent for a moment. "How is that possible? How did you attend school without a last name?"

"I never went to school," I said softly, more heat blossoming in my cheeks.

"How old are you?"

"I'm eighteen."

Felix looked at me as though he thought I was lying. More silence and then: "Eden, do I need to call the police? What happened to you?"

My gaze flew to his at the word *police*. "No! Please, no. I… No one is looking for me. I'm not a runaway or anything. I just…I don't have anyone anymore. They're all…gone now. Please, no police." My voice broke on the last word and I looked at him pleadingly, ready to run if he went for a phone.

Felix considered me thoughtfully for several moments before he finally said, "What can you do, Eden? Do you cook? Clean?"

I shook my head. "I wasn't allowed to do any of that. I

can play the piano," I said hopefully. It was pretty much the only thing I could do.

Felix raised his brows. "Is that so? Well, as it so happens, I have a granddaughter who's been asking for piano lessons. Are you skilled enough to teach her?"

I nodded slowly. "Yes. Yes, I could teach the piano."

"All right, then. This is the arrangement I propose—you're hired. Room and board is included in your salary. And your job involves nothing more than teaching my granddaughter, Sophia, the piano. Is that clear, Eden?"

I nodded, feeling something that felt a little like hope spark inside. I was going to be safe, warm, fed? I let out a silent exhale. I might at least have that.

"Then it's settled. I'm going to assume that because of where you were lined up last night, you don't have anything other than what you came with?"

I shook my head, looking down at the clothes that hung off my body. "I'm sorry. Once I work for a little bit, I'll be able to afford some different clothes...ones that look nicer..." I trailed off, embarrassed, but Felix waved his hand in the air.

"I'll advance you money for new clothes. Marissa will go out today and pick you up some things. You met Marissa last night."

I nodded and then studied Felix for a minute. He was older, probably in his sixties, I'd guess, but he was still a good-looking man, with bright blue eyes and a full head of salt-and-pepper hair. "Felix, I don't understand. Why are you doing this for me?" I finally asked him.

He studied me momentarily and then turned his gaze to several pill bottles I hadn't noticed before, sitting on the side of the table. He picked up one of the containers, unscrewed the cap, and threw back a pill. I couldn't help notice that his hands were shaking as he brought a glass of water to his mouth. Was he ill? He set the glass of water back on the table. "Because I made the wrong choice yesterday when I saw what happened in my store," he answered, his brow dipping. "When I saw you again, leaving the line for the shelter, I recognized it as a second chance to do the right thing. I made the wrong choice once before too, Eden, and I never got a second opportunity to correct that one. Does that make sense?"

"I think so," I said quietly.

He nodded. "Okay, good, then we each benefit. You have a place to stay and I have a new piano teacher. Speaking of which, I'll need to get it tuned. It hasn't been played in years." Sadness appeared in his eyes for a second and then it was gone as he scooted the chair back and came to his feet. "You rest and relax today. Tomorrow, you'll meet Sophia. Marissa is here all day if you need anything."

"Thank you," I said softly as he walked past me, gratitude and relief filling my chest and causing me to suck in a sudden breath. Behind me, his steps slowed, but he didn't say anything, and a few minutes later, I heard a door close down the hall.

I spent the morning in my new room, reading the books I found on the nightstand for the escape they brought and curling into a ball and crying when I couldn't hold back the tears.

Around lunchtime, I heard Felix arrive home. Soon after, the doorbell chimed and then I listened for the next hour to the sounds of the piano being tuned.

When a knock came at my door, I opened it and Marissa was standing there with a smile on her face. "Lunch is almost ready, dear, and the piano is tuned if you'd like to try it out."

"Thank you, Marissa. You don't have to make me food though. I can come to the kitchen."

Marissa waved her hand as she walked away. "It's no trouble."

"Marissa?" I called, nerves fluttering.

She turned. "Yes, dear?"

I cleared my throat. "Felix…um, does he…allow you to go out?"

Marissa tilted her head, her brow creasing. "Go out? You mean out of the house?"

"Yes. I mean, if you want to. Does he allow it?"

"Yes, of course. I'm free to do as I like, as are you." Her expression turned to one of concern.

"Okay," I said softly.

Marissa just kept looking at me for a second before she nodded and turned away.

I walked to the living room, where I'd seen the large grand piano earlier, and sat down at the bench, taking in a big breath before setting my fingers on the keys. The feel of the smooth ivory simultaneously felt like coming home, and beginning anew—the dawning of a new life I had no idea how to define and hadn't sought, yet one I would have to live all the same. *Without him.* I closed my eyes, tears escaping from the corners to slide slowly down my cheeks.

When I heard someone speaking, I opened my eyes, listening to the words being spoken in another room. Despite the sound of the piano, I could hear them clearly, the acoustics in the ceiling delivering the voices straight to my ears.

"She's good," I heard Felix say quietly.

"She's better than good, Felix. Where does she come from?" another man asked, the one who had tuned the piano, I assumed.

9

"I don't know. She hasn't told me. She seems so very sad, though. Lost."

There was a pause before the other man said, "I knew another piano player who brought that same quality to the music she played."

"Sadness?" Felix asked.

"More than that. A broken heart," the other man said.

And then no more was said as the music filled the empty space around me, drifting from my fingers, but originating in my heart, the longing in my soul, from all the shattered places inside me. And each note echoed the same name—*Calder, Calder, Calder.*

Calder

The street ten stories down swayed below me, the promise of the hard smack of concrete and then blessed oblivion calling to me so sweetly, the same way her music once had. I didn't want to resist. I hoped I'd register at least a few seconds of unfathomable pain before I floated away. I deserved it. I didn't want a death that didn't include misery. *Had she suffered? Had she called my name in the dark as the water covered her and then filled her lungs with burning, suffocating terror?* A sob, a loud gulp of tortured breath, escaped my throat and I took another swig from the half-empty bottle in my hand. It slid down my throat in a slow slide of fire. *Fire.*

"Calder." I heard Xander's voice behind me, low and filled with fear. "Brother, give me your hand."

I shook my head back and forth swiftly and swayed precariously on the ledge where I sat. Just a small tilt forward, even the intention of a tilt, and I'd plunge to my death below. *To her.* "No, Xander," I said, my words slurring slightly. I was drunk but not too drunk that I couldn't think clearly enough. Or I thought so anyway.

"What are you doing, Calder?" Xander asked, sitting on the ledge a little ways down from where I was. I squinted over at him. His voice was even, but his eyes were wide with panic.

"I hate to do this to you, brother. But it hurts too damn much. It was my fault. I don't deserve to live," I told him.

"Then why are you alive?" Xander asked, his voice smooth and gentle, like a lullaby. My mom used to sing me lullabies when I was a little kid and couldn't sleep. Of course, my mom had also stood by while my dad tried to set me on fire. But I wouldn't think of that. I couldn't because it still made me feel like I was burning even though the flame had never touched me. My shoulders sagged, and I felt the wetness on my cheeks as a breeze blew by.

"You know what I think? I think you're alive because you're *meant* to be alive. For some reason, you're *meant* to be here. You're the only person who made it out of Acadia that day. The *only* one. And I, for one, refuse to believe there's not some purpose to that. I refuse to believe you didn't reach your hand up through that god-awful wreck of water-covered destruction so I could pull you out of there. And I want to help you discover what that reason is, Calder. Take my hand again. Take my hand, brother, and let me help you."

I turned my head his way again, grief sweeping through me even more swiftly. I took another fiery sip of alcohol.

"You carried me for twenty miles on your back once," he said, his voice breaking at the end. "Twenty miles. And if you hadn't, I would have been at Acadia that horrific day too. I would probably be dead now. Would you have left me that day? *Did* you leave me that day?"

I frowned. "No," I said. "Never."

"Then take my hand. Let me carry you this time. It's my turn, Calder. Don't deny me that. Whatever I have…"

"I know," I choked out. I bent my head forward and gave in to the anguish, my shoulders shaking in the silent sobs that wracked my body. When some of it had passed, I whispered miserably, "Fuck." I wiped my sleeve across my face and threw the bottle to the side. I should have gotten myself more drunk, but I didn't have a taste for the shit. "This life feels so damn long," I said after a minute.

"That's because you're hurting, and it seems like it won't ever get better."

"It *doesn't* get better. It never gets better."

"It will. You have to try. Calder, you have to try."

"I've been trying! For four months, I've been trying."

"It's going to take longer than four months. It just is."

I let out a deep breath and stared at the sky beyond. In the distance, I could see it was full of fury, dark, rolling storm clouds moving ever closer. Soon the whole sky would break open, just like me, and the rain would fall.

We were both silent for a few minutes, my head swimming. "Any news on the identification of the other bodies?" I finally asked.

"No," Xander said. "You know I'll let you know if there is." Xander watched the news, listened to the reports about Acadia. I couldn't bring myself to.

"They still haven't mentioned anyone who made it out?" My voice cracked on the last word.

Xander shook his head, his expression filled with sympathy.

"The footsteps you saw in the mud…"

"No, brother. And that could have been…just, I don't know. Please, Calder. Take my hand."

I turned away, looking back out to the gathering clouds.

Xander watched me for a few minutes and then glanced back at the now-broken bottle of whiskey I'd thrown. "You can't keep numbing things if you want to move forward."

I straightened my spine slowly. "I don't drink to numb things," I said, meeting his eyes. I knew mine were half-lidded and swollen. "I drink because it makes me *feel* everything more deeply. I drink for the suffering."

"Gods above," Xander muttered, shaking his head. "Then even more reason to stop. You don't deserve that."

"Yeah," I choked out. "I do."

"It wasn't your fault, Calder. None of it was your fault."

I shook my head back and forth, not able to form the words in my heart. It *was* my fault. She wasn't here because I hadn't been able to save her. I'd failed her. And I longed for her so desperately that some days I couldn't even move. The grief felt like it was tearing my insides open, and the only escape I could think of was death. But what if…? "What if taking my own life takes me somewhere other than where she is?" I asked, my voice barely rising above the wind.

Xander was silent for a minute. "I don't know if that's how it works. I want to tell you it does, so you'll come off this ledge, but you know I'd never lie to you under any circumstances. The truth is, I just don't know." He hung his head but kept his eyes turned upward, glued to me.

I looked away, back out toward the sky.

"Calder, I'm not going to say I know what you're

feeling, but I'm missing people as well. And Eden was my friend too."

I let out a harsh exhale and gave a small nod. Xander had lost his parents, his sister, his brother-in-law, his friends... "I know."

"Let me help you. And please don't leave me totally alone. I'm not saying that to pile on more guilt. I'm just saying that because it's the gods' honest truth. I'd miss the hell out of you and I'd be alone. Please don't do that to me."

I looked over at him, took in the face that had always been a constant in my life since before I could remember, saw the grief and fear clear in his eyes. I breathed out a long, shuddery sigh and reached my hand out to him. He moved slowly but gripped me so tightly that, in that moment, I knew if I lunged myself over, he'd come with me. He wasn't going to let go. I felt the tears start flowing again, and we sat that way for a minute, just grasping each other. Finally, I began turning as I let go of Xander's hand and swung my legs around, my feet landing on the solid roof now in front of me. Soft raindrops hit my face, as gentle as a kiss.

I crossed my arms over my knees, my back hunching and my head falling forward. And I cried. Xander moved closer and his hand gripped my shoulder, but he didn't say a word. The rain continued to fall, soaking the back of my T-shirt, running down my neck and mixing with my tears. After a while, my tears ceased. The rain had become nothing but a light mist in the air. I sat up and stared, unseeing, at the door that led downstairs, to our rathole apartment, and then let out a shaky breath. I was so tired. The alcohol mixed with the ache inside me made me want to sleep. And maybe tonight I could do it without the haunting dreams.

"You know what I'm gonna do tomorrow?" Xander asked.

I shook my head. "With you, there's no telling," I said, swiping my arm across my wet face.

Xander chuckled. "There's my boy," he said, and I could hear the love in his voice. "I'm gonna stop into that art supply store I pass every day and I'm gonna buy you some supplies. Maybe painting would help. What do you think?"

I ran my hand back through my wet hair. "I don't know if I could," I said honestly. "It might hurt." I paused. "Then again, everything hurts."

"I'll get the supplies and let you decide, okay?" he said, gripping my shoulder again.

"We really can't afford art supplies."

"Sure we can. I've been meaning to take off a few pounds anyway."

I let out what might have been an imitation of a chuckle and shook my head.

"Come on in," Xander said. "We have two cans of those beans you love so much."

"Oh Gods," I said, grimacing, but when he stood, so did I, following him inside, away from the edge, away from Eden, but never away from the ache that lived in my soul and always, always would.

BOOK TWO

CINCINNATI, OHIO

"No man or woman born…can shun his destiny."

—Homer, *The Iliad*

CHAPTER ONE
Eden

Three Years Later

"Eden? Uh, Miss...I'm sorry, I don't have your last name written down here." The lawyer, Mr. Sutherland, leafed through the papers in front of him.

"Yes, what is your last name anyway?" Claire, Felix's daughter, asked sharply. She leaned forward in her chair to look around Marissa to where I was sitting. "I don't think I've ever been told."

I blinked, snapping back to the present. I had zoned out for a minute, my mind conjuring up the many times I'd tried to engage Claire and her brother, Charles, in small conversation over the years, even through the early days of my anguish, even in spite of the overwhelming grief I was trying to cope with day by seemingly never-ending day. I had only ever been met with disdain. And now Felix was gone, and here we were, sitting together in his lawyer's office, where we'd been called to collect the last things he'd been working on from his sickbed. My eyes darted to Marissa at the question about my last name. Marissa glanced at the watch on her wrist. "Mr. Sutherland, I hate to rush you here, but I know Eden has a lesson and I have another appointment this afternoon."

Mr. Sutherland cleared his throat. "Yes, of course. We're basically done. Mrs. Forester, I just need you to sign here and my secretary will put a copy of the documents in the mail."

Marissa leaned forward and signed the papers he slid in front of her and then dropped the pen in her purse.

I scooted to the edge of my chair, clutching the large envelope Felix's lawyer had given me, the one with my name written across the front in Felix's handwriting, the bold penmanship that made my heart clench with ache and loss. *Oh, Felix, I can't believe you're gone.*

"Now wait a minute here," Charles, sitting to the right of his sister, said. "What exactly is she getting in that envelope? We need a breakdown of—"

"It's nothing more than a personal letter," Mr. Sutherland said impatiently. "I assure you, Charles. The same thing that's in each of your envelopes." He nodded to the large envelopes Claire and Charles were each holding on their laps.

"All the same, if we could just inspect it—" Charles started.

"I'm sure Miss"—he glanced at me and then back at Charles—"I'm sure *Eden* would kindly appease you by showing you the contents if it would mean wrapping this meeting up." Mr. Sutherland looked annoyed.

I let out a breath and stared at the attorney, my heart picking up speed. This letter was all I had of Felix—I wouldn't let them take it. I didn't even want them to rifle through it. It was mine in a world where nothing else was. Marissa put one hand on my knee.

Like a whisper, it came, as it sometimes did: *Be strong, Morning Glory.*

I stood, holding the envelope against my chest like a life preserver. "No, you may not inspect it," I said just a little shakily. "If you were so interested in your father's personal affairs, you should have asked him while he was *still alive*. You should have shown up to even one of those Sunday dinners he invited you to, called him back once in a while to chat, spent more than three minutes picking up Sophia after her lesson." I looked pointedly at Claire. "I tried to get to know you. I wanted to be your friend." Hurt overcame me and I paused, filling my lungs with a deep breath. "But you weren't interested. And that's okay, I guess. But now, you do *not* get to inspect this envelope, because although you don't believe it, I loved Felix." I paused again, swallowing down the pain that welled up in my throat, taking in their shocked expressions. I had never once dared to speak to them with anything other than meek agreement. I gentled my voice but still made sure it was strong and clear. "Felix was a father figure. You don't know anything about me because you never cared to know, but your father was someone who helped me when I needed it more than you can possibly imagine. You have no idea how much that meant to me, no idea." I looked back and forth between their narrowed eyes. "The answer is no, you may not inspect this envelope," I repeated.

The lawyer said it contained a personal letter. To someone else, that might not have been much, but it was all I would ever have of Felix. I didn't have much of anything, but I had this, and two people who disliked me, who had chosen time and again not to show me an ounce of kindness, were not going to take it away. I hugged it to me more tightly, staking claim.

"Now hold on a minute here," Claire said, standing and pointing a finger at me. "You don't know anything about us either. You don't get to stand there and judge us, you little gold digger."

"Claire, Charles—" Marissa started.

"Gold digger?" I repeated incredulously, interrupting Marissa, disbelief rolling over me. "I never took a dime from your father that I didn't earn. Not one dime."

Mr. Sutherland stood from behind his desk. "Everyone, please, these situations can get heated. I understand that, but really, let's remember this is about Felix's last wishes. He split his entire estate between you"—he nodded to Claire—"and Charles."

Claire and Charles glared at him and then turned their suspicious eyes on me. "Fine," Claire said. "Take your envelope. It's all you'll ever get. And we want you out of our father's house in two weeks. If you wish to continue tutoring Sophia on the piano, you'll do it from somewhere else."

My skin prickled with heat, but I did my best to tamp down the hurt. I had come a long way in the last three years. I was no longer the unskilled, timid girl who'd arrived broken and hungry on Felix's doorstep. I'd learned that I possessed a little more strength than I'd ever imagined, and I'd gained two friends in Felix and Marissa. Yet somehow, I'd ended up alone. Again.

I pressed my lips together, not willing to rock the boat any more than I already had. I cared very much for Sophia, and I didn't want them to take her away from me—even if I did only see her twice a week. I comforted myself with the knowledge that although they disliked me, they knew I was a good piano teacher. Sophia's results spoke for themselves.

Plus, I was desperately going to need the income.

"Well then," Mr. Sutherland said, rounding his desk, apparently spotting a good opening to shuffle us out of his office. Who could blame him? "Thank you all for coming in. Felix was not only a good client but a good friend. He'll be missed."

Marissa stood and lowered her eyes and nodded. "Yes, he will," she said, taking my hand and squeezing it as I gave her a tremulous smile. We followed along behind Claire and Charles.

Mr. Sutherland showed us to the door, and we said our thanks to him one more time, ignoring each other. Just before he closed the door behind us, I turned and he paused. "Raynes," I said softly. "My last name is Raynes."

Mister Sutherland looked at me quizzically and then smiled, giving a nod. "Good day, Miss Raynes."

I turned to Marissa, taking her hand in mine. Claire and Charles were already halfway down the hall in front of us.

Once I was back at Felix's house, sitting on my bed in the room I'd woken up hungry and grief-stricken in three years before, I opened the envelope with shaking fingers.

Inside was a manila folder with a letter paper-clipped to the front. It was dated one month earlier, right before he'd become so ill, he was only lucid part of the time.

Eden,

If you're reading this, then I'm gone. I fervently hope me writing this is just a safety measure. I hope I'm able to give you this information myself, but with my health, I

*have to take precautions. I have to make sure you're not
left with nothing. I can't bear the thought of leaving you
here with as many questions as you arrived with. I'm not
a man who finds it easy to express my emotions, but I
want you to know how much I've grown to love and care
for you over these past three years. And I like to believe
you see me as a father figure and that you've come to care
for me as well. This is my attempt at caring for you when
I'm no longer there.*

*I believe your parents' names are Carolyn and Bennett
Everson.*

I gasped and dropped the folder to my bed. The corners of
two eight-by-ten glossy photos slid out and I stared at them for
a second before reaching forward and pulling them all the way
out. My heart stopped for a brief millisecond and then took up
what felt like an irregular beat in my chest. I lifted the photo
on top and gazed at it. It was my mother. I knew it was. A blur
of misty images danced through my mind—a ring of laughter,
the smell of flowers. *That face.* It was my face, only older. *She's
alive? My mother is alive? How?* Before looking at the second
photo, I snatched Felix's letter back up and read the rest.

*I believe you were abducted, Eden. And I have questions
only you can answer about why you didn't know that. I
hope I can ask you them myself once I'm done gathering all
the information I can for you. But as I write this letter, this
is all I do have. If I'm gone, I hope it's enough.*

*I started this investigation a few months ago, and when
I came across the photo of Eden Everson on the missing
children's database, I suspected instantly it was you.*

Your parents reported you missing fourteen years ago. It

was all over the news for months, especially sensational because your father was a suspect in the case. He had been involved in a business scandal earlier in the year, and he was also apparently connected to someone who may have been responsible for your disappearance, but public details on that are scanty. In any case, he vehemently denied having any part in your kidnapping or knowledge of your whereabouts to his dying day. He took his own life, but in his note, he still declared his innocence and his grief. After your father's suicide, your mother went into hiding. I can only imagine that after everything she'd endured, being in the public eye was too much to bear.

My investigator found her and discovered that in recent years, she'd remarried and her name is now Carolyn Collins. Her second husband passed away last year. She never had any other children. Her address is in the envelope.

With the help of a good friend who owns Cincinnati Savings and Loan, I've also opened an account in the name Eden Everson. I know that you've saved all the money you've earned from me so you'll be fine until you can get an ID in your real name and access the money I've left for you. It was the only way I considered that wouldn't involve Claire and Charles.

I only wish I had started this investigation sooner, but you, your music, the smile you put on Sophia's face brought so much light into my home, and I was selfish with you. I wanted to provide comfort and healing—I hope I at least did some of that. I hope I was a temporary shelter in a storm. And now, my dear Eden, it's time for you to continue on your journey. It's time for you to take that brave step out and find your people, your life, your destiny. I know in my heart it's a beautiful one.

All my love, Felix

Sadness, shock, and hope warred within me. I swiped at the tears running down my cheeks and swallowed the lump in my throat. *Felix. You did save me—in so many ways I can't even count,* I thought as I pictured the scared, emotionally broken girl who had stepped off that bus here in Cincinnati three years earlier. In some ways, I was still that girl, but I had also learned to draw upon the strength Calder had seen in me. I liked to think that somehow he knew and was proud. Somewhere he was looking down and calling me his brave morning glory.

Felix had rescued me, given me a home, a purpose, and a safe place to grieve. I'd never divulged to him or Marissa where I'd come from, not even when I saw news coverage about Acadia, where no one had come out alive. But they knew I was emotionally damaged, and they gave me the space I needed to work through some of it in my mind, in my own time. And though much of the last three years had passed in a daze of pain and longing, because of Felix and Marissa, there had been love and comfort too.

And he'd given me back my music and the pride that my sweet little student now loved the piano as much as I did. She had helped me grasp the hope that there were still small pieces of happiness in this lifetime. Not many, perhaps. And they were fleeting. But they were there—and they helped me survive.

Once I got a handle on my tears, I pulled the second picture from the folder and blinked down at the handsome blond man. I tilted my head, trying to recall his face, and although there was a small spark of recognition, I had nowhere near the emotional response I'd felt when I looked at my mother's photo.

I set it down and began reading through the rest of the

paperwork. It all corroborated what Felix had written in his letter, although the scandal my father had been involved in wasn't spelled out.

At the bottom of the pile lay the photo from the missing children's database. I stared at it for long minutes, my heart galloping. It was me, no question. Eden Everson. My name was Eden Everson. *Is. Is Eden Everson.* "My name is Eden Everson," I whispered. The name felt foreign on my tongue.

I was a missing child. I had been stolen. Shock rang through me like a gong. *Hector had lied to me. Hector had kidnapped me. All those years...all a lie.* I sat there for a minute simply staring at the wall and letting the truth sink in. My parents hadn't died in a car accident. He'd taken me from them.

The last page at the back of the folder was an address in the Hyde Park section of Cincinnati. I folded it up and tucked it in my purse sitting next to me.

When I went to put all the papers back in the envelope, I felt something hard at the bottom and opened it wide, tilting it upside down. The locket I'd brought to Felix's shop three years ago fell out. I let out a small breath, gripping it tightly before bringing it to my chest and holding it there. *Oh, Felix. You kind, sweet man. I'll miss you forever.*

A sudden knock at my door made me startle. "Come in."

The door opened and Marissa peeked inside. "I just wanted to let you know I'm home, dear."

"Thank you, Marissa." I licked my dry lips. "Marissa, can I ask you something?"

Marissa came inside and sat on the end of my bed. "Have you been crying?" she asked gently.

"A little, yes. I'm okay. Felix, he wrote me a letter and he... Did you know he was investigating my past, where I came from?"

27

Marissa looked surprised. "No. Did you ask him to?"

"No…I…I'm not upset about it. In fact, he found my parents."

Marissa's eyes widened. "Your parents? I thought you said your parents were dead."

I nodded and bit at my lip for a moment . "I thought they were. They're not. Or at least, my mother isn't."

"What are you going to do?"

"I think I'm going to go to her," I said. *I think.*

Marissa studied me for a few seconds but didn't ask more questions. It was her way. I knew she'd never pry unless I indicated I was ready to speak more on a subject. "You know I wish I could offer for you to stay here…" Her face filled with regret.

"I know, Marissa. I do. It's okay. I have some money now, enough to rent a room for myself. And I have a skill, and a reference." I met her kind eyes. "I know you'd let me stay here if it belonged to you." I grabbed her hand in mine and squeezed it.

Her eyes filled with more sadness. I knew she'd miss me as much as I'd miss her. "Have you found an apartment yet?"

"I've checked out a couple. I just need to decide on one." They were all small and run-down. I couldn't afford much, but it would be mine.

Marissa nodded. "You just let me know when you're ready."

"I will." Marissa was going to rent my new place in her name since I still didn't have identification. *Not yet anyway.* A world of possibilities swam in front of my eyes and I could hardly put them all in order. *I have a name.*

"Eden…" Marissa began before she brought her lips together, blinking tears from her eyes. "Three years ago when you first came here, you asked me if Felix would let you go out of the house if you wanted to."

I took a deep breath and studied my fingernails. When I met her eyes, I said, "Yes. I remember."

She nodded. "Felix would have never prevented you from doing anything you wanted to do. But it seems…well, it seems that you've held *yourself* captive here since then, rarely ever going out, holing yourself up in your room much of the time." Her kind eyes were filled with sympathy. "I just hope you'll see this change not only tinged with sadness but as an opportunity to begin truly living. I have so much faith in you. *Felix* had so much faith in you."

My heart constricted tightly. I wondered if I was ready for that. I wondered if I'd *ever* be ready for that. I gave Marissa a smile. "I'll try," I said.

She offered me a small sad smile in return.

"Will you tell me about him?" I asked after a moment. I had always wanted to know what made Felix's eyes fill with that far-off sadness he allowed through when he thought no one noticed. I wondered what had happened between him and his children and why they were so filled with bitterness.

Marissa studied me for a minute. "You remind me of her in some ways. Only you have a strength she never did."

"Her?" I asked.

Marissa looked out the window, her eyes going misty. "Lillian, Felix's wife."

Lillian. I'd seen her picture in the house, but no one had ever talked about her.

Marissa was quiet for several moments and I thought she might not answer. But then: "Felix's parents were immigrants. They ingrained in him a very strong work ethic. Work came first. Supporting your family came first." She paused for a second, obviously remembering. "When he married Lillian, I immediately noticed she was a delicate girl, sweet but always in need of reassurance. She lit up under Felix's attention. And she dimmed when he wasn't around. And he often...wasn't around." She pursed her lips and paused.

"Lillian made it known to Felix she felt ignored, I suppose. I heard their fights, and I heard her tears long after he had left the house. But for Felix at the time, work was his priority. His business was growing into a big success, and that's what he nourished. Lillian withered. So many times, I stood with her as she stared out the window when he'd promised to be home for dinner...her birthday, their anniversary. Their children grew and began having their own lives as well, and Lillian's loneliness increased. And then the diagnosis came. She had cancer. By the time they found it, she didn't have much time left. Seemingly, she was here one minute and gone the next." She shook her head, tears springing to her eyes.

"Oh no," I whispered. "I didn't know."

"He never talked about it." She turned to me. "The thing is, after that, he changed. Work wasn't his focus as much anymore. He devoted time to his family." She shrugged. "Of course, some things happen too late. His children harbored resentment. They weren't willing to forgive. Felix...he never quite forgave himself either." She gave me a gentle smile. "When you came along, he saw it as a second chance to nourish a wounded heart." She shook her head. "Of course, he never said that, but I...I saw it. You saved him too, Eden."

I wiped at a tear that was making its way slowly down my cheek. "He was a good man," I said softly.

Marissa nodded. "Yes." She stared off into space, her lips

tipping. "Isn't it funny how we're all just bouncing around in this crazy world, our own stories, our own hurts, all weaving together, changing outcomes, sometimes good, sometimes bad? Well"—she patted my knee—"I'd like to think you and Felix came together for a reason and you each healed a little because of the other."

I nodded. "Yes," I said, trying not to choke up. "I don't know where I'd be without him. I don't know where I'd be without *you*."

Marissa squeezed me tight and then stood up. After she'd closed my door behind her, I fell back on the bed thinking of what she had said about our varied stories and how we were always affecting other lives—every moment of every day—whether we meant to or not. I closed my eyes and pictured people walking around trailing bright white light behind, some of those lights meeting, tangling, changing colors as they combined. And in my despair, the possibility brought me comfort.

CHAPTER TWO
Eden

I stood in front of the ornate black door pulling gulps of air into my lungs and letting it out slowly. I was trembling, my fists clenched at my sides. *What if Felix was wrong? What if he was right, but she rejects me? What if…?* I hadn't even told Marissa my plans. I'd taken the bus and walked the rest of the way to the address Felix had left for me. I'd felt like I needed to do this on my own, and if I changed my mind, only I'd know.

I stood there, staring at the brass lion's head knocker, trying to talk myself into using it. It looked intimidating in and of itself, never mind the fact that I was already shaking like a leaf, fear pulsing through my blood. *Be strong, Morning Glory.* I took a deep breath and used the knocker to rap twice. As I waited, I looked over my shoulder, down the long set of stairs leading to the street. This area of Cincinnati was filled with elegant older homes, the yards lush, the trees huge and ancient. My head swiveled back toward the door as I heard footsteps coming toward me from the other side.

It swung open and she stood there, my mother. I knew her immediately. Not only because of the photo I'd seen, but because the *feeling* that swept over me was the same sensation I'd felt when I'd tried to recall her for the past fourteen years. I started trembling even more. *I know you. I belong to you.*

I blinked, just taking her in. She was a little taller than I was, probably five foot five or so, and her blond hair was cut into a straight bob that ended right at her jawline. She was wearing a pair of darker jeans with a white sweater. She was beautiful, and distantly familiar. *She is real. She is alive—* standing right in front of me. I wanted to laugh and cry and run away and launch myself at her.

She cocked her head. Her mouth opened and then closed as she took me in, a look coming over her face that I wasn't sure how to define. "I'm sorry… How can I…?" She paused and blinked at me. "Do I *know* you?"

"I'm Eden," I said so softly I wasn't sure I had actually spoken. "I think I'm your daughter," I squeaked out.

The woman's eyes, *my mother's eyes*, widened and she stumbled backward, bringing her hand to her chest. "Molly," she called weakly, her voice breaking as she turned her head slightly to someone who must be inside. "Oh, Molly…" And then she swayed as a young blond woman ran up behind her, catching her in her arms as my mother collapsed.

"Oh my God," the girl named Molly cried out. "Carolyn!"

I rushed in and helped Molly lead Carolyn to the couch in the large family room right off the foyer. "I'm so sorry," I murmured, bringing Carolyn's feet up on the couch. "I didn't do that in a very sensitive way. God! So stupid, Eden. I was just so… I didn't think." I had prepared myself for this, at least as much as I could. But she hadn't had any warning whatsoever.

33

I looked down worriedly at Carolyn, who was lying on the couch, her eyes now open, as she stared at me in shock.

"Holy shit," the pretty girl named Molly murmured. I looked over at her to see her staring at me. "You can't be," she said, and then shook her head slightly as if she was attempting to wake herself from a dream. "What's happening here?"

I took a deep breath. "Should we get her a cool washcloth or something?" I asked, nodding down at Carolyn.

Molly blinked as if just remembering Carolyn was there. "Oh, right, um, sure. I'll be right back."

Once Molly had left the room, I sat down on the couch next to Carolyn and I took her hands in mine. She was still staring at me, her large blue eyes wide, her mouth parted as though speechless. "I'm sorry to show up out of the blue like that," I whispered. "I should have called first…"

Her hands gripped mine and a tear rolled slowly down her cheek. Her chest rose and fell in quick inhales of breath and her mouth opened and closed, but still, no words came. "I know how you're feeling," I said softly, squeezing her hands back. "It's okay, I know."

"How? Where?" she breathed out. Before I could answer, Molly came rushing back into the room and knelt down on the floor and put a damp white washcloth on Carolyn's forehead.

Molly's eyes shot to mine. "Are you really *her*?" she asked. "Like, how? My *God*! Do we need to call someone? What's the protocol here? Jesus!"

"I'm sorry." I offered her a small smile. "I didn't even ask. Are you my stepsister?" I remembered the letter Felix gave me telling me my mother had never had more children, but perhaps her second husband had. My thoughts were tumbling all over each other.

34

Molly shook her head. "No, I'm your cousin." Her eyes widened. "Oh my God! My cousin is alive." She put her hand to her chest and took a deep breath, composing herself. "Um, I've been living with Carolyn since my mom, her sister Casey, passed away five years ago."

"Oh, I'm so sorry." I frowned. "It's so nice to meet you." *This feels surreal.* Molly stared back at me as if she was thinking the same thing.

I looked back at Carolyn and she pulled on my hand so I would help her sit up. She came up slowly, breathing out and leaning back on the couch as the washcloth slipped into her hands and she gave it to Molly. We both watched her carefully as her eyes swept over my face, down my body, and back up to my face. "Eden," she said. "My precious girl. My daughter."

I nodded. "Yes."

"You're so beautiful." She raised her hand, her fingers brushing my cheek as she touched me tentatively and then pulled away.

Her eyes moved down to the locket I wore around my neck and she gasped. "The locket!" she cried. Her eyes flew back to mine. "Your father and I gave you that for your sixth birthday." Tears spilled from her eyes and coursed down her cheeks and her hands trembled as she reached forward to touch the small round piece of jewelry.

I nodded, tears coming to my eyes too. I had known it was mine the minute I saw it in Hector's drawer.

Molly, who had stood up, returned now with a small glass of amber liquid from the bar on the other side of the room. She handed it to Carolyn, who wiped her cheeks, glanced quickly at the shot, and then downed it in one gulp before relaxing back into the couch again, her eyes returning to me.

Next to me, Molly was downing a shot as well. She met my gaze and tipped her head toward the bottle asking if I wanted one. I shook my head and returned my attention to Carolyn—*to my mother.*

"How? Where?" Carolyn asked again, only this time her voice was stronger, calmer. "Eden. Eden." Her face crumpled. "Did anyone hurt you?" She grabbed for my hand and I grasped her back. "Please tell me no one hurt you. Were you safe? Please tell me you were safe." Her voice sounded pained, desperate.

Had I been hurt? *Yes.* Had I been safe? *No, not at all.* But I didn't say that because the explanation of both answers was complicated and required more than I had in me to give right at the moment. Instead I said simply, "Hector, I was with Hector."

Carolyn clenched her eyes shut for a few seconds. "You escaped from Acadia," she whispered.

"You saw it on the news? You saw Hector?" I asked.

She nodded. "There have never been pictures of Hector Bias, which I'm sure you know, and I didn't know him by the name Hector. But I recognized the description of Acadia. I notified the police on your case, but they said"—she moved her head from side to side again—"there were so many bodies…so many of them unidentified." Her eyes flew up to mine. "How did you escape before…?"

"I didn't," I said. "I was there."

"You were… But *how?* How did you survive that? And how did you find me?"

"I'll tell you all of it, all I can remember anyway." I squeezed her hand, relishing the fact that I was touching my mother. "I want to know what you know as well, and I have so many questions too." I hoped Molly didn't really see the need to call anyone, especially the police. I wasn't ready for that course of action yet. I needed time to prepare.

"Yes, Eden," Carolyn said. "Whatever you need. Eden... my daughter..." She started to cry, and as her gaze washed over me again, her cries turned to sobs. Molly sat down on the couch and leaned over to hug Carolyn. I watched them for a moment and then they both grabbed my shirt and pulled me toward them. We sat crying and hugging as the world somehow continued to spin around us.

———

Twilight descended on Cincinnati as we sat together on the poolside patio. All around me potted flowers perfumed the air and the water sparkled in the dwindling light. I turned to my mother and Molly. "And that's where I've been living for the past three years, with Felix and Marissa. I've been teaching piano. I have several clients now and earn some money, enough to get by..." I trailed off as I took in their shell-shocked expressions.

It was the very first time that I'd uttered a word about Acadia since I'd stumbled away from it that day...and though I'd relayed it all in a colorless voice, my emotions carefully tucked away, for me, it was another small survival.

"My *God*!" Molly said. "That's..." Her gaze swung to Carolyn. "She's been ten minutes from us for the past three years now."

Molly's statement hit me in the gut and I could tell it affected Carolyn the same way. I wasn't sure how to feel. In one sense, the knowledge that we'd been so close and not found each other brought a certain grief with it, but in another sense, if I had found my mother right away somehow, I'd have missed out on my time knowing Felix. And I couldn't wish Felix away—I couldn't.

Carolyn grabbed for my hand again and squeezed it. I'd noticed she seemed not to be able to stop touching me. Perhaps she was still convincing herself I was real and solid and not about to fade to mist before her eyes. "Oh, my sweet girl, you lived through hell, Eden. Truly, you survived hell." Grief passed over her face, but she took a deep breath, paused, and continued. "Like I said, I went to the police when I heard about what happened at Acadia, but of course, your body wasn't found there... I knew though, I *knew* that Hector Bias was the man who had taken you, even though they could never identify him in order to show his face on the news. I thought my deepest fears had come true— that he had killed you at some point." Her shoulders curled forward slightly. "Everything about Acadia just sounded so familiar. Hell, truly hell."

I lowered my eyes. "Not all of it was hell," I said. "Sometimes I was scared, and I was very lonely...for a time. But"—I raised my eyes to hers—"some of it I wouldn't give up for anything in the world."

Carolyn's face crumbled, and she shook her head vigorously. "No, *none* of it should have happened. None. It was all my fault that Hector took you. All of it."

"Carolyn," Molly said, "we've all told you that's not true."

She continued to shake her head. "No, it is true. It is."

"Carolyn—" I said.

"Mom," she interrupted, "please call me Mom. You always called me Mom."

Mom. I felt the words flow through my insides, a breeze of calm, setting me at ease. "Okay, Mom." Emotion welled up as the word fell from my lips. *I am still loved. I belong to someone again. Perhaps I'm not going to be alone after all.* "Mom, will you tell me what happened?" I asked. "How Hector—"

38

"Yes. I'll tell you all of it. But, Molly, will you get a bottle of white from the wine fridge? I think this requires it. Eden, would you like something to drink? Water? Pop? Apple juice! You always liked apple juice." There was almost a pleading in her expression.

I nodded, holding my confusion at bay. Did grown-ups drink apple juice? At Acadia, only the children of the council members drank apple juice. There were still so many small questions I didn't have answers for. "Uh, sure. That sounds...good."

"Oh, and how rude of me. I didn't even offer you dinner—"

"No," I said, "just the juice, please. I ate before I came here."

Molly stood up and walked toward the french doors off the patio and disappeared inside.

"Okay," Carolyn said. "Well, if you change your mind, of course, this is your house too." She patted my cheek. "You'll move in tonight, of course."

"Oh...I, well. We'll talk about that—"

She shook her head vehemently. "No, Eden, please. I can't bear it. I won't be able to sleep another night if you're not under the same roof." She started to cry quietly again. "Now that I have you back, I'll die if you don't stay."

"Carolyn...Mom," I said, "I'm not going anywhere." I offered her what I hoped was a reassuring smile. "I'm back, and I'll never go away again."

"Promise me," she said, her voice cracking.

"I promise." Molly reappeared and handed me a glass of apple juice and then set a glass of wine in front of Carolyn. "Thank you," I said.

Carolyn took a long sip of her wine and leaned back.

She looked out over the pool. "Your father helped build an investment firm from the ground up. It was very successful. We suddenly lived a lifestyle we had never dreamed of… cars, houses, vacations…" She waved her hand in the air. "We learned that all the material things meant nothing in the end. But of course, at the time, it seemed like everything we'd ever dreamed of." She was quiet for a minute, looking lost in thought. "Anyway, one of your father's coworkers was caught stealing money he was supposed to be investing. There have been higher-profile cases like it on the news in recent years, and everyone has heard of those, but back then, I barely understood it."

"So my father wasn't the one stealing?" I asked.

She shook her head. "No, but he had looked the other way. He knew what was going on and his failure to act allowed the crime to continue. His failure to report what he knew resulted in hundreds of people losing their life savings. In the end, the entire company and all who ran it were disgraced." She let out a heavy sigh. "The details don't matter so much, Eden. Trust me, I knew them all and they still didn't help me make sense of it, other than to say that it came down to greed—levels of it, yes, but all greed in the end." A brief look of pain skittered across her features as if she was living back there for just a moment.

"Your father took it hard. Not just the loss of his job, all the *stuff*, but the disgrace. The regret of his inaction. The shame ate at him like a cancer. And that's when Hector came along."

My eyes flew to hers.

"Hector first presented himself as a man who had lost everything and understood what we were experiencing. At first we were skeptical, naturally, but…the more he talked…

told Ben, your father, that it wasn't his fault, that the greed of society had seeped into his soul…well, it sounds ridiculous now. But at the time and with how far we'd fallen, I guess we were searching for something to save us, *anything*…"

I thought back to all those empty-eyed souls who would come to sit before us at Temple month after month. I pictured the desperate hope in their eyes at the promise of redemption Hector was offering. "I understand, Mom. I do," I said, my voice pained.

She looked at me sadly. "Of course you do. I'm sorry for that."

"It's okay. I'm okay. Please go on," I said.

She sighed. "Well, your father, he became almost obsessed with Hector, although at the time, *we* knew him as Damon Abas. Your father was intrigued with this society that Damon…*Hector* had started, this place where there was supposedly no greed or sin, no pain or competition. This community had begun being built several years earlier, but Hector had spent that time constructing the buildings and finding the first people who would live and work there. Hector and your father talked nonstop about how it would all operate…the necessities people would require down the line, what was working, what wasn't." She chewed at the inside of her cheek. "Even with the talk of gods and visions and other things that were difficult to believe in…it healed something in your father for a time, gave him something to cling to, a purpose, an escape, and so for that, I was so very grateful. I ignored my suspicions about Hector… I did just what your father had done—I looked the other way because I was benefitting from it." Tears welled in her eyes again. "I guess if you choose to trust a snake, you deserve his venom."

"Carolyn…" Molly said, but Carolyn shook her head and wiped at her eyes.

"Anyway, Hector reached out to your father specifically because Hector had this idea about a council. He described them as a group of men who understood what it was to fall in the 'big society' as he called it—a group of men who had personal knowledge about the evils of our culture—men who could guide and mold this 'land of plenty.'"

I thought about what I'd learned from the news reports on the Acadia council—things I hadn't understood when I'd lived there. Apparently, according to family members who knew the men, Hector had gone around the country recruiting those who had been disgraced in one way or another and were desperately looking for a place to find respect again, to reclaim some small measure of the power they'd once had. *Like my father.* And of course, there was the financial gain. Hector was paying them a yearly salary—far more than any of them had been making in their previous jobs. The police had investigated where the money trail originated, but apparently Hector had known how to hide it because that was still an unknown. The Acadia property had been paid for in cash and put in his false name as well. They'd never found anything to clue them in to Hector's true identity.

And of course, the council had been chosen to benefit Hector in a myriad of ways as well—a judge, *a police officer…*

An emotional storm billowed inside me as we discussed Acadia, and how it had first been constructed and conceptualized. It had been hell on earth. But… it had also been my home. It had been where I fell deeply in love. And just picturing it sparked a longing to *be* there that was so intense, it shocked me because it had also been the place where life ended. Of course, I knew very well that it wasn't the place I longed for but a person. But for me, that's where he'd always be, and that was a confusing, heartbreaking reality that I hoped to someday come to terms with. And maybe understanding Acadia would help at least a little in that endeavor. "What happened to make my father see Hector for who he really was?" I asked after a moment.

"You," my mother said quietly. She looked off behind me as if she was recalling something specific. "He had met you, but one day you ran in while your father, Hector, and I were talking, and you had a sundress on. Hector saw the birthmark on your shoulder and he got this look." She visibly shivered. "The look in his eyes...it was...*hungry*." She paused. "Things changed after that day. Your father saw the way Hector looked at you, the way Hector became obsessed with you. He had this idea that *you* were the key to this journey to the afterlife the gods had planned for the people that would live in this perfect utopian society of his." She shrugged. "After that, your father started distancing himself from Hector...made excuses when Hector asked to come to our home. I had hoped your father was on his way back to being the man he had been. But then one day, we came home from a hearing about your father's old company, and...you were gone. The nanny we'd left you with thought you were playing in your room. Just like that, you were gone. And then"—she sucked in a breath—"your father was too."

I scooted my chair out, stood up, and leaned over to hug my mother as she cried in my arms. I wiped the tears from her cheeks and then hugged her again. After a minute, I returned to my own chair. "I'm so sorry," I whispered. "Everything you've been through... I'm so sorry." I knew that when it came to unthinkable grief, the best someone could do for you was recognize and acknowledge your pain because there was no taking it away.

My mom sniffled. "Your father, Eden. He wasn't a perfect man. He had made a terrible mistake. But he loved you more than anything in this world. It broke him to lose you. And he simply couldn't put the pieces back together."

I pictured the man in the photo Felix had given me, the man whom I recalled so very little of, the man who'd made a terrible mistake and gone searching for mercy from the devil himself. We both sat quietly, my mom and Molly sipping their wine, me thinking about everything I'd been told in the last hour. It would take me a long time to organize all the pieces. But I knew it all started with Hector's true identity, and as far as I knew, there were no leads on that. "Hector told you his name was Damon?" I murmured.

"Yes. Damon Abas. Another false name."

I nodded. I wondered if the police would *ever* determine Hector's real name. Now that I knew more about him, it was almost as if he had simply materialized at my parents' house that day so long ago looking to recruit his first council member for his 'land of plenty.' "Did the police look for a place like Damon Abas had described once I was taken?" I asked.

"Oh yes. Damon...*Hector* had indicated Acadia was here in the Midwest, somewhere close by. He never disclosed the location and we had no reason to press the issue at the time. We figured we'd learn more when we began planning our relocation. The police scoured every community that was anywhere *near* the description Hector had given us. They came up empty. I never realized how many alternative societies are out there, most of them completely under the radar. It was like looking for a needle in a haystack. And of course, we had no real name, no photographs of the man." She sighed. "Now that I know about Acadia, I see so clearly how well it matched Damon's description of his planned community and I imagine the police do too. As for the whys and the hows of what he did, there are so many things to understand. Half of me wants to know everything there is to know, and the other half wants to wash my hands of it and thank God you're back where you belong."

I nodded and offered a smile, feeling joy in the word *belong*. Finally—the thing I'd been searching for my entire life.

We talked for hours. My mom had many more questions about how I'd been treated in Acadia. I told her of my loneliness and confusion. I spoke of Mother Hailey and felt a pressing on my chest. I didn't speak specifically of Calder or Xander. I couldn't—not yet. But I did tell her there'd been happiness for me there too, and that I'd had friends. And I filled her in haltingly on more of the horror I'd experienced at the end—most of it at least. My mom cried some more and so did Molly.

We filled each other in on what our lives were like now, about what it'd been like for me to reenter a new and different society, about Felix, and the things my mom had done to keep my memory alive all the years I'd been gone.

Finally, as the hour grew later, I covered my mouth to stifle a yawn. I was emotionally exhausted. "I'm sorry," I said, shaking my head. "It's been a long day. I should get going. Do you think you could give me a ride?"

"You'll do no such thing!" my mom exclaimed, setting her wineglass on the table. "Please, Eden, I meant what I said. Please stay here. Please."

"Seriously, Eden, she has rooms to spare upstairs. And you said you were looking for a place..."

45

"All right. That would be wonderful, actually. Let me just call Marissa and tell her. She's going to be thrilled. Really, I can't wait for you to meet her."

"Meet her? I'm going to squeeze her so hard. She's been taking care of my baby!"

I breathed out a small laugh. "Thank you, Mom." I looked over at Molly. "Thank you too, Molly. You made today so much better than I ever could have dreamed."

We all stood up and hugged, my mom shedding a few more tears, and then Molly showed me to my new room, in my new home, and brought me a few of her things to borrow until I could retrieve my own the next day.

When I'd slipped into bed, my mom came in and sat beside me on the mattress, gazing down at me in wonder and running her hand over my hair. "My little girl," she said softly. She hummed to me for a few minutes, a look of awe-filled joy in her expression. "My beautiful Eden," she whispered, "I never thought I'd see you again."

"I love you, Mom," I said. "I never forgot you."

She caressed my cheek, a tear escaping her eye. It rolled slowly down her cheek as she said, "Oh, my sweetheart, I love you too. I never thought I'd get the chance to tell you that again in this life. We have so much lost time to make up for."

I lay there after she closed the door, looking around in the dim light from the moon outside, reeling at how life could change in an instant.

All my life I'd dreamed of my mother, held on to the belief that I'd been loved before. And now I had her back. I said a silent thank-you to the God of Mercy, hoping against hope that being back in my mother's arms would help heal another piece of my broken heart.

CHAPTER THRFF
Eden

The day I stumbled away from Acadia, the day I lost the love of my life, I thought I'd never feel happiness again. I didn't think I'd ever care about anything. Nothing mattered and all I could do was hurt. Just breathing felt like enough.

I'd heard it said that the only way through grief is to grieve. Sometimes I felt like I'd done a decent job of that, and other times, I saw something or remembered something or *smelled* something, and the pain would hit me so hard, I almost felt like doubling over with the blow.

I'd been living at my mom's house for a month, and like I'd hoped, the stability and love I had found there was a balm to my heart. Not that I hadn't found some measure of peace with Felix, but it wasn't quite the same. I didn't *belong* to him. For the first year I'd been there, the only thing I'd been able to do was manage my anguish. For the two years my mind could focus on anything *other* than my grief, I had focused on earning and saving money, attempting to build something of my own that would allow me to feel safe. I didn't imagine I'd ever have more than a few fleeting moments of happiness, but I craved safety, security, and that seemed at least possible, so that's what I worked toward. I had known Felix was ill the day I arrived at his house, and losing him had been a constant worry for me, for more reasons than just the fact that I grew to love him.

Every morning during those first weeks at my mom's house, I woke up in my pink, frilly twin bed—the comforter still preserved from my childhood room. It felt like, again, I had woken up to a whole new story and I was a different main character, stumbling through unfamiliar territory, trying to understand my new role and play it well.

I had expected that not having to be concerned constantly with how I would take care of myself and survive on my own would help me heal even more. But in fact, the lack of that particular anxiety allowed my mind to spend time probing areas I'd somewhat successfully neglected up until then, like skirting around the edges of a fading bruise only to find the pain remained. *I hurt.* It felt like I ached all the time that first month at my mom's house. I *still* hadn't yet told my mom or Molly about Calder because I simply didn't know if I was strong enough to talk about him to anyone. It was another step I'd have to feel ready to take—I figured I'd know when that time came. But my mom didn't seem to want to discuss Acadia very much anyway. We'd talked about it that first day, but any time I made any reference to it now, she changed the subject. I wasn't sure if she was trying to protect me from the sadness she thought it brought me to remember it, or if she herself preferred to pretend it didn't exist. I suspected the latter.

My mom had a piano in her living room, and so I started back up with a couple lessons. And if I didn't have a lesson, I played anyway. Some days it helped more than others.

When I wasn't playing the piano, I filled my time by walking through my mom's neighborhood, admiring the old homes, browsing through shops with no intention of buying anything—acquainting myself with the outside world in portions I controlled. I visited Marissa, finally telling her where I'd come from, and I looked things up online I still didn't understand. In a nutshell, *I existed*. Was this the life I was meant to be living? *Was this my destiny*...to walk through all my days feeling a never-ending void deep inside, this constant wanting? If I was moving when the question arose in my mind, I would stop and pause, the very small whisper of a feeling telling me it wasn't. *What then?*

Although my mom didn't seem to want to discuss grown-up topics with me, it seemed she was constantly where I was, always reaching out to touch me, looking at me with fearful eyes, as if I could evaporate into thin air at any second. I understood it, and part of me appreciated her continual mothering. After all, I'd lived without any for so long. I had yearned for a mother's love for what seemed like forever. But another part of me finally had some freedom and I wanted to attempt to figure out who I could be on my own. I wanted to be treated like the twenty-one-year-old woman I was, not the child she often seemed to still want me to be. The one she'd lost. We were both struggling with the dynamic between us. I guessed that would just take time.

Sometimes I wondered if I'd always be a captive, even if in very different forms: first with Hector, then by the fear Clive Richter created, then of my own doing, and now by my mother. The motivations were different, I knew that of course, but it still felt as though I'd never be free to be myself, or even to begin learning who that might be. I'd only ever experienced that with Calder and I only ever would, and that knowledge brought deep despair because it was another level of loss.

One beautiful early fall morning, I woke up just after dawn and took my coffee out on the patio. The air was cool, so I grabbed a throw sitting on the edge of the couch. I wrapped the blanket around my shoulders and sipped the strong, hot liquid I'd grown to enjoy with Felix as I admired the chrysanthemum- and ivy-filled planters. I could tell the garden was my mother's therapy. It was clear she nourished it as if it was her own heart—a tangible thing to keep loved and well cared for. Perhaps we all craved something like that. For me, it was my music. It was where I went to fill up and feel alive. Its beauty was always waiting, even when the world felt ugly, the notes clear and orderly in the midst of chaos.

When I had finished half my cup of coffee, Molly came stumbling outside in a pair of yoga pants and a long-sleeved T-shirt. "Hey," she mumbled.

"Good morning. You're up early."

"So are you. I thought I might go to the Zumba class at the gym. It starts at seven. You in?"

"Zumba?"

"Yeah, it's this Latin-based dance workout. It's really fun. You should come."

"I'm not up for fun at seven in the morning."

Molly snorted. "Maybe you're right." She eyed me over her own cup of coffee.

"So are you okay with the garden party Carolyn has planned?"

My mom was planning what she called a "very small garden party" for a few of her very closest, most trustworthy friends. She had agreed not to call the police just yet, but she was bursting to tell those she loved I was home. I couldn't bring myself to deny her that. I gnawed on my lip for a minute as I considered Molly's question. "It makes me a little nervous," I said. "But I'm trusting Carolyn."

Molly nodded. "I think it'll be fine," she said, but then paused. "The party part anyway. However, you might want to be aware that Carolyn has setup plans."

"Setup plans? You mean with a…man?" I swallowed. That was the very last thing I wanted.

"She has this grand scheme to make you fall in love with her neighbor's son, *Bentley*."

"Bentley?" I looked around as if this mysterious Bentley might suddenly appear.

"Yeah, Bentley Von Dorn—that's a mouthful, right?" She snorted. "He's actually very good-looking, but he's completely horrible in every other way possible." She gave an uncomfortable and short-lived chuckle that also held some note of…something I couldn't exactly discern.

I raised a brow. "My mom wants to set me up with someone horrible? Well, that's nice."

She shrugged and I detected a pink tinge in her cheeks that had to be connected to this horrible person named Bentley she was currently speaking of. "Oh, well, *horrible* might be an exaggeration," she said. "Distasteful is probably a better word. And I'm sure Carolyn has no idea." She looked down at her fingernails, studying them, that pink tinge deepening. "Anyway, heads up. I'd stay away." I watched her skeptically for a minute but didn't say anything. I had a feeling there was a lot more to Molly's take on Bentley than she was saying and that perhaps Molly didn't think he was horrible at all.

As we sat there under the covered patio, soft raindrops

began to fall. I watched them, the sadness approaching me slowly, like a hesitant friend. Just the talk of a setup, dating, the subject of love in general, made me melancholy, a hopeless ache descending. *I'd never have that again.* Not ever. Calder had been my one true love, the other half of my heart. He was gone now and so was that part of my life.

There's a spring. I'll wait for you.

I felt Molly's eyes on me as I stared out over the raindrop ripples on the surface of the sparkling pool water.

"I wish you'd share it all with us, Eden. Maybe it would help. You've been here for a month now, and I hope you know that we already love you so much."

I met her eyes, surprised she had read my mood so well. Surprised and touched. "I know," I said quietly, "and I love you both too. And just being here, *having you*, has helped me so much. I can't even tell you."

"I know, but that's not what I meant. I meant I wish you'd let me help you with your sadness. Perhaps—"

"No one can help with that," I said gently. "I wish you could." I looked back out at the rain. "I know Felix found you and my mom for me, but I like to think *he* guided me to you." I paused. "If that kind of thing is possible."

"He? Who?" Molly asked, grabbing my hand in hers.

His name caught on my lips. I couldn't say it, not yet. But I kept talking because the rain was falling, my words were suddenly flowing and somehow I needed them to. "Sometimes I imagine the rain is him," I said. "If I'm alone, I turn my face into it"—I mimicked raising my face to the heavens—"and I can *feel* him. I'll never have a place where I can visit him, and so I'm with him in the rain." I met Molly's questioning gaze. "But then it takes me back there too. I never know which I'm going to get."

"Acadia," she whispered.

I looked out across the pool again and nodded. "I've heard it called a cult so often on the news. And I guess it was." I bit my lip for a minute thinking of all the horror that had taken place there in those final days. "To me it was home though. I loved people there. And that's the hardest part."

"Oh," Molly breathed as though a puzzle piece had clicked into place. "There was a boy," she said.

"Yes."

"And he—"

"Yes," I said.

"Oh, Eden. No wonder. You were in love and then you lost him. Oh, I'm so, so sorry."

I nodded, a single tear escaping my eye.

Molly leaned forward. "Is there any chance that he got out too? I mean, you didn't go to the police…"

I shook my head, wiping the wetness from my cheek. "The whole place was flattened. Underwater. I know you probably saw it on the news, but to be there…" I shivered, wrapping my arms around myself. "The water and then the collapse. No."

"Oh God. Oh, Eden."

She stood up and hugged me, and when she took her seat again, I still felt sad, but somehow lighter too. I'd spoken of him. Finally, I'd done it and though it had hurt, it felt like a small victory too.

My mom walked through the patio doors a few minutes after we'd wiped our final tears away. "Good morning, girls," she singsonged. She was fully dressed, coiffed, and looking like she'd been awake for hours. She came over and kissed me on my cheek, bringing her face close to mine and gazing at me with a smile on her face for a good ten seconds. Her powdery, floral scent wafted all around me.

I couldn't help but smile back at her, my mood lifting just a little more. "What?" I asked.

"You!" she said, pinching my cheek. "You bring joy to my day. And you're so gorgeous, even with bedhead." She grinned.

Molly snorted. "Well, gee, what am I? Chopped liver over here?"

"Oh," my mom said, standing and clapping her hands together. "You're gorgeous too. I'm just used to you." She went over and kissed Molly and pinched her cheek as well. "I have so much to do before the party," she said, taking the seat across from me.

"Do you really think your friends will be discreet?" I asked. "I mean, these people can definitely be trusted not to go to the police, right? Until we're ready?"

My mom's eyes widened. "Oh yes. I've sworn them all to secrecy for now. They know exactly how much I've suffered, and now how much you've suffered too. They would never betray me that way." She paused, looking concerned. "But, Eden, we'll have to tell the police you're back at some point, my darling. They'll want to close the case, investigate, and whatever it is they do in situations like this."

I frowned. "You can't get in trouble for not telling them right away, can you?" I asked.

Molly cut in. "I can't think of any law you're breaking, no, and I highly doubt they'd do anything about it anyway. How would that look? Anyone in their right mind will understand that you've been traumatized enough." She glanced at Carolyn. "Still, you can't live with it hanging over your head. The sooner you get the whole hoopla over with, the sooner you can move on with your life."

"Hoopla," I whispered. I'd fixated on my fear of the police, but I hadn't considered the fact that I'd be in the public spotlight. But of course I would. Everyone would want to hear about the girl who escaped from Acadia, the missing child who'd been reunited with her mother.

"Oh yes, it will be a media circus. You have to be prepared for that." Carolyn frowned slightly. As I studied her face, sympathy filled me. If anyone was familiar with a media circus, it was her, I imagined.

I nodded, even more determined now to put off going to the police. *Police.* As always, just the word alone had fear skittering down my spine. *A captive to fear.*

"Well, anyway," Carolyn said brightly, "we can talk about all that after the party. We'll make a decision together."

I smiled, but I was still a little concerned. "Okay. So speaking of this party, I thought you said it was a very small intimate group of friends?" ·

"Oh, it is, just twenty. But my garden parties are infamous, so I have a reputation to uphold." She winked. "Plus, since it will be chilly, there's more to do. Heat lamps, twinkle lights… It's going to be beautiful. It will be like making up for all the birthday parties I didn't get to throw for you."

I laughed softly. "Okay." I started to stand and Molly and my mom did too. "I'm going to go in and take a shower," I said.

"All right. I've laid your outfit out on your bed," my mom said.

I turned back toward her. "Outfit?"

"For the party."

I heard Molly groan, and my eyes darted to her. She widened them slightly as if to say that Carolyn had really lost her mind. What could it hurt though? I smiled at my mom. "Thanks, how nice of you."

"Of course, darling."

"Eden," Molly called when I'd turned toward the door once again. "It was so nice talking to you." She smiled warmly if not a little sadly.

"You too, Molly," I said.

I went upstairs to my room, trying my best not to gasp out in horrified shock when I saw the sheer, light pink, sleeveless dress with the huge flower at the neckline. I held it up in front of me, my eyes widening as the flower seemed to grow before my very eyes. *Well.*

As I stared at it, a feeling of rebellion gripped me. *This is not the same*, I reminded myself, picturing a white lace dress that had been chosen for me to wear against my will. *This is not the same.* Even so, I hung the dress up in my closet and closed the door firmly behind me. I didn't want to look at it right then.

CHAPTER FOUR
Eden

I scrolled through the internet page in front of me, taking a few notes here and there when something seemed important but mostly reading the content and pausing when I needed to digest something. The information filled my mind, blocking out everything else and bringing with it the peace I craved—at least for the moment.

A knock sounded at my door and I snapped my laptop closed. No one would understand this obsession—certainly not my mother. Molly peeked in and smiled. I breathed a sigh of relief and set my laptop aside as she closed the door behind her.

"You know what you need?" she asked.

"So many things, I don't even know where to begin."

She laughed softly. "No really. You need a night out."

"Oh no, no. I don't do bars. And I don't even have an ID anyway." I shook my head, leaning back on the pillows propped on my headboard.

"I'm not going to a bar. I'm meeting a couple friends

from school and we're going to see this local artist who's been getting a ton of buzz."

I stood and grabbed my laptop to put it on my desk under the window. "An artist?" Molly was a junior at the Art Institute and studied fashion marketing, and she had plans with her classmates often.

She nodded, plopping herself down on my bed. "Yeah. It's his opening night, but my friend Allie got into a sneak peek for students and so she gave me her two tickets for tonight. She said he's hot as sin too." She raised a hand. "Not that you're up for looking at guys or anything, but you know."

I gave her a wry smile. "It's okay, Molly." I caught sight of myself in the mirror and sighed. My hair was a mess and I hadn't bothered with a stitch of makeup—which I could use because I looked pale and tired. I picked up a brush and attempted to tame my bangs at least. A moment later, Molly came up behind me and gathered my hair and started twisting it into an updo. I tossed the brush down, grateful for the help.

She met my eyes in the mirror. "I just think this might be a safe thing to do, you know, to practice being social."

I stared back at her for a minute, thankful to have found a female friend my age. She understood so much more about life than I did. And part of me did want to at least be social… to have a few friends. To learn how to laugh again. I just wasn't sure I was ready just yet. I'd barely begun opening up to Molly. "I guess it's obvious I need practice," I said on a sigh.

Molly picked up a pin and stuck it in my hair, giving me a gentle smile. "That's only natural, Eden. And after what you've been through…well, it's going to be a process, you know? And I completely understand that you need to start out slowly. I've been looking for an opportunity to help you get out, and I think this is perfect." She pulled some strands loose around my face and then studied me momentarily, appearing pleased with her efforts. "There. Perfection. Put on something that makes you feel pretty and meet me downstairs in a half hour."

"I don't know. I'm kind of just wanting to curl up with my laptop tonight. Plus, Carolyn has that big garden party planned for tomorrow. I think that will be enough social practice right there."

"But they're not your peers. They're your mom's friends. It's not the same." She put her hands on her hips. "And curl up with your *laptop*? Now that's just sad. And isn't that what you've been doing all day?" She tilted her head. "What do you do on there anyway?"

"Oh, I'm just, you know, trying to catch up. Everything is so different in the outside world."

A sympathetic look softened her expression. "I can only imagine. You don't have to navigate it alone though, Eden. I can help."

"Thank you, Molly. I really do appreciate it. You've been so kind to me." I walked over to my desk and started organizing the papers I'd printed out earlier that day.

"So then," she continued, "I'm not taking no for an answer about tonight. You need to see the desert spring guy. His paintings are full of so much light! And that's only from the brochure."

I turned toward her slowly. "Desert spring?" Of course, I had never told her, or anyone, about Calder's and my spring. I gave her a confused frown, slightly jarred by the description after we'd *just* been talking about Calder recently.

59

"Yeah. I don't even know if such a thing really exists. But he paints pictures of this perfect spring with towering rocks on all sides of it. It looks like some sort of paradise or the Garden of Eden, and this girl—just the back of her, over and over, but"—she gazed up dreamily—"they're so real and so romantic. He's truly gifted, I'm telling you."

An artist...*an artist?*

My blood ran cold and every one of my cells surged forward at once. I heard my own voice as if it was coming from outside of myself. "A girl?" I swallowed heavily. "Tell me more."

Molly's smile faltered as she took me in, obviously troubled by whatever she saw on my face.

"What's his name?" I demanded, my lips trembling. *It couldn't be. No way. It couldn't be. Stop even thinking this, Eden. The thought alone is going to destroy you. There are lots of artists in this world...surely more than a few paint springs. But desert springs? And a girl...?*

"Eden, what's wrong?" Molly asked, her look of concern deepening.

I took the few steps to her and grabbed her upper arms and gave her a slight shake. "What's his *name*?"

"Storm. He calls himself Storm. Just that. A made-up name I'm sure, and it kind of sounds like a stripper." She laughed nervously. "But I wouldn't mind him taking some of his clothes—"

"Where's the brochure?" I asked. "I need to see the brochure."

"Eden. What's going on? Are you okay?"

I sucked in a breath, attempting to calm myself, but failing. "Please, Molly, just show me the brochure."

"I'm sorry, I don't have it here. I looked at Allie's at school, but I didn't take it with me."

My heart thundered in my chest and I let go of her and took off the robe I'd been wearing all day. I grabbed some jeans lying at the end of my bed and pulled them on. My whole body was shaking and I felt like I was at risk of having a seizure of some sort.

I reached into my closet and grabbed the first shirt I laid eyes on, something navy blue or black. Dark anyway. It took me a couple tries to get my head through the neck hole and I started crying with the overwhelming emotion paired with the frustration of trying to get dressed. In the background Molly was saying something, and when I finally pulled the shirt over my head, her words registered. "You're scaring me. What's going on? Is it the guy? Storm?"

Pulling the shirt over my head had made my hair fall out of the updo Molly had just done and so I ran my hands through it quickly, all of it tumbling down my back again. I took several deep breaths, but the shaking continued. "I need you to get me down to that gallery," I said shakily. "I need you to drive me there right this minute."

Molly's face was a study of confusion and worry. "Okay, whatever you need. Let's go."

I nodded jerkily and slipped on some flip-flops. It was far too cool outside for flip-flops, but I hardly cared. *Don't think. Just don't think until you get there. You might be crazy. If you are, it's okay. It's okay. You'll be okay.*

I practically ran down the large staircase and flung the front door open, Molly right on my heels. I heard my mom's voice behind us as I ran out the door. "We're going to that art thing!" Molly yelled back at her.

"Oh, well, okay. Bring her right back—" Carolyn's voice was cut off as Molly slammed the door behind us.

I jogged down the short set of stairs to the garage on

the side of the house and waited at the passenger side until Molly clicked the remote car lock. Once Molly had backed the car out and pulled onto the street, she turned toward me. "Do you want to tell me—"

"No, Molly, I'm sorry. I will once we get there. But right now I feel like I might throw up. Please, I just need to sit here." I gripped my hands in my lap, squeezing so hard I could feel my fingernails cut into my skin.

Molly nodded and turned back to the road.

Fifteen minutes later, we were downtown. As we drove past the gallery where the showing was, I turned, looking at the huge line formed outside. I saw a flash of green in the paintings in the window and squinted to make sense of them, but we were in motion, too far away, and the people lined up were mostly blocking my view.

"There should be parking in a garage right around the corner," Molly said.

I put my hand on the door. "Let me out here, please. I need to get out here."

"Whoa. No jumping out of the car while it's moving! I want to go in with you anyway, Eden. I'm worried about you!"

I shook my head, trying to get control of my breathing. The surface of my skin was hot and prickly, and I couldn't feel my extremities. "I'm okay, I promise. I just really need to get out here. Please. At the next red light, I'll hop out."

Molly pursed her lips. "All right, fine. But I'll be about five minutes behind you, okay?"

"Okay, thank you." I let out another big exhale, clenching my hands in my lap to stop the shaking. I swallowed the bile trying to make its way up my throat and practiced the breathing I'd gotten so good at right after I'd left Acadia and needed to control my emotions enough to function.

Molly's car came to a slow stop at the red light several blocks from the gallery and I reached over and squeezed her shoulder and then hopped out of the car and made my way across the street to the sidewalk.

And then I must have run, although I don't remember. Suddenly I was at the end of the line of people waiting for the gallery show to start, and I was hot and breathing heavily.

Oh God, oh God, oh God.

It can't be. It can't be. It's all a strange coincidence. It has to be.

I started weaving through the waiting people, some shooting me dirty looks, a few telling me to get back to the end. I ignored them. I needed to get to the front window.

I had to see. Oh God, I had to see.

Several people were leaned back against the glass of the front display window and I stood on my tiptoes to see above them but wasn't tall enough. "Excuse me, I'm sorry, I need to see in there," I said, my voice quivering. The people blocking my view all looked at me curiously, but began moving out of the way, like a curtain opening.

I held my breath and fisted my hands.

And there it was. *Our spring.* In vibrant. Living. Color.

I gasped out a loud sob and reeled, my hand coming up to my mouth and tears springing to my eyes. The world grew bright around me, and adrenaline exploded through my body.

Yes, it was our spring. I recognized every rock, every shrub, every blade of grass.

And I recognized myself.

I was standing tall and proud, *powerful* and sure, in front of a huge snake looming at me from our rock domain. My head was held high, my shoulders squared, my hair cascading down my back and covering my nakedness with only the backs of my shoulders and legs on display. My face wasn't visible, but it was me.

My gaze moved down to the small plaque beneath it to the title of the painting. *The Snake Wrangler.* I laughed out a strangled sob and then brought both hands to my mouth and simply stood crying for several minutes until I was in control enough to move away from the window and through the people to the gallery entrance.

No one tried to stop me, no one told me to get to the back of the line. They just parted and let me through, shooting me looks of confusion and surprise. I was crying outright now, not even attempting to hide my tears.

I couldn't have if I'd tried.

He's here. I can feel him.

Oh God, oh God, oh God.

At the front, a man in a black suit looked at me in confusion, his gaze sweeping down my jean-clad body and landing momentarily on my flip-flops. "I need to get in there," I said, drying my tears quickly with the sleeve of my shirt, my voice still coming from somewhere outside of me. I thought it sounded strong though, unwavering.

"I'm sorry. You need a ticket. All these people have tickets." He inclined his head to the line formed behind us.

"Here you go," Molly said, suddenly appearing beside me and holding something out toward the man. "Two early entry tickets." He took them, his eyes moving back and forth between us. He glanced at the tickets quickly and I held my breath, but then he nodded toward the gallery, granting us entrance.

I rushed to the glass door and pulled it open, scanning the surroundings. As I took in the art hanging on every square inch of the gallery walls—our spring, morning glories, and *me*—over and over, everywhere, always the back of me or a very slight profile, but always me. Excitement, fear, adrenaline, and extreme anxiety coursed through me. But mostly awe. I felt as though my heart was beating through the walls of my chest. I felt like I might fly out of my skin. I looked around wildly.

Where is he? Where is he?

Molly's hand clamped down on my arm, and I gratefully leaned in to her for support. "Come on," she said quietly. "He's gotta be close."

"Yes," I squeaked.

He has to be close. There's a spring. I'll wait for you. I'll be there.

We walked around a wall of art, and when we came out on the other side, there he was. The whole world faded away and it was just him. *Calder. My Calder.*

He was alive. He was *alive.*

I felt the tears coursing down my cheeks again and all I could do was stare, drink him in, allow my mind to try to make sense of the reality right in front of me.

He was talking to a small group of people and as he turned his head toward me, a smile on his lips, his eyes blinked and widened, his smile vanishing as his face drained of color. A glass he was holding in his hand went crashing to the floor as the people around him gasped and moved away. His expression was a mixture of confusion, shock, and disbelief. And then very suddenly, his face went dreamy as though he realized he was sleeping and was going to experience it for as long as he could. He tilted his head, his eyes fixed on my face as he began walking toward me, the people around him stumbling out of the way as he merely bumped them aside with his movement, his feet crunching over the glass on the floor. I couldn't move. I was rooted to the spot.

I heard Molly breathe out, "Oh my God," next to me, but I didn't turn her way. My eyes were locked with Calder's.

When he made it to me, he tentatively reached out his hand and felt my cheek, one of his thumbs swiping at a tear. He brought his hand back and looked at the moisture on his fingertip in confusion, and then his gaze flew to my face as he let out a small, guttural sound in the back of his throat. His mouth opened and closed, and his head whipped around the gallery as he took in all the people gaping at us before he met my eyes again. His expression seemed to clear as he grabbed my face in his hands and let out a tortured gasp, his eyes going wild. "How?" he croaked out. "How, how, how?" He shook his head back and forth, his hands squeezing my cheeks so tightly that I cried out.

I covered his hands with my own and we both sunk to the floor. Calder's wide eyes roamed my face and his breathing came out in sharp bursts. "You're real," he kept saying over and over. We were both on our knees on the gallery floor, Calder's hands running down my shoulders, my arms, shaking me gently. I squeezed his broad shoulders with my hands too, convincing myself he was really there. Really real, really alive.

"Eden, Eden, I don't understand," he choked out. "How, how?"

Suddenly people were pulling us somewhere. I stumbled up, as did Calder, our eyes never leaving the other's as we were guided along and a door was closed. I could smell coffee and something sweet and hear the voices of the people who had come into the room with us. But I couldn't look away.

"You survived," Calder said. "God, you survived. How, Eden? How?"

"I floated," I said, tears coursing down my cheeks. "Just like you taught me. I floated."

Tears were flooding his eyes too. "There was no air though. No one survived. There wasn't any air."

I squeezed my eyes shut tightly and shook my head, not able to form words, my head not clear enough to think about anything other than him...here, right in front of me.

Instead, I grabbed Calder's hands in mine again. We were both trembling, the adrenaline draining from our bodies. Behind me I heard lots of voices in hushed tones. "I know, there's so much, so much, and your art." I started to cry softly again. "Your art, oh my God, Calder. It's so beautiful." I breathed out a small sob. "You're an artist."

"Where are you living, Eden? Eden." He gave his head a shake as if the words coming out of his mouth didn't sound real to him, as if he was still trying to convince himself this wasn't a lucid dream.

"With my mom and my cousin, Molly," I said.

His eyes grew impossibly wider. "Your *mom*? Eden—"

"Hey, what's going on in here? People outside are—" I turned toward Xander's voice just as he stumbled back against the wall. "Holy shit," he breathed out, and then, "Holy shit!" He rushed toward us and grabbed my shoulders. "Holy shit. Holy shit." He threw his arms around both Calder and me, and we stood there crying and squeezing each other until Xander pulled away and blotted at his own eyes with the cuff of his shirt. "How, Eden?" he finally managed, his eyes roaming over my face with a look of wonder.

I opened my mouth to speak when a woman's voice came from behind us. "Maybe we can all have coffee after the show and go through the details?" she said very calmly. We all turned around, and I wiped my eyes and attempted to get my breathing under control as I took her in. She was beautiful with dark brown, shiny hair that hung smoothly to her shoulders and large green eyes.

"Madison, I'm canceling tonight's show," Calder said, looking back at me, his eyes scanning my face again as though if he took his gaze off of me for longer than a second, I'd disappear.

Madison put her hands on her hips. "Calder, this show could mean everything for your career. Don't do that. It's only three hours. Three hours you'll never get back."

"Eden," Molly said gently from behind me, "let me take you home, honey, and you can call, uh, *Storm*, after his show. Right after his show, okay?"

"Calder," I said, not looking away from him. "His name is Calder." He was even more beautiful than I remembered him: his dark silky hair longer, his bone structure more defined, a slight scruff on his jaw, and his deep, dark eyes pools of joy as he stared back at me.

The woman named Madison let out a loud sigh. "Well, that sounds like a good idea. This is a huge shock. Both of you can get yourselves together and we can all have a nice little reunion after Calder wows the crowd and makes a huge name for himself."

We? I looked back at Madison and held my hand out. "I'm Eden," I said softly.

Madison glanced down at my still-shaking hand and then took it in hers. She stared at me for several long seconds. She had said this must be a shock—*she must know who I am. Does she know I'm the girl in all of Calder's paintings?* After a long pause, she said, "I'm Madison, Calder's girlfriend and the owner of this gallery."

My heart jolted and I swallowed heavily, my eyes flying

to Calder. He closed his briefly and opened his mouth as if to speak, the color draining from his cheeks again, his eyes agonized and full of regret. "Eden..." was all he managed.

I took a deep breath, looking over at Xander, whose expression was equally incredulous and now also pained. Xander's gaze slid to Calder. "Whatever you need," he told him simply.

"I want to cancel it," Calder said. "Madison, I need to talk to Eden. Now."

I shook my head. "No. It's three hours. We'll talk afterwards, all right?" I managed a smile, drawing in another big shaky breath. "Us, you and me, we can wait three hours. This show won't wait." It seemed utterly ludicrous that we would do anything other than hold on to each other for dear life right now, but even in my shocked, confused, joyful mind, I recognized he had a life that I wasn't a part of anymore. A terrible sense of grief gripped me at the knowledge that he had a girlfriend, but I drew my shoulder higher and focused on him right in front of me. *He is alive.*

"Will you stay here and wait for me?" he asked.

I glanced at Madison, who had a worried look on her face, her lips pursed. I couldn't bear being in a room, or even a building, with Calder's girlfriend for three hours. It would kill me. "No. I'm going to let Molly take me home and I'm going to get cleaned up and I'll come back in a few hours, okay?" I brought my hand back up to Calder's cheek and he leaned into it. Madison cleared her throat, and I brought it away but didn't glance at her.

"No, Eden, no. I just... I need... I can't let you walk out of here. No."

"Calder," Madison interrupted. "I have to *insist* you stay here for at least a couple hours. *We've* hired all these people.

They're all depending on you. And you have a contract with the gallery. Just a couple hours, that's all," she finished.

"I'll take her," Xander said, glancing between us. "I've got her. I'll keep her safe, brother. Okay, Calder, yeah?"

Calder let out a long sigh and then nodded, appearing half-stunned and half-miserable.

Xander gave a succinct nod. "All right. I've got her. Trust me? I'll text you her number and her address, and I'll send yours to her phone too. I've got her."

Calder brought his hand to his head and gripped his hair, bringing his lips together in a thin line.

I took a deep, calming breath. I was still shaking slightly and my brain seemed to be filled with white noise. "A few hours," I whispered.

Calder simply stood there—his expression one of anguish—his hand still shaking too as he reached out to touch me one last time before letting his hand fall away.

"Okay. Thankfully only a few people from the gallery saw that, so not much damage control to do. Lori, will you open the doors again and just explain that—" The door closed behind me, shutting out Madison's voice. I walked out of the gallery on wobbly legs. People were flowing through the doors now, and I only noticed a few curious glances my way. Xander held me on one side, Molly on the other.

Outside, it had started to pour down rain, and the people in line were pressed up against the wall and window of the gallery, taking cover under the small overhang.

"Well, this came out of nowhere," Molly said, stepping back under the cover of the doorway.

There was a brief discussion about whose car I'd ride in, but none of it registered, and when Xander took hold of my arm and pulled me along, I let him and then we both ran through the rain.

He helped me up into some kind of dull red, beat-up truck, and I leaned back in the seat as he got in the other side and started the engine. I ran my hands quickly over my partially wet hair and then gripped my jean-clad thighs. My mind and my body were weak with the toll of emotions slamming into me so fast and furious that I could hardly make sense of them all. Calder was *alive*. Calder was *here*, in Cincinnati. Calder was selling his art. Calder had a *girlfriend*. I clenched my eyes shut with the pain that knowledge brought.

"I didn't mention to your friend that I don't have a license," Xander said, running his own hand through his wet hair and then down his shirt. "I didn't know if she'd let you ride with me. The whole no-ID thing really tends to get in the way…" He trailed off, glancing over at me, a look of incredulity still on his face. He turned on his windshield wipers and my heart took up the same rhythm as the squeak of the blades clearing the water off the glass.

I shot him a smile. "Believe me, I know. And Molly, she's not my friend; she's my cousin."

He looked at me questioningly as he pulled into traffic.

"I found my mom," I said in answer. I couldn't even remember now if Xander had been in the room when I'd told Calder.

Calder.

Xander's gaze remained on the road, but I saw them widen. "What? How? I…" He shook his head in wonder. "My God, Eden, and *how*? How did you survive? Holy shit."

"I'll tell you all of it, Xander, when we get to my house. I think I need a couple of shots or something."

Xander glanced at me and let out a small chuckle. "Yeah, you and me both."

"I can't believe I'm driving away from him right now," I said almost to myself.

"I know it probably feels all kinds of wrong, but this show, Eden, it could be his big break. It's just three hours, and it'll give you both a chance to get some equilibrium back."

I nodded and then reached out and set my hand on his shoulder briefly. "I looked for you," I said. "After Acadia... once I got to Cincinnati. I looked for Kristi and for you. I was still searching for Kristi as of today." Just earlier, I'd been sitting on my bed, searching online for any information... How was this the same day?

Xander looked over at me in surprise. "She left for college. Remember she was leaving—"

"I know. I even got her last name from the ranger station once I finally got the nerve up to call. I thought the police might... I didn't even know, but anyway, she was already gone obviously, but they gave me her last name. That's all they'd give me though. Smith. Her last name is Smith." *Of all the luck.*

Xander chuckled softly. "Yeah, not the most uncommon name."

"No. I quickly learned that. Do you know how many Kristi Smiths there are in colleges all over the country? Some not even listed." I sighed. "I knew though, Xander, I *knew* she wouldn't leave you drifting alone through the world. I knew she must have helped you. I still wouldn't have ever stopped searching for you."

Xander frowned. "I actually lost touch with her. We didn't have phones for so long, and when we moved apartments, I couldn't find her number. I searched everywhere,"

He glanced at me with a look of regret. "You would have been out of luck even if you'd have found her. She wouldn't have known how to reach me."

"I'd have known that Calder was alive though," I said. "And I'd have known you were both in Cincinnati." I let the weight of that reality—all the grief I could have avoided—fall over me for a second.

Xander reached over and grabbed my hand. "Thank you for looking for me."

"I was so worried about you," I said sadly. "I knew you had heard about Acadia and I could only imagine how you were feeling…and I thought you were mostly all alone out there."

Xander's gaze hung on mine for a moment. "Only I wasn't."

I let out a small half laugh, half sob. "No, you weren't. Oh my God." Tears spilled from my eyes and I swiped at them.

"He was supposed to meet me at the bus station on your birthday," Xander said quietly. "We had talked about taking a bus to Cincinnati on your eighteenth birthday. It was the only connection any of the three of us had to anywhere and we knew we needed to leave town. He probably didn't even have time to tell you that plan."

I shook my head, staring at his handsome profile, so familiar and yet still different—older, more manly. Xander kept staring straight ahead at the road where the blurry lights of Molly's car traveled right in front of his truck. The rain continued to fall in sheets. It wasn't letting up.

"You guys never showed," Xander said, his jaw tensing as his shoulders sagged. "I went back the next day too, and I sat there and waited for you. I thought maybe it had taken you a little extra time and I didn't want to miss you. But when I realized you hadn't been able to get out of there, I knew something had gone wrong. I just had no idea…" He shook his head slowly, as if denying his own memories. When he looked over at me, I saw the anguish in his eyes. "I waited for Kristi and she drove me out there the very next morning—I didn't know, I had no idea. I'm so sorry." His voice caught on the last word and his expression was filled with so much pain and regret.

"Xander," I said, reaching out to him. He grasped my hand in his, squeezing it tightly. "None of us knew how irrational Hector had become. You couldn't have known. And honestly, if you had shown up any earlier, you may have very well been among all those people. You showed up to save Calder. That's what matters now."

Even in profile, I could see that he carried the weight of every what-if scenario imaginable on his back. And no one's back was strong enough to withstand that type of weight. Xander had broken at least a little. But Acadia had broken all of us in ways both big and small.

I left him there. I couldn't even let myself go there in my mind. At least not right then.

"Tell me how." I took a deep breath. "How did he survive?" The last word came out on a squeak and caused Xander to glance over at me worriedly before looking back at the road.

"The cell he was in. I know you'd never been in there, and I hadn't either, but Calder described it to me as a solid, little cement box. Some water flooded in, but there was a drain in the floor and that kept it low—thankfully—because he was mostly passed out. He doesn't remember much. And of course, he hates himself for that. There's not a lot Calder doesn't hate himself for."

Xander was quiet for a minute, and another tear slipped down my cheek. "The whole thing collapsed, Eden, you know that. Flattened. When I got there, the water had receded, but there were body parts sticking up from the rubble and just..." He grimaced. "It looked like the depths of hell." I recalled the lifeless, bloated bodies floating in the cellar. The images had haunted me for three long years. I wasn't sure they'd ever go away.

"It was," I said. "That's exactly what it was."

He squeezed my hand again. "It looked hopeless. But then I heard this very small banging and I followed the sound. I pulled as much debris away as I could, and there he was, half-dead, shot, bloody, swollen, beaten, oxygen-deprived, in shock, but *alive*, sitting in the corner where the drain was, a space barely big enough for his body. It was like a fucking miracle. He was banging a small piece of concrete against the floor, over and over again. He was mostly out of it, mumbling about springs and Elysium and you and Mother Willa."

He lapsed into silence as we turned onto my street and I waited for him to continue. "We got him out of there and back to Kristi's friend's house. Kristi even delayed her move to help us and make sure we were okay." He sighed. "I was so scared of the police. After Clive...but now, if I had called them...if you had seen Calder on TV, this would have been different." He shook his head. "Kristi tried to convince me, but I wouldn't listen and Calder begged us not to too, once he was coherent. There was so much we didn't understand then, so much that terrified us."

"Xander, I didn't call the police either. I still haven't called the police even though my mom... Well, that's another story, but I know. I know."

He pulled behind Molly into my mom's driveway. "Clive is still out there," he said.

A shiver went down my spine. "I know." I opened my mouth to go on, but my mom swung my door open and offered me her hand, putting an umbrella over us and practically pulling me out of Xander's truck. It seemed she'd been watching for us to return home. Molly must have called her from the car.

We ran through the rain into the house, and after we'd dried off with a towel, Xander and I sat in the living room drinking hot tea instead of the shots we had talked about. Suddenly, I was chilled to the bone. I felt like I'd never get warm. But somewhere underneath the shock and the sadness that both our lives were so different now, there was a current of wild joy that ran through my bloodstream.

He is alive.

My mom introduced herself to Xander, but then Molly, thankfully, pulled her away so that Xander and I could talk.

I told Xander everything I'd been through since we got in Clive's police cruiser that fateful day. Xander got up and hugged me several times, and my mom fluttered in and out of the room worriedly. Molly pulled her out again a few times, but I shook my head to let her know it was okay. I could see how much she needed to feel useful to me, in even the smallest of ways, and perhaps she needed to hear this as well.

Xander told me that he and Calder had been doing construction work, mostly—anything where they could get paid under the table. They'd both gotten good at it and so far hadn't been between jobs for long. It paid their bills. And I had to admit that a fierce pride flowed through me as I listened to how they'd survived.

"I worked and supported us for the first year," Xander said, his eyes darting to mine and then away. "Calder, he... he didn't do much other than lie around with this blank expression on his face." He ran his hand through his hair. It was a little longer now too, and it suited him. He was quiet for a minute, seeming to be lost in the recent past. "I thought he was in shock, you know, and obviously grieving profoundly. I was too," he said quietly, letting out a harsh exhale. "After his wounds were healed, I did what I could for him, which at the time wasn't much more than keeping him fed and hydrated." He paused again, so long I thought he wouldn't continue. Pain pulsed through me, and a lump formed in my throat, but I held the tears at bay. I felt like I'd already cried a river.

"One day, I came home from work and he wasn't there. I looked everywhere and all I found was a receipt for a bottle of whiskey that he'd gone to the store and bought, trying to self-medicate, I guess. I finally found him up on the roof, at the very edge, swaying and crying." Grief flooded Xander's expression and I sucked in a breath. "I talked him down, dragged him back inside, got him settled down. A few more minutes though, Eden, and..." He trailed off, and I reached out and put my hand on his knee, gripping it. "If he hadn't jumped, he would have fallen."

"I know that pain," I said. "I know. Thank God you were there."

Xander nodded. "He should be the one here right now," he said.

I shook my head. "No. I hated leaving him, but after everything, I'd never forgive myself if he didn't have this opportunity again. His art. *His destiny*," I finished on a whisper.

Xander pressed his lips together. "It saved him once, you know. After that day on the roof, I didn't know what else to do. I went to an art store and spent money we didn't really have to buy every supply I could think of. I brought them home and he didn't seem interested, but the next day I came home and he'd painted something. I recognized it as part of that spring where you two always met."

My heart squeezed tightly.

"Each day I came home, he'd painted a little bit more. After a while, it was all he did. You. Over and over and over. It was like it was the one thing that brought you back to him, at least in some way."

But he never painted my face, I thought, wondering why. *Had he been unable to?*

"I'm the one who encouraged him to take an art class at the community college. The teacher there saw his talent and called her friend Madison, who owns the gallery he's at tonight." I saw the guilt in his expression but he didn't need to feel guilty. Everything he'd done, he'd done in love. "She was very obviously interested in him, right from the beginning. I mean, more than just his art. I encouraged it, Eden. I encouraged him to try to find some happiness with her. I encouraged him to give Madison a chance. Truth be told, I practically pushed him to it." He grimaced and looked down.

"You couldn't have known," I said softly, my heart hurting. "You're his friend. You love him. You were only trying to help him move forward." Tonight had been his opening night at Madison's gallery. If I was doing the math correctly, did that mean they'd been together a few months? Half a year? I didn't ask Xander. I didn't think I wanted to know.

Xander scrubbed a hand down his face. "Yeah. And now? God, this is all so incredibly unbelievable."

I laughed softly and raised my teacup in the air, furrowing my brow at the ridiculousness and tragedy of it all. If I didn't laugh, I was going to cry more tears I didn't think I had.

"Calder, he's...the same, but he's different. It's like he's been so damned destructive recently. He bought himself this beat-up motorcycle and he drives it without a helmet, too fast. He volunteers to do the roofing on our job sites, not because he enjoys it but because it's the most dangerous part." He brought his eyes to mine. "It's almost like he doesn't actually want to take his own life, but he doesn't fear death either. He tempts fate at every turn by taking these crazy risks." I could see in his pained expression how much it affected him. I couldn't blame him. Calder was all he had. But I understood the way Calder felt too. I hadn't found myself at the edge of roofs, or racing down roads without a helmet, but I wasn't fearful of death either. I'd found myself hoping for a short life because I believed he waited for me beyond the veil between us.

Xander's phone suddenly dinged, indicating a text. Xander shook his head as if to bring himself to the here and now and glanced down at it. "He's home," he said.

"Already?" I glanced at the clock on my mom's mantel. It'd only been two hours since we'd left the gallery.

"I'm surprised he lasted that long," Xander said, standing. "Come on, I'll drive you." He took me in a hug and said softly, "I'm so damn glad to have you back, Eden." His voice was choked with emotion. I hugged him back tightly.

Despite my mother's hand-wringing, I got back into Xander's truck and hugged him again when he dropped me off in front of Calder's building, and then gave him a short wave right before I entered Calder's main doors. I waited for the elevator for a minute, my mind reeling. I didn't know if Calder was off-limits because of Madison, but I desperately needed to be in his arms. I needed *him*. But questions and doubts crowded my thoughts. Had he found a way to do as Xander encouraged? Had he moved on? Or was I the only one who hadn't? When the elevator didn't immediately arrive, I ran up all fifteen flights of stairs.

CHAPTER FIVE
Calder

The apartment was dark. I sat in the only chair I had, a rickety wooden one left behind in a closet by the previous tenant. There was a sharp buzz vibrating through my blood and my fists clenched and unclenched on my thighs. I'd gotten ahold of my emotions just enough to make it through two hours of the gallery event, every minute an exercise in pure mind over matter. My body was tensed to run across the city to Eden. *She is alive. My beautiful Morning Glory is alive.* My thoughts spun and I breathed out a harsh exhale as a mixture of astonishment and euphoria slammed into me for the hundredth time in the last couple hours. My skin felt clammy and I couldn't seem to catch my breath.

A light knock sounded and I bolted out of the chair and flung my door open. I gasped out a sound of desperation as I pulled Eden into my arms and we stood there together in my doorway holding each other again and just breathing, hers harsh and rapid as if she'd just run up the stairs. I didn't even know how long we stood there as her breathing slowed, but after a while, Eden pulled away and I managed a small smile that felt more sad than anything.

"Your show. Were you okay?"

I nodded and led her inside, closing the door behind us as she dropped her purse on the floor. "Actually, no, not really." I scratched the back of my neck. "Watching you walk away from me…that was ridiculous, Eden. I should have cancelled it. Really." I let out a small humorless laugh. "It was ridiculous." To go on with a scheduled event—regardless of *what* it was—in the wake of discovering the love of my life was alive? *Ridiculous* didn't even describe it.

She released a breath. "The timing was just…" She trailed off, obviously not knowing how to finish that statement. I didn't either. There was no timing that wouldn't have caused the world to split beneath my feet and so I simply nodded.

We stood there in the dim glow of the city lights coming in through the large windows, just staring at each other. She was so unbelievably beautiful. And she was real. Not a dream. Not paint put on canvas to form a picture from my memory.

"Do you have lights?" she asked after a minute, tilting her head and looking around the barely lit room.

"No, not yet. I got a rental deal on this place from a guy I work with. I've been fixing it up in exchange for low rent and no application process…the whole ID thing." I scratched my jaw. "I don't have the wiring done yet."

She nodded, her eyes moving around the large open floor plan. "I forgot to ask Xander where he lives," she said.

"He has an apartment about ten minutes from here. I asked him to share this place, but he thought it was time for us to get some space."

Our eyes met and we were both quiet for a minute. *What*

are you thinking? I used to know by your expression what you were thinking. "Eden…"

She licked her lips and then opened her mouth as if she was going to say something but then closed it on a frown. Then her face crumpled and she heaved in a big shaky breath. "This is…strange, and it hurts. It's like we… And you have a…you have a…" Her shoulders shook in silent sobs.

At the sight of her tears, pain hit me in the gut, propelling me toward her so I could wrap her in my arms and pull her body against mine. "I'm so sorry. So sorry," I kept repeating.

I felt her shaking her head at my chest. "No, no, you thought I was dead, I know. You were trying to move on with your life, I know."

"No," I said loudly, almost shocking myself with the intensity of the word. "No," I repeated. "I hadn't moved on, Eden. I'd have never moved on. Not ever. I just… I don't even know. I wasn't trying to move on. I was just trying to survive. I was trying so hard not to want to die all the time. I'm so damn sorry."

We stood there in the darkness, holding each other, moving our hands down each other's bodies as if trying to convince ourselves the other was real, not just a ghost or a dreamy apparition, a figment of our grief-filled imaginations.

I listened to her quiet breathing, pain and joy warring inside. "You still smell like apple blossoms," I whispered, inhaling the beloved scent of her, the one I never, ever thought I'd smell again—not in this lifetime.

I felt her smile against my T-shirt as her hand clenched the fabric next to where her cheek rested.

"You smell different," she murmured. "Like laundry soap."

I smiled, but it felt stiff. I couldn't stop feeling like I would wake up at any moment and the feeling scared the hell out of me. We were both silent for several more minutes. "We have so much to talk about," I said. I needed that. I needed her words, and the description of how she'd survived to make it real for me, to help me understand.

"I know." But neither of us pulled away, and neither of us asked any questions. I felt her heartbeat, steady and sure. Her softness pressed into me and she was real and solid and *alive*.

My own heart rate sped up and something shifted, the molecules in the air spinning faster around us. Eden lifted her head and gazed into my eyes and then before I had even decided to do it, my lips were on hers and we both moaned, a mixed sound of desperation and relief. My tongue entered her warm, wet mouth, and she pressed her body to mine as we tasted each other, refamiliarizing ourselves.

We began tearing at each other's clothes, shaky, desperate, with no finesse at all. I walked her backward until she slammed up against the wall, a whoosh of breath coming up her throat. I drank it down, pressing firmly into her. She pressed back against me, gripping handfuls of my hair and tugging.

I pulled away and removed my shirt in one swift movement and then lifted Eden's over her head too. I unbuttoned my jeans and let them fall, and Eden tripped over her own feet as she bent to remove her own jeans. I caught her, going down sideways to the hardwood floor. We hit with a thud and both grunted in discomfort. Under other circumstances, it might have been comical, but for me, in that moment, there was only fear and desperate love and an achy, clawing need. It was almost as if we both wanted to open each other's skin and crawl inside, bury ourselves so deeply that it would be impossible to ever separate us again.

When we were completely undressed and skin to skin, we both sighed again, and our kisses grew slower, deeper, some of the flailing urgency quenched, at least for that moment.

I held her face gently in my hands, one elbow supporting me on the floor as I leaned over her. She brought her hand down and gripped my erection in her fist, and I groaned and ground myself into her hand. It had been so long since I had felt this way—it was still the same. Eden still brought out the same fiery arousal in me that made me feel as if the sun was kissing the inside of my skin.

She pulled me on top of her and wrapped her legs around my hips. We were both trembling, the sounds we were making small gaspy declarations of our joy, or distress, or raw want. I didn't even know—maybe all of those and even more.

The fullness of our history—the confusion and the misery and the love—swirled around just at the perimeter of my mind, speeding up my blood, my fear, my longing. Then all the excruciating anguish of the past three years without her invaded my thoughts. It was too much, too much, and I grasped her so I wouldn't drown again.

My desperation to push into her body—to find the refuge I'd only ever found in her—twisted me inside out. But I took a steadying breath.

I would protect her this time.

I broke from her mouth and reached for my jeans, where I took out my wallet and with shaking fingers, removed a condom. I looked back at her and ripped it open with my teeth. Her eyes registered what I was doing and grew shiny with grief. Her face crumpled and her shoulders started shaking slightly as more tears fell. "I'm sorry," I whispered, my voice cracking. "I'm sorry." Whether it was because the condom was an acknowledgment of the agony she'd endured because we hadn't known enough to be careful the first time, or whether it was simply the fact that I had one at all, I wasn't exactly sure. I could only figure it was probably a mixture of both.

"I know, I know," she whispered. It was as if Eden heard my internal thoughts and was answering both concerns. As if she still knew my heart well enough and forgave me for the ways I'd failed her. My Morning Glory. Once I'd rolled the condom on, she pulled me down to her again and kissed me deeply. When I plunged inside of her, she broke from my mouth and tipped her head back on a gasp. *Oh God, oh God.* The feeling was exquisite, blindingly beautiful. *She* was exquisite. My vision grew blurry, stars burst before my eyes. I grunted and began to move, the pleasure so intense, goose bumps broke out on my entire body.

"Eden, Eden, I was dead without you. Oh God, I've been walking around like a ghost—half in this world and half in the other. Eden…" I moaned out the words, all of them flowing together so that I wasn't even completely sure if I'd said them out loud or if they'd just flown through my own mind in a burst of firing synapses.

Eden pulled me closer, clenching her legs around me tighter and moaned out, "Yes, yes." I didn't know if she was answering me or just moaning out her pleasure. I licked up the side of her neck, the sweet and salty taste of her skin exploding on my tongue. I wanted to devour her. I groaned and pumped inside her harder and faster, our skin slapping together and her back making loud contact with the wood beneath her. She gripped handfuls of my hair, pulling roughly as she cried out my name.

And then we were nothing but a tangled, gasping, moaning blur of skin and heat and mouths and thrusting pleasure. Everything about it was surreal. Somewhere far off in the distance, my brain registered the strange harshness of how we were going about this, but it felt so necessary to my existence that I didn't investigate the thought. I *couldn't* investigate the thought. I had my lost love in my arms. Nothing else mattered. I just let the relief wash over me, our joining bringing a calm I needed so desperately I was practically animalistic in my pursuit of it.

I felt Eden tense under me as she arched her head back and cried out her climax. Her hands came to my back and she scraped her fingernails down my skin so hard, I was sure she had drawn blood. For some reason it inflamed me even further and I swelled inside her. Her breathy sounds of dwindling pleasure brought on my own, and bliss swirled in my abdomen, moving downward until I tensed and jerked inside her, groaning into the sweetness of her throat.

We both lay there for several long minutes, our breathing slowing, our heartbeats taking up an even, steady rhythm. I leaned up and looked at her, her expression gentle but still sad. I smoothed the hair away from her face and kissed her again softly before I slid out of her and rolled over onto my back, bringing her with me.

Again, we lay there together for several minutes, my hands running up and down her arms as she held on to me tightly. When I registered I was still wearing a condom, I said softly, "Let me get rid of this real quick."

After I'd cleaned myself up and wrapped a towel around my waist, I stood against the bathroom wall, just trying to get control of my racing heart, massaging my chest as if something inside had broken. Or perhaps was piecing itself back together, the scar fibers forming—always a reminder of the time I'd lived without her.

When I came back from the bathroom, Eden had pulled her clothes back on and was standing in front of the floor-to-ceiling windows, staring out at the night. I stopped and watched her for a moment, her profile bathed in moonlight and city lights. The vision of her swam and then solidified and I moved closer, eager to touch her again. Needing to touch her.

"It's how I've always loved you best," I said, stepping right up to her and brushing her hair over her shoulder as she turned.

She cocked her head to the side in question.

"Under moonlight," I explained.

She smiled softly.

"For a minute, standing there, I thought you were a vision and I had made this all up in my mind. Will I ever stop thinking that?"

"I don't know. I don't know how this works. I never imagined—"

"Didn't you ever think I might be alive? Even for a minute?"

She shook her head. "I saw the wreckage, Calder. I watched it all come crashing in. I saw the bodies, the water still covering it all. I…" She took in a big shaky breath. "That was the moment I died inside." Her eyes widened in horror as if she was picturing it, feeling the emotions of that moment again. Instinct made me reach out to her and grab her hands. "There was no way…" She choked out a small sob. "I left you there," she whispered, misery etched into her beautiful features. "Oh God, Calder." She brought her hand to her mouth. "I left you there." She shook her head back and forth as if in denial. "I'll never, ever forgive myself. As long as I live, I'll never—"

I pulled her toward me and held her against my chest. "Shh," I said, rubbing my hand over her hair. "There was no way you could have known. I saw the wreckage on the news. I wouldn't have had any hope either. I promise you, I don't blame you for assuming no one could have survived that." She nodded but still looked miserable when she pulled away. "Let's go sit," I said, leading her toward the wall to the right of the windows. "I'm sorry I don't have any furniture."

She sat down on the floor and leaned back against the wall. I dropped the towel and pulled on my discarded jeans and went and sat down next to her and then pulled her against me. When my back hit the wall, I could feel the sting of the wounds she had caused with her fingernails. I wanted to sigh with the somehow wonderful feel of the pain, proof she existed. I realized in that moment that it had been the same with the emotional pain too. All these years, something in me had *grasped* on to it, not ever wanting to let it go. Truthfully, a big part of me had wanted to dive headfirst into the anguish and drown in it. I had wanted it to torture me, bury me alive. A part of me craved it because it was all I had of her.

She wrapped her arms around my waist and leaned into my body. I took a minute to let my soul rejoice, closing my eyes and breathing in the scent of her hair.

"Xander told me how you got out," she said in a whisper.

I nodded, pulling her closer, allowing myself to remember. "When I was dragged to that cell, I was mostly unconscious. I...well, you saw the state I was in. I'd been shot too. I didn't even realize it until I tried to stand. I lost a lot of blood, but I only have a scar to show for it now."

I sighed, going silent for a minute as Eden waited. "I thought I was going to die. I figured it was a given. And I almost felt a certain...acceptance. I regained consciousness here and there, and I heard the screams. I just kept thinking that you were out there somewhere among them, and it tore my guts out, Eden. I don't even want to go back there in my mind to describe it to you."

She squeezed my waist and said very quietly, "It's okay, you don't have to. I know."

I felt the sadness settle around me. "I'm so sorry. What you went through. And I wasn't there."

She looked up at me and put her fingers to my lips. "There was literally not one more thing you could have done. You fought with all your might, everything you had in you. You don't think I know that?"

"And it wasn't enough," I choked out.

She let go of my waist and turned toward me and put her forehead to mine. "It *was* enough. We're both here. Do you see that now? It was enough. Whatever we did, it ended up being enough. We've already forgiven each other. Maybe we can manage to forgive ourselves now too."

Tears were running down Eden's face again and she swiped at them. "Hector put us both in the only two places in that hellhole where there was enough air to survive. The gods forgot to mention that little tidbit of information to him." She let out a very small laugh.

I supposed there was some humor in that. I chuckled too. "The cave-in," she finally said. "Were you conscious then?"

"No. After the screaming, I don't remember anything until I heard Xander's voice above me. He says I was banging something and that's how he knew where to look for me in the debris, but I don't remember that. The next thing I knew, I was waking up at a friend of Kristi's." He grimaced. "I didn't even want to be alive. I was so damned pissed I was alive. I think I still was until about two hours ago."

Eden sighed, shaking her head and bringing her hand to my cheek again for a second before bringing it away. "I know about that too," she whispered.

We were both silent, just staring into each other's eyes for a few moments. "Tell me the rest," she said.

"Kristi's former roommate was a medical student. She told him a story about me being in a gang. Anyway." I sighed, running my hand through my hair. "He fixed me up the best he could, and a week later, Xander and I got on a bus and came here."

A look of grief passed over Eden's features and she shook her head slowly. "Three years and we've been in the same city all along."

I felt the same grief and regret fill my chest. "Yeah" was all I could manage to croak out. "Eden..." I started. "You know it was my water system that caused the flood, right?" I already figured she must. The reenactment of what the police thought happened that day had been on the news over and over again. Of course, they weren't there. We were. And only I knew that they had gotten a few things wrong.

Eden's expression gentled. "It was *Hector* who caused the flood. He just happened to use your water system to... deliver the water from the rising river right over the cellar so that when the rain came..." She trailed off, not finishing that thought.

I put my head down and massaged the back of my neck. "I *built* that system." I looked up at her. "And, Eden, Hector didn't rig it. I'm the one who kicked it over. It wasn't Hector, it was me. I kicked it over in a fit of rage. I caused the flood."

Eden blinked, understanding dawning. "Oh, Calder," she whispered.

"It was my fault. If I hadn't done that, all those people—"

"Stop," she said, her voice rising. "You didn't do that on purpose; you had no way of knowing that would happen. That is not your burden to bear." She brought her fingers to my chin and tipped my face up so that I was looking straight into her face again. "That system was your longing for more, Calder. That system was beautiful, despite what happened. I'll never believe anything different."

Guilt and love washed through me simultaneously— guilt for my part in the tragedy that day, and love for who she was and what was shining out of her eyes. "Still my Morning Glory," I murmured.

Her eyes moved over my face, filled with tenderness. After a short pause, she continued. "And the thing that wasn't on the news? The thing that only I know is that Hector swallowed the key to the cellar. *He swallowed it.* He didn't just lock the door; he swallowed the key." She let out a small disgusted laugh. "He was never going to let those people out, whether they wanted out or not. And, Calder, most of them, even at the end, they didn't. *They believed.* That's no fault of yours."

He'd swallowed the key? I didn't know what to feel about that piece of information. On one hand, it filled me with horror, and on the other hand, it brought me a small measure of peace about my own part in the tragedy. Xander had told me again and again that it wasn't my fault, but seeing the same thing shining out of Eden's expression, fierce and honest, brought me a peace I'd been longing for. My brave, sweet Morning Glory.

"Tell me how you got out," I finally said.

Eden sighed and looked out the windows, and an

expression that I had trouble reading came over her face. "Thinking back, it doesn't seem real," she said. And then she told me everything that she'd gone through that night, floating in the pitch-blackness as the screams and calls for help ceased in gurgles and death on the other side of the wall right next to her. My heart bled and a lump rose up in my throat so large I thought it might choke me. I felt horrified, sick—my gut was wrenched—and yet beyond that was *pride*. I was so proud of her. And not only had she survived but she had done so using the knowledge I gave her. Somehow, a part of me had been there in that room with her. I'd given her a sort of key and I hadn't even known it. The thought soothed me.

She told me how she'd come to Cincinnati, about Felix and Marissa, about teaching piano, finding out about her mom, going to her door, and I listened to it all, incredulous and in awe of her strength, bowled over by her resilience. "I thought you were strong," I told her. "But I didn't know the half of it."

She smiled and then looked around my apartment. "Xander said you two have been doing construction work. Is that where you learned to do what you've done around here?" She waved her arm, indicating the room around us.

I cleared my throat, taking note that she was changing the subject. Maybe we both needed it. It was a lot to process. It might take a lifetime to process. "Yeah. I do more roofing now actually."

A worried expression crossed her face. "Xander mentioned that too." She paused for a minute. "But now your art—"

"I haven't made a dime off my art yet."

"But you will," she said, her voice full of conviction.

My cell phone, sitting on the floor next to us, buzzed and lit up, and I glanced at it and saw Madison's name come up and the message I'm worried. Come home on the screen. I reached over quickly and turned it off, but when I looked back at Eden, her eyes were on the phone and I could tell she had seen it. Her gaze moved slowly to mine, full of hurt, and I wanted to throw the damn phone through one of my windows.

"Eden..."

"Home? You've been living with her?"

"No. I mean...shit. I was staying with her while I was finishing up this place—just temporarily. As you can see"—I waved my hand around the dim apartment—"it's not exactly habitable."

Eden bit her lip, her eyes large pools of sorrow. "Do you love her?" she asked so quietly I almost couldn't make out her words.

"No. I don't. I..." Gods, *God*, this was awful, horrible in every way possible. I wanted to scream and smash something. I took a deep breath. "I love *you*. I'll never love anyone except you."

"But you're with her," she said. It wasn't a question, just a statement, and she said it matter-of-factly. "You thought I was dead, Calder. I understand."

"No! I don't want you to understand. It's not understandable. I don't even understand it."

Eden sighed and then stood, stretching her legs once she did. I leapt up too. "We have so much more to talk about," Eden said as she smiled sadly. "We could talk for days and still not have told each other every bit of what we've gone through. But, Calder, right now, we both need to get some sleep." She walked over to her purse and took a phone out and texted someone, the girl who'd been with her at the gallery, I assumed.

"Sleep here," I blurted, moving toward her and gripping her arms as she turned around. There was no way I could watch her walk out my door. The thought of it alone filled me with terror, just as it had earlier at the gallery. "Stay with me. Don't leave." *What if I never see you again?*

"I'm not leaving you. I'm just not going to sneak around with you. You have a life." She bit her lip, looking down. "I don't blame you for that. But—"

"I know," I said, feeling as if my heart was breaking open in my chest. "We deserve more than that."

"Yes," she said.

My phone buzzed again and I clenched my eyes shut for a moment.

Eden glanced at the phone. "You need to go *home* too," she said quietly. Her voice had a hitch at the word *home*, and it felt like a splinter to my heart.

"I want you, Eden. I've never wanted anyone except for you. I'm so damn sorry for this situation."

Eden looked to the side. "My mom is throwing some small late-afternoon garden party tomorrow for me." She paused. "Just some really close friends who can be discreet about me returning. Anyway, I should be done with that at seven o'clock or so. Maybe we can get together?" she asked, running her tongue over her bottom lip.

"Yeah, of course. I mean, anything, just tell me. Tell me what to do here," I said, noting the desperation in my own voice. "I don't know what to do here."

She studied me for a minute and then she nodded. "I'll call you when it's over."

"Okay." My phone buzzed again and I almost went over to it and smashed it beneath my foot.

Eden must have seen the anger on my face because she said softly, "She's innocent in this situation too."

I stared at her. *Still so compassionate.* And I knew she was right. I let out a harsh exhale and said, "I know."

Eden leaned forward and kissed me softly, and it was everything I could do not to grab her by her shoulders and force her to stay in my apartment. I felt desperate and miserable and joyful all at the same time.

Eden's phone dinged and she looked down at it. "That's Molly," she said. All I could do was nod. She gave me one last smile and then we moved together, wrapping our arms around each other and just standing that way for what seemed like a long time but not nearly long enough. When she finally pulled away, she turned without meeting my eyes and then the door clicked behind her.

I walked slowly through my apartment, finally sinking down to the floor against the same wall we'd sat against together. I spread my legs out straight and just breathed. I couldn't think of much else to do.

After a while I reached for my phone and texted Madison, telling her I was staying at my apartment. Then I turned it off. I pressed my wounded back against the wall, closing my eyes in relief at the small flash of pain. That's where I finally fell asleep close to dawn.

———————

I woke up with a stiff neck and a pounding in my head. I sat up slowly and realized that the banging was actually coming from my front door. "Hold on!" I yelled, my voice cracking like it usually did first thing in the morning. I stood and massaged my sore neck as I walked toward the door and then opened it. Madison.

She walked inside, looked around, then turned and faced me. "Is she here?"

"No," I said, walking toward the kitchen, where I had a small battery-powered coffeepot and some coffee. I went about the business of brewing a pot as Madison stood silently at the counter and watched me. Once I was done and the smell of coffee began filling the room, I leaned against the counter, facing Madison. "I'm sorry," I said.

Hurt skittered across her features and she nodded, looking down.

I walked over to her and took her in my arms, hugging her to me. "I'm sorry," I repeated. I didn't know what else to say.

We stood there for a while like that until her hands started roaming up my back, kneading the muscles, and her lips came to my throat, feathering kisses along the skin. I pulled away. "Mad…"

She dropped her hands to her sides, letting them hang loosely there. "What? I can't touch you anymore?"

I ran my hand through my hair, took a deep breath, and met her eyes. "No. I'm sorry, no."

"Why?" she asked, her expression pained.

I felt like the biggest asshole on the face of the earth. "Because if you touch me now, I'm cheating on her. And I would never cheat on her." I grimaced. It was the truth, but I hated hurting Madison. She'd been nothing but good to me and I cared about her.

Her mouth gaped open. "Cheating on *her*? You're fucking cheating on *me*! Did you fuck her?"

My jaw tensed. "Stop, Madison."

"Stop? You asshole! What should I stop? Should I stop wanting you? Should I stop fighting to keep you? Would you have me just slink out of your life so it's more convenient for you to be with *her*?"

"I meant stop making this worse than it already is! Don't you think I know what a *fucked* situation this is? Don't you think I know what an asshole I am? What am I supposed to do here? For the love of the fucking gods! *God! Fuck!*" I turned and walked back around the counter, putting my palms on its surface and leaning forward, hanging my head.

"You're supposed to stay with me. You're supposed to see that she's your past and I'm your future. You're supposed to realize that all the two of you are going to do is drag each other back *there*, back to hell. Is that what you want? Someone who you look at each day and remember only tragedy and trauma? Whose very *face* you can't even paint because you can't bear to look at it?"

I raised my head and studied her face. She was beautiful, there was no doubt there, but her face didn't make my heart clench with fierce love. Only one face did that. Only one face ever had, since the time I was ten years old. Only one face ever would.

"I do paint her face, Madison. I just don't share it."

Madison's expression fell and another stab of guilt hit me. She took a deep breath. "Still, all she'll do is remind you of the worst day of your life."

"That's not how it would be, Mad." But deep inside, her words affected me. *Is* that how it would be? If not for me, for *her*? Did *she* deserve to move on? Explore her own life without me and without the grief she'd been carrying? She had shared a little of how her life had been, but it sounded like she had little purpose or direction. Was she able to move forward? Did she deserve a chance to find out?

Madison let out a sound of frustration. "You don't think that now, but it is exactly how it would be." She frowned. "At least take some time. You don't have to feel a duty to be with her. You don't *owe* her anything, Calder. You can still be friends, but come home with me. Please. Take some time."

I stared at her, not saying anything for a few moments, not knowing *what* to say as confusion made my brain buzz. "I'm sorry," I finally repeated. I moved forward and took her hands in mine across the counter as I tried to come up with the right words. "I know Eden and I, we went through hell together. But...it wasn't all that. In fact, it wasn't even mostly that." I drew my hands away and raked them through my hair. "I don't even know if I could explain to someone who wasn't there, what it was like for us."

I had told Madison about Acadia, but not all of it. She knew what I'd gone through, and I appreciated the fact that I'd been able to talk about some of it with someone other than Xander. I trusted her. But how could I tell her what I'd experienced with Eden? It wouldn't be right, and it wouldn't be kind, and somewhere inside, I wanted to keep it for myself anyway. It was *ours*—Eden's and mine, and to me, it was sacred.

"You don't need to explain it to me. I see your art. Every day, I see your art," she said. "Do you think I don't know how hung up on her you are...were, whatever? I just... Please, take some time to think about this. Take some time to consider things once your emotions have settled. Please, baby." A tear ran down her cheek and I swiped it away with my thumb.

I took a deep breath, turmoil swirling through me. I knew she saw my art, or some of it, at least. But did she really see *me*? Did she see how I ached? How I felt incomplete? Empty? I turned to get two cups out of my cabinet and poured us both coffee and handed one to her. "I didn't exactly plan any of this," I said. "It's just..."

"I know," she said, looking down at her coffee before bringing her eyes back up to mine. "I'm here to help, okay?"

I wasn't exactly sure what she meant by that, but I nodded. "Thanks."

Madison sighed and then picked up her coffee cup and took a sip. She looked away from me, back out the windows. "You sold every piece last night," she finally said softly, still not looking at me.

I took a step back. "I sold every piece? What?"

Madison met my shocked gaze. "Yeah, every damn one. Sold out. And you leaving was actually a brilliant move. You're 'unattainable' now, a 'sensitive artist' who can't stand crowds. Brilliant. It's like I planned it myself." But her smile dwindled. I knew it hadn't ended in a way she would have planned.

"Mad—"

Madison shook her head and set her practically full cup of coffee down. "I'm going to go now. Call me later, okay?" She stepped around the counter and kissed me on the cheek before turning quickly away.

"Wait, Madison," I said, setting my own cup down and walking quickly around the counter. "Please know that I never, ever wanted to hurt you," I said lamely as she turned toward me. "You've been so good to me. I'll never stop appreciating all the ways you helped me, and I don't just mean with my art."

She closed her eyes and pulled in a deep breath, seeming to need the moment to work out her response. When she met my gaze, there were tears in her eyes, but she gave me a nod. "Talk to you soon." Then she turned on her heels and walked out my door.

I stood staring at the closed door, trying to sort through my emotions. Was Madison right? Did Eden and I have a future? Out here, in the world, was she better off without me? I had failed her once. I wouldn't do it again. I scrubbed my hands down my face and went back to the kitchen to finish my coffee and figure out my life.

CHAPTER SIX
Eden

The hot shower water cascaded over my head, my mind focused on Calder as I rinsed the shampoo from my hair and then distractedly washed my body. My thoughts were a twisted knot of confusion and I'd felt on the verge of tears since I'd left the gallery the day before, not entirely from sadness or despair but just from the barrage of emotions that continued to rise in unceasing waves. It was overwhelming and exhausting, and though it was already past noon, I'd stayed in bed until just a few minutes before.

I had put my phone on my bedside table, expecting Calder would have at least texted me when he woke up. He hadn't and I wasn't sure what to think about that.

As I pictured the frantic sex we'd had the night before, I paused in the process of applying conditioner to my hair. He'd cheated on his girlfriend with me. That was the truth of it and yet…something about that description made me scream inside. How on the gods' green earth could he and I ever be classified as cheating? I groaned and leaned back under the water. The thing was…it hadn't even seemed like sex exactly. Or at least, it hadn't felt like the point of it was sexual satisfaction. It was more like a desperate clawing need to be joined in any and every way possible. *And it might have been last time we ever touch intimately.* The thought made me weak with anguish and I put a hand on the wall to hold myself steady.

Once dried, I stood in front of the mirror in my underwear and bra, turning on the hair dryer and beginning to dry my long hair. I met my own eyes in the mirror. "He's alive," I said quietly to myself. "And that might have to be enough."

Calder had moved on with his life. And if he was happy, could I really ask him to throw it all away for me? We had loved each other once, *desperately*. I didn't doubt that. And for me, he'd always, *always* be the love of my life. But we were different people now. Fate had ended us. Could we pick right back up where we left off? Was it even possible? Grief made my heart constrict tightly and I set the hair dryer down and leaned against the sink, just drawing in one breath after the next. Had I found him only to lose him once more?

I took a few minutes to collect my emotions and then pulled my hair up into what I thought was a sleek ponytail and straightened my bangs. That humongous flower on the dress my mom had bought wasn't going to allow me to wear my hair down if I didn't want it to get eaten alive by it.

A knock sounded on my door and I called, "Come in." Molly opened the door, beautiful in a deep-blue strapless dress, her hair curled and hanging loose. I took in her elegant beauty. She looked like a woman, and I was going to appear as an overgrown child in the little girl dress my mom had chosen. But I couldn't muster up very much annoyance over a silly outfit when my heart was so filled with confusion and pain.

Molly hugged me and then stepped back. "Are you okay?" she asked, taking me in worriedly.

"Yes." But then my carefully held expression crumbled and I shook my head no.

"Oh, Eden," Molly said, hugging me again. "I can't even imagine what you're going through. It's unbelievable." She pulled away, holding my arms. "But he's alive," she whispered. "You were just telling me about him, and now you've found out he's alive. If that isn't a miracle, I don't know what is."

I nodded, sniffling. "I know, I know," I said. "And that's what I have to focus on. The rest…"

"Yeah…the rest." She chewed at her lip. "That's going to be the hard part."

I nodded, inhaling a breath and letting it out slowly.

"Do you think you'll be okay going to this party today? I filled Carolyn in on what I know about Calder and told her she should cancel the event, but she thinks it will do you good." Molly sighed. "Carolyn has a tendency to see things the way she wants to see them sometimes. She means well…mostly."

"I know. And thank you. And maybe the distraction of the party *will* do me good. The other option is to stay in bed all day and cry. My emotions are such a jumbled mess. I don't even know what I'm thinking from one minute to the next."

"I can only imagine, Eden." She frowned. "Do you think you'll talk to Calder today? What did you decide last night?"

Molly had picked me up from Calder's apartment, but I had been too weary and overwhelmed to even speak. I'd gone straight up to my room and fallen into bed, needing nothing more than the temporary respite of sleep. "I told him I'd call him after the party." I frowned, trying not to tear up. "I thought he'd have at least contacted me by now though." I felt tears prick my eyes. "It's complicated, I guess. He has a girlfriend. He practically lives with her."

Molly's grimace was slight. "God, Eden, I'm sorry. I heard the girlfriend part. I didn't know he lives with her. Still though, obviously he chooses *you*, right?"

I glanced away. "I don't know. I mean…I think maybe, but how will I know for sure I'm the one he really wants? He says he doesn't love her, but would he tell me if he did? Does he now feel some sort of an obligation to be with me? We're both different people now. God, I'm still trying to wrap my mind around the fact that he's alive, he made it out."

"It's a pretty unbelievable story," Molly said. "Jaw-dropping, actually. And I haven't even heard all the details."

I opened my mouth to speak when Carolyn breezed into the room. "Good morning, Eden sweetheart," she said, coming over to me and hugging me tightly. "Are you all right?" Her eyes moved over my face as if looking for signs of damage.

"Not so much, Mom. But I think I will be."

"Well, of course you will be." Her eyes were large pools of sympathy. "This party will be the perfect thing to get your mind off that boy."

That boy. I frowned. "I don't want to get him off my mind."

She waved her hand around. "Well, you know what I mean, of course. As wonderful as it is to know that your friends survived that awful flood"—she shivered—"he's involved with another woman and has moved on with his life. That must be awfully disappointing. But, darling Eden, you have your whole life in front of you. It's for the best that you move on too, don't you think? Find a nice

105

boy who doesn't remind you constantly of that terrible, terrible place?"

"Do you mean remind *you* of that terrible, terrible place?" Molly asked sharply from behind her.

Carolyn blinked at Molly, hurt registering in her expression. "I think it's best for all of us to look to the future, not to the tragedy of the past," she said.

Molly let out a breath. "I didn't mean to be harsh, Carolyn. I just think we need to let *Eden* decide what's best for her life. We need to let Eden decide what she's ready to move on from and when."

I gave Molly a small grateful smile. In such a short period of time, she had become not just a cousin but more like a very dear sister. Something I had never had. Somehow she knew me well even though we'd never met before a month ago. I knew she had my back and it helped me to be more patient with Carolyn.

"Well, of course." My mom's gaze returned to me. "I just hope you'll let me, as your mother, help and guide you too, my darling girl. I like to think I've come by some wisdom in this long lifetime of mine. And I've missed out on mothering you. Please, have it in your heart to let me do some of that now."

"Of course I do. Thank you, Mom." I gave her another quick hug and then turned to my dresser, where I intended to grab the tights my mom had bought me.

My mom and Molly both gasped and I turned back to them, startled. "What?"

"What happened to you?" my mom cried out.

"Huh?"

My mom led me to my mirror and turned me around. I looked over my shoulder, my stomach dropping. There were bruises and finger marks all over my back, my thighs, and my shoulders. "Oh, uh…"

Molly started laughing softly, and when I glanced at her in the mirror, she smacked her hand over her mouth.

My face felt hot when I turned toward my mom. Hers was as white as a ghost.

"Can we just pretend you didn't see this?" I asked.

Her lips became a thin line. "Did he hurt you?"

"No!" I shook my head vehemently. "He would never hurt me. Mom…things just got…um, intense. There were a lot of emotions involved in our…reunion. God." I put my head in my hands. "Can we please just set this aside. Physically, I'm fine. I promise."

She stared at me for a minute and then let out what sounded like a resigned breath. "As long as he didn't intentionally hurt you," she said.

"No, I promise you. Never."

My mom seemed to consider something for a minute and her expression softened. "Eden, darling." She took my hand in hers. "You and I should have a nice little mother-daughter talk. Boys will want things from you, honey, and—"

I groaned. "Mom. I'm aware of what goes on between men and women when they're in love."

Disappointment clouded my mom's expression. "Oh. Okay. Well, we'll chat about that a little more another time. Get dressed and meet me downstairs. The guests should be arriving in a couple hours, and I have a few things I was hoping you girls would help me with."

Molly gave me one last sympathetic look and left the room too. I checked my phone and my heart dropped to see there still weren't any messages. Did Calder regret the night before? Had he started questioning his feelings for me? Had he reconsidered what he'd said about always loving me?

I retrieved the outfit my mom had picked out and started to get dressed. I pulled on the tights first—tights! As far as I knew, only little girls and ballerinas wore tights. Then again, I wasn't exactly up-to-date with current fashion trends. In fact, Marissa had bought every piece of clothing I owned. I pulled the sheer white tights up my legs, doing a little jumping dance to get them up as high as possible. Then I pulled on the dress and zipped the side zipper. The flower came right under my chin and I batted at it with both hands as it tickled my neck and jaw. The growl that came from it was probably me, but maybe not.

I slipped on the pale pink heels that were sitting by my bed. They were actually pretty and not high at all, but I wobbled slightly when I walked in them. My mom probably hadn't considered the fact that this was my first pair of heels. I practiced walking around my room for a few minutes, and when I felt competent enough that I wouldn't tumble down the stairs, I made my way to the kitchen where I heard my mom's and Molly's voices. When I walked in, they both looked over at me, my mom gasping happily and clapping and Molly gasping less than happily and bringing her hand up over her mouth.

"Oh, Eden, you look beautiful," my mom said.

I shifted from one foot to the other. "Thank you, Mom. Thanks for the dress."

My mom came over and took my hands in hers and then spun me around. "It's perfect." She futzed with the flower, frowning slightly and then smiling when I assumed she got it to lay the way she wanted it to.

"What *is* that?" Molly asked as she approached me. She

messed with the fabric flower, batting at it like I had when it sprang out of whatever position she'd tried to wrangle it into.

I leaned toward her. "Don't anger the flower," I whispered, raising my eyebrows at her and then glancing down at it, feigning wide-eyed fear.

She snorted and my mom put her hands on her hips. "Oh stop it, you two. That flower is perfectly lovely. It's elegant and feminine. It makes a statement."

"Yeah, it says, 'I'm *craaaaa-zy.*'" Molly raised her voice and sang out the last word in a high soprano.

I burst out laughing. Molly started laughing too, and Carolyn set her hands on her hips and pursed her lips at us. "Oh fine then, if you don't like the dress," she said, looking away. "It's just that you had one similar when you were four and it was your very favorite. You wore it all the time. I just thought…"

I got control of my laughter, feeling suddenly guilty. I didn't like the dress, but my mother's intentions weren't bad. And I hoped it was just a phase—she was still learning who I was *now*. I was hard-pressed to reject motherly affection, even if it felt a little misguided. "Oh no, no, really, it's very… pretty. I'm just not used to dressing up. I'll get used to it in no time." I smiled at her. "Really."

She hugged me tightly. "Thank you." She pulled back, bringing her hands together. "All right, we're ready early, but there's so much to do. The florist delivered the flowers and they're in the refrigerator in the garage. Do you think you and Molly could start putting together the centerpieces?"

"Yes, we'd love to," I said, looking at Molly. Her eyes were still on the flower at my chin. I cleared my throat and her eyes snapped to mine.

"Oh yes. Right. The three of us, I mean, uh, the *two* of us would be happy to."

I pressed my lips together to hold back the laugh that threatened and then pulled Molly with me toward the garage as my mom called behind us, "The vases are in the lower cabinet next to the refrigerator."

Molly and I assembled the centerpieces as I talked a little bit more about what had happened with Calder the night before and divulged some of what it'd been like for us in Acadia. Talking about it now didn't hurt quite as much. *He is alive!* I checked my phone repeatedly during the day but there wasn't a call or a text from him. How surreal to be thinking of getting a text from Calder. He hadn't even known how to use a phone three years ago. I wanted to talk to him about all the ways he'd experienced culture shock after leaving Acadia. And I wanted to share with him all the ways in which I had too. Thinking about the boy I'd known and first fallen in love with caused an ache to lodge in my chest. Calder was back, he was alive, and yet…he'd never, ever again be that boy. Whether or not he was ever mine again, I'd lost that version of him forever and that *hurt*.

Of course, I wasn't the same either. I'd changed too.

I was interrupted in my thoughts by the peal of the doorbell. The company that was going to set up the tables, chairs, and heat lamps had arrived. I helped direct the setup and pretty soon the caterer was there. The next few hours went by in a blur of activity.

I quickly went upstairs to freshen up and check my phone again. There was one text and I held my breath as I slid my screen open.

Xander: How are you doing? Just checking in because I can. Still surreal. :)

I smiled and texted him back quickly.

Me: Doing okay. Surreal on my end too. I can hardly believe it.

As I was putting my phone away, it dinged and I picked it right back up.

Xander: Have you heard from him today?

I frowned as I typed back.

Me: No

I waited a second and then:

Xander: You will
Me: I hope so. I'll text you later.
Xander: Sounds great

Was Xander right? Would I hear from Calder? And if so, why so late in the day? Was he working up the nerve to tell me he'd chosen Madison after all?

I brought my phone downstairs and left it on the counter in the kitchen so I could check it here and there.

Then the guests began arriving and I was introduced to my mom's friends who fawned over me and hugged me, most with tears in their eyes.

Marissa brought Sophia with her, and we had a small hug fest in the front foyer, even though I'd seen them both recently. My mom, who had met Marissa when I first moved in, hugged her, and cried like she did each time she saw her.

We all went out to the garden, which was beautifully decorated with tables in white linens and the vases we'd arranged full of orange lilies, deeper orange and yellow roses, and sprays of tiny green berries I didn't know the name for.

Twinkle lights had been strung up in the trees and sparkled in the late-afternoon sun. The sky would be growing dim soon and the heat lamps would be turned on. The whole garden had a magical feel to it, but I felt empty inside. I had longed for Calder for so long, believing I would never see him again in this lifetime, but suddenly I *could*, and I was still longing for him. I tried my best to keep smiling, to tamp down the despair the swirled inside me. Was he with *her* right now? Had he decided that he'd moved on from me, and that it was best we both keep moving forward? *Was* it best? He'd never experienced anyone else except me—well, before her anyway. Maybe it was selfish not to let him figure out what he wanted now that there were more choices than just some naive girl down at a spring who worshipped the ground he walked on. We were out in the world now—the big society—and there were women like Madison in it. I grabbed a glass of champagne off a nearby tray and sipped at it, pulling at the flower-beast at my chin.

"You look like you're about to make a run for it," I heard next to me and turned to a tall, good-looking, blond man who was smiling at me.

I gave him a smile in return. "Is it that obvious?" I took another sip of the champagne and grimaced slightly at the strong, unfamiliar taste.

"I don't think anyone else has noticed," he said, glancing around at the women in small groups laughing and chatting, my mother in the middle of one. She glanced over at me and waved. I'd noticed that her eyes were never off me for long. I gave her a thin smile.

"I haven't seen your mother look this happy in, well, since I've known her." The man said as he turned more fully to me. "By the way, I have the advantage here. I know your name. I'm Bentley Von Dorn."

"Oh. Yes, my cousin Molly mentioned you're our neighbor. Nice to meet you."

A look came over his face that I couldn't quite read. "Oh, Molly, yes. I can only imagine what she had to say." He paused for a minute, his eyes scanning the crowd, for her I assumed. *Very interesting.* He gave his head a small shake. "Anyway, it's an honor to meet you, Eden. You're even more beautiful than your mother said. And believe me, she gushed."

"Thank you, Bentley. That's very nice of you to say."

"Well, I know it's true since I can only see a quarter of your face behind that flower, and I can still tell you're beautiful."

I laughed. "It's ridiculous, isn't it?" I finally managed, giving the flower a suspicious glance.

Bentley reached out and moved it slightly and it sprang back to its original position. "Ouch," he said withdrawing his finger and frowning. "I think it just bit me."

I laughed again, some of the tension and loneliness lifting, at least to a manageable level.

I chatted with Bentley, noting that once his eyes found Molly, they rarely moved away, and then I chatted with several of my mom's friends. I finally relaxed a little, although that same low buzz of anxiety I'd felt deep in my blood ever since I'd left Calder the night before never went away. Everyone was nice and welcoming, and we all enjoyed dinner as early evening settled around us, the twinkle lights sparkling brighter now that the sun was dwindling, and the heat lamps warming the cool air. I sat between Bentley and Molly, pretending to listen to their banter, but really my mind was focused on Calder. It was such a beautiful evening and I wanted desperately to be spending it with him.

I snuck inside and checked my phone, but there was still no call. It was close to seven, but I decided to wait to call him until the party was wrapping up and I was free to leave if he asked me to. *He might not, Eden, and you have to prepare for that.*

As dinner was cleared and dessert was being served, my mom made her way to the patio area where the string trio had been playing since the beginning of the party. A couple workers from the catering company set up a white screen next to her as she stood in front of the guests seated at the tables on the lawn. Everyone grew quiet as they turned to give her their attention.

"Thank you all so much for coming today," she said. "This last month has been"—she brought a tissue to her eye—"the happiest month of my life. I feel almost like I did when I first brought you home from the hospital." She smiled tenderly in my direction. "I can't stop looking at you, marveling at your beauty and the miracle that you're in my arms." She sniffed and brought the tissue to her nose. "I couldn't spend another minute without showing you off, just like I did then, to all those I love, my closest friends." She swept her arm around indicating the guests before her.

"Last week I started going through my old picture albums." She gave her head a slight shake. "I haven't been able to do that. All these years and I haven't been able to do that. But now, looking through them has brought me so much happiness. It reminded me that even though I didn't

114

get *all* the years, I got some of them, and they were beautiful, just like you. I don't know what you were like when you were ten or fourteen or sixteen." She sniffled. "But I know what you're like at twenty-one, and I never, ever thought I would." I picked up a napkin and dabbed at my eyes, moved by the love shining so clearly from my mother's eyes. "And now we have the rest of our lives to make up for the time that was taken from us."

She moved a little farther to the side as a picture of me as a baby appeared on the screen. My own gummy smile stared back at me. That photo was followed by one of me as a toddler, two bottom teeth on display as I grinned, a piece of birthday cake oozing out of my chubby fist. I laughed and sniffled. I didn't remember ever looking at these photos—I had never thought I'd see pictures of myself as a child. There certainly would never be any from Acadia.

More pictures scrolled by: the first day of school, my flaxen ponytails tied with pink ribbons, Christmases, me sitting on a pony at some kind of fair, both my mom *and* my dad in many of them, their arms around me. I didn't have any specific memories of those events, but just seeing what a happy childhood I had warmed me and brought with it a gratitude for where I was right that very minute, despite all I had lost.

I was loved. I had been loved all along. By my mother and, despite all his mistakes, by my father. And *by Calder*. All my life, someone had loved me. I knew enough now to understand that not everyone in this world was lucky enough to say that. My shoulders lowered as a feeling of peace came over me and I knew that, *somehow*, everything would be okay. The details of how and why were a mystery, but sitting there in that sparkly, fragrant, festive garden, overflowing with love, I knew. I might talk myself out of it later, but in that moment, I heard the whisper, and I *knew*.

And then he was standing there, at the very edge of the garden, almost like a fantasy that had suddenly materialized.

A soft gathering of butterflies fluttered between my ribs and I blinked, afraid to believe my eyes, my gaze running over him from head to toe. He was wearing a pair of dark gray dress pants and a white button-down shirt with a darker tie. His hands were in his pockets and he walked closer as the slideshow ended. The guests began clapping and I heard a few sniffles and felt their eyes on me but I couldn't look away from Calder.

"I know what she was like at ten," he said, turning to my mom. She gave him a small confused smile as he walked closer. I'd never seen him looking more beautiful than he did right then. *Calder Raynes is in front of me wearing dress clothes.* The moment was dreamlike, unreal. I watched him with bated breath. "She was a brave little dreamer, who had an unbreakable spirit."

He came to stand next to my mom, but his eyes were trained on me. Somewhere next to me, I heard several women murmur, "Oh *my*," and "Well."

Calder looked at my mom, asking silent permission to continue, and she gave him an affirmative tip of her chin. "Fourteen was when she really started to glow, and suddenly, I couldn't look away. I wanted to. Because where we came from, it was a dangerous thing to notice." He paused. Every person in that garden hung on his every word, seeming to collectively lean forward in anticipation of what he would say next. "Any time she was in the room, it was like the whole place was bathed in her light." He tilted his head, looking thoughtful for a second. "Does that sound like an exaggeration? Maybe overly dramatic, poetic words from a boy who has loved her his whole life?" He shook his head. "They're not. It's simply the truth. Eden blossomed into a woman of grace and courage before my very eyes, despite that there wasn't anyone there to help her do that. She never let go of her innate strength, and it's the thing that makes her the most beautiful in my eyes."

Calder walked toward me, joy flooding my heart and tears pricking my eyes as he came closer. "When she was sixteen, she had the power to take my very breath away. And she did it often. She made me miserable and blissful and everything in between." He moved between two tables a few in front of mine. "I didn't know a lot about the world at the time. And as it turns out, I knew even less than I thought I did. I led a simple life. I bathed in a river until I was eighteen years old."

There was a collective sigh from the women around me and I breathed out a small soggy laugh. "Well, that's not an unwelcome vision," an old woman next to me said a little too loudly.

"But what I did know was that I loved a girl. And I knew I loved her in a way I'd never, ever recover from. I knew I loved her to the very depths of my soul. And I knew she loved me the same."

He stopped and looked back at my mom. "I also know what it feels like to lose her. I know what it feels like to have a piece of your heart missing." His voice lowered and he cleared his throat. My heart swelled and tears coursed down my cheeks. "I know what it feels like when the person who's your whole life is stolen from you and each day bleeds into the next in a blur of misery and longing."

My mom swiped at her eyes and hugged her body as

Calder turned back to me. "And I know what it feels like when your life is unexpectedly, *miraculously* returned to you." He paused. "We lived through things so horrific and unfathomable that most of the time, I can't even bear to retell it all to myself. But what I've been thinking about all day today is the beauty we experienced, the love, and the wonder. I needed so much just to sit with that because somehow in the midst of the immense grief, I'd blocked out all the light, and there was so much of it, wasn't there?"

He reached the place where I sat, and I turned away from the table as he knelt down in front of me. I let out a small strangled sob, nodding yes and smiling through the tears as I brought my hand to his cheek. "I'm sorry for interrupting the party," he said. "What I really came here to ask you is whether you wanted to go bowling with me."

I blinked and dropped my hand. "Bowling?"

"Yeah, it's this game where you knock down pins with—"

"Yes, I know what bowling is," I interrupted, laughing softly. "I'm caught up."

He grinned. "I just thought, you know, I've never had the chance to take you on a proper date, and I had a feeling you'd like to bowl."

I laughed, leaning forward and placing my forehead on his. After a minute, I pulled away just a little bit and whispered so only he could hear, "Madison?"

He released a breath. "Did you even think it was a choice, Eden?" he whispered back. "For *me* it's not. I...I want to make sure it's not for you either."

A fresh batch of tears coursed down my cheeks as I shook my head back and forth. "It's not. It's not a choice for me either. For me, it will always be you."

Relief filled Calder's expression before he leaned forward

and kissed my tears away. "Also, Eden?" he said after a few moments. "That's a really large flower."

"Shh, it's finally sleeping. Don't wake it."

We stood and continued hugging and kissing and wiping away tears as the people around us clapped and let out a few whistles. I laughed up into Calder's handsome, beloved face and he smiled tenderly into mine.

I saw my mom approaching us in my peripheral vision and pulled away from Calder. "I'm Carolyn," she said, her voice wobbly.

"I'm Calder." He reached out for her hand and there was an awkward moment when their hands missed because they were both staring at me, and then Calder went in to hug her and my mom turned to me and we all sort of collided. Laughing, we finally wrapped our arms around each other, standing there in a group hug as my mom and I sniffled back our tears.

When we pulled apart, Calder said, "I was wondering if I could take your daughter out tonight?"

"Well…" my mom started. She looked around at all the people staring anxiously at us, waiting for her to answer. They were obviously invested in this now too. She took a deep breath and focused her gaze on Calder. "Yes. But please bring her right back, okay? And take care of her?"

"I promise," Calder said.

My mom leaned in and kissed my cheek and then I took Calder's hand as he led me toward the back door. Before I went inside, I pivoted and waved at everyone and called, "Thank you all so much." And then we entered the house to the sounds of the group calling out their warm goodbyes.

CHAPTER SEVEN
Calder

Eden's hand felt warm and right in my own as we stepped into the deserted kitchen, the sounds of the party fading behind us as I closed the door.

"I should change first," Eden said, turning and gazing up at me. "This isn't exactly bowling attire." She swirled her finger toward the enormous flower at her chin and gave me a teasing tilt of her lips.

I smiled back and then both of our smiles dwindled in tandem. For a few seconds I allowed myself to get lost in her eyes, those deep blue pools I never thought I'd get to gaze into again. I let the moment soothe my wounded, battered heart. "Want me to wait here, or—"

"No, come with me," she said, but neither of us moved. We stood there gripping each other tightly for several minutes—just seeming to need to orient ourselves to the reality of the here and now—before she pulled me by my hand through the large shiny kitchen.

I loosened my tie as we climbed the stairs, and Eden

led me down the wide hall to her bedroom. She closed the door behind us and immediately started unzipping the side zipper on her dress as I took off my tie and stuck it in my pocket. Eden let her dress pool around her feet, murmuring a "thank God," as the stiff fabric flower fell away from her chin. I chuckled softly and then moved my eyes slowly up her body. I hadn't taken the proper time to drink her nakedness in the night before. She was still slim, but she looked more womanly now, her hips just slightly fuller, and her small breasts firm and round in the white strapless bra she wore. My body surged to life, pressing uncomfortably against my new dress pants, the ones I'd bought just an hour ago so I could show up looking appropriate for her mom's party.

I'd spent the day just as I told her, reliving the beauty we'd experienced together. I hadn't had it in me to go there in my mind over the past three years, and I had needed it even more than I'd realized. I had needed to spend time with the *us* we had been in order to feel ready to move forward into our future. I'd gone to Madison and told her. It hadn't been easy, but I owed it to her to be honest immediately. I had never envisioned a future with her. I'd never been able to. And perhaps part of it was that I was simply too hung up on Eden to see a life ahead with anyone. Which wasn't fair. I should have given Madison all or nothing at all. And it had never been in me to give her my all. I'd have to live with the regret I felt for hurting her.

Eden rolled her tights down her legs and tossed them aside and then glanced over at me and paused, appearing suddenly uncomfortable. "Is it strange that I feel self-conscious in front of you?"

I approached her and took her hands in mine. "We have a lot of reacquainting to do, Morning Glory. There's no handbook for this. I doubt if there's even a self-help book that could touch what we've gone through. We're on our own here."

She searched my eyes. "Are we going to be okay, Calder? Do we even have a chance?"

I thought about that for a second. I had promised her so much before, vowed that I'd protect her, that we'd be okay…and I'd failed. I breathed deeply to force the guilt from my lungs, the anger and loss—and self-hatred. All the emotions I'd been grappling with for years. "We're going to try our damnedest, Eden. That's all I can give you. That's all I can promise."

"That's enough," she said. The trust I could see in her expression humbled me. After everything…she could still look at me like that? *How? Why?* I opened my mouth to ask her, but she leaned forward and kissed me. Her lips were soft and sweet just as they always were in my dreams. And though she'd been stolen from her family, isolated from friendships as a child, left to largely fend for herself in a strange city while still recovering from the harsh, brutal death of me and our baby… Despite all she'd suffered in her life, despite my failure to be there for her when she'd needed me, she still offered herself selflessly and without hesitation. That strength that I'd spoken of in the garden was still there, only somehow, against all odds, even brighter and more solid than it'd been before.

I took the expression of love she offered me like the gift it was, opening my mouth and sliding my tongue against hers. We kissed deeply, Eden tilting her head and moaning sweetly into my mouth. I felt desperate to feel her skin against mine. But we were here in her mother's house with a party still going on downstairs. I wanted to get her back to my place where I could take my time with her. We deserved that.

I broke the kiss and pulled away regretfully. I wanted her badly, but we also needed time together in this new world beyond physical joining. It felt necessary to experience a new normal together where we talked and laughed and simply walked through the world as the people we'd become rather than ghosts of who we were.

"So," she said pulling away and grabbing a pair of jeans lying at the end of her bed, "this bowling thing…how good are you?"

"Oh," I said, sitting down on her bed, "I've never bowled. Xander and I used to go to this bowling alley on Monday nights a couple years back." I paused, recalling the shell of a person I had been, sitting there blankly watching people whoop and laugh and pour beer from pitchers. "We were dirt poor," I said. "They had this all-you-can-eat nacho bar." I made a gagging motion. "I swear if I never see another vat of orange cheese for as long as I live, it will be too soon."

Eden laughed, but there was sadness in her eyes. She opened her dresser drawer to get a tank top and pulled it over her head. I leaned back on her pillows, turning my face to the side and inhaling the clean apple blossom scent of the fabric. If I had anything to say about it, my own sheets were going to smell like that tomorrow and every day for the rest of my days.

She closed her drawer. "No more all-you-can-eat nacho bars for you, famous artist," she said. She walked to her closet and opened the door just a crack and reached inside.

"Hardly famous," I murmured.

She grabbed a shirt and then turned her head and regarded me for a moment. "You will be though," she said, like it was just a certainty.

"I—" My words halted and my blood ran cold when I caught a glimpse of what was in her closet. "Eden, what is that in there?"

Eden shut the door quickly. "Nothing," she said. She licked her lips nervously, holding the shirt over her breasts. "Just, um, some research I've been doing."

I stood and walked over to her, putting my hand on the closet door handle.

"Calder..." Eden reached for my hand. I halted, but her hand fell away from mine and she stepped back, breathing out a resigned breath.

I opened the closet door and there on the back of it, covering every inch of space, were newsclips of Acadia, pictures of the council members they had found and identified. There was a photo of Clive Richter—the face of the demon who had originally caught my attention when I glimpsed it from the bed—that she must have printed out from somewhere online, a rough sketch of who I was guessing was supposed to be Hector, and countless small notes written in Eden's handwriting. Toward the middle, there was something that looked like a timeline. My gaze darted from one side of the corkboard she'd adhered to the back of the door and all the items pinned to it and then to the other.

"What are you doing, Eden?" I asked. Even to my own ears, my voice sounded flat. *What is this?*

Color stained her cheeks and she looked away. "You don't have to sound like I'm a nutcase. I'm just...researching. I'm..." She made a small sound of frustration. "I'm gathering knowledge. It helps me feel in control. It helps me feel less scared, I guess. Less..." She ended with a frustrated shrug.

I studied her. "Morning Glory," I finally said, taking her in my arms again. "What are you trying to find here?"

She shook her head against my chest, her arms trapped between our bodies where she still held on to her shirt. After a moment, she stepped back and pulled the black top over her head. "They haven't been able to identify Hector," she said quietly. She reached back and took her hair out of the smooth ponytail it was in and ran her fingers through it as it fell over her shoulders. "And I just thought, if I could figure out who he was, where he came from, you know, it would help me see him more as a man and not a—"

"Monster?"

Her eyes met mine. "Yes."

"I get it, I do. You know more than anyone on planet earth, I do. But this"—I waved my hand over at the board with all her research pinned to it—"this can't be good for you—to spend so much time with *them*, it can't be healthy, Eden."

She crossed her arms as she looked over at the board. "I thought it might help me figure out who your parents were too," she said. "They're still not even close to identifying so many of the bodies."

I grabbed her hands and held them in mine between us. "You don't need to do that now," I said gently. "I'm here."

"Yes. But you still don't know who you are," she said. "If you can find out where your parents lived before Acadia, you might have grandparents somewhere…aunts, uncles, *family*."

I looked off behind her. "I don't think I was born in Acadia anyway."

Her brows came together. "What do you mean?"

I told her haltingly about what Mother Willa had said to me all those years ago, about how Maya was born at Acadia but that I was not. And then I reminded her of the things Hector had said at the end about how he had *brought* me to

Acadia. Granted he was as mad as a hatter, but… "My coloring, it was so different than my parents' and my sister's," I said. Even before I'd questioned anything else, I'd wondered about that. A dull ache throbbed in my chest as I pictured Maya, but I pushed that aside for now. "And learning that *you* were abducted makes it even more plausible that I was too, doesn't it? Clearly kidnapping was yet another crime Hector wasn't morally above committing."

"Well, then this is even more reason to look into the people who raised you—"

"After three years of nothing? The likelihood of finding out information on them is slim to none," I said. Even picturing their faces, hearing their voices in my mind, made me feel sick and conflicted. I'd loved them and they'd betrayed me so horribly. "And I'm sorry, but I can't…I can't go back there, not even in my mind, all right? I can't. Not yet."

She put her hand on my arm, and just her touch was soothing. I let out a sigh. "Let's start fresh, Eden. Let's leave all that behind, at least for now. You don't need it anymore. I'll help you take it down."

"No. Not yet. I'll do it in my own time, but not yet." She motioned to the bottom of the board. "But I can take all this down. It was my attempt to locate Kristi so I could find Xander."

I glanced at the lists, some items crossed off, notes next to others. It looked like they were names of colleges printed from the internet. My heart squeezed with both sorrow and pride. And I understood that this project was her attempt to grasp a small modicum of control in a world where everything felt confusing and unsteady. Maybe it wasn't my place to suggest that she give it up now. She'd always sought knowledge, hadn't she? And in the end, it'd saved her life. I grabbed Eden and squeezed her to me again, putting the overwhelmingly fierce love for her into that embrace. *Morning Glory. Morning Glory.*

When we let go of each other, she shut her closet door. "I'll take care of that later," she said. "For now, take me on a date, Calder Raynes. It will be my first, you know."

"I'm all your firsts," I whispered, "and all your lasts."

She smiled. "And I'm all your firsts."

I felt a stab of pain at the fact that she wasn't all my *only*s anymore. Another thing I'd have to learn to forgive myself for. And I only hoped she'd be able to as well. "Come on," I said, taking her hand. "Oh, and grab some socks."

We descended the stairs, listening to the low hum of voices still coming from the garden. I had borrowed Xander's truck, so I didn't have to drive Eden around on my motorcycle. Plus I didn't even own one helmet, much less two, and there was no way on earth I'd ever risk Eden's safety. And suddenly, I was a little more concerned about my own. I squeezed Eden's hand as I helped her up into the truck, the feeling of disbelief sweeping over me for the millionth time. I rounded the truck and climbed into the driver's seat, turning the ignition.

"It's so odd to see you behind the wheel of a vehicle," she said, flashing me a quick smile.

I chuckled. "I know what you mean. Do you drive?" I asked as I pulled onto the street.

She shook her head. "I haven't yet but Molly offered to teach me."

I nodded. "I'm impressed that you learned how to use a computer," I said, thinking about all the detailed research she'd done on Acadia.

"I saved up for one and bought a laptop about six months

ago. I realized if I was going to find Xander, I'd need one. Calling around places was getting me nowhere."

"Did you call the ranger station?"

"Yes. That's how I got Kristi's last name. But they wouldn't tell me what school she went to—if they even knew, but I figured they did." I saw her shrug in my peripheral vision. "For all they knew, I was some weirdo." She paused. "I was so paranoid to even call there. It's so hard not knowing exactly how things work…what's safe and what's not. Sometimes I still feel paralyzed with fear." She ended on a whisper. "A computer seemed safer than the phone, more anonymous."

I reached over and took her hand.

"Anyway," she went on, "I do other online research too. And I read. I've been learning about politics, religions— trying to understand what different people believe, what feels right to me."

I made a small snorting sound. "How can you believe in anything anymore?" We'd been lied to our entire lives.

She was quiet for a minute, and I felt the weight of her eyes on me in the dim interior. "Sometimes I don't. I'm still working on that too."

"What else do you research?" I asked, to change the subject.

"Um, all kinds of things. Just trying to understand the big…I mean, the world. You know."

"Yes, I do know. Xander keeps trying to get me to buy a computer—and open a Facebook account. He tells me about it. Of course he uses a take on his name—Zander with a Z or something—because he's paranoid too."

"Of Clive Richter," she guessed accurately.

I nodded, frowning. It seemed that the terror of Clive

Richter finding us had been our constant companion over the past few years, dictating so much of what we did and didn't do. I wasn't even sure what he *could* do to us now, but I refused to find out. "Xander seemed upset he could never participate in this 'Throwback Thursday' thing, where you post pictures from the past, because he'll never have any of those." I attempted a chuckle that died a quick death. Xander had actually seemed bothered by it.

"Do *you* care about that at all?" Eden asked. "I mean, for yourself?"

Did I care about not having one single photo or keepsake from my childhood? I thought about it for a second as I pulled into the bowling alley parking lot, switched off the engine, and leaned back in my seat. "Not really." On a list of things that caused me heartache, that one didn't even make the top twenty.

She watched me for a couple beats and then nodded. "And who are Xander's Facebook friends exactly?" she asked with a raise of her brow.

I chuckled. "I don't know, guys he works with maybe? The women he sees. There are definitely enough of those." I stared out the front windshield. Xander had his own way of coping with the demons that haunted him and the loneliness I knew he struggled with.

"I went on Facebook looking for Kristi, actually, but it didn't pan out," she said after a moment. "I thought about opening an account, but at the time I figured I'd just be 'Eden No Last Name' and my status update would always be the same—*Life sucks, feeling suicidal.* I didn't think I'd get a whole lot of friend requests."

I let out a burst of laughter and then tried to suck it back because what she said was terrible but I could also tell it was true. But when I glanced over at her, she had a small amused smirk on her face and so I grinned and then laughed harder.

She laughed too, until we were both laughing so hard that tears were in my eyes and she was doubled forward.

The laughter brought on a huge surge of unexpected emotion that hit me like a tidal wave. I leaned forward on the steering wheel and continued to laugh until I realized there were tears running down my cheeks and my laughter had turned to shaking.

"Come here," Eden said, and I could hear the tears in her voice too.

I moved over on the seat and grabbed her to me so tightly that she sucked in a breath. How long would it be that our emotions would bounce from one extreme to the other? How long until I wasn't vibrating with the fear that she'd be taken from me all over again? "I missed you so much. So fucking much," I choked out. "Oh God, Eden, my Eden. Oh my God, I wanted to die without you." I tried to hold the tears back, but something had taken over—maybe the laughter had broken yet another dam of long-suppressed grief. I didn't know. But I was helpless to stop it and so I just gripped her to me and inhaled her comforting scent and cried like a damn baby into her chest as she stroked my back. I felt her tears hitting the back of my neck. It was the first time I'd cried since Xander dragged me off that roof.

We clutched each other for what seemed like a very long time until my heart slowed to a steady beat and I listened in awe and thankfulness to the sound of hers under my ear. "Just for the record," I finally mumbled, "this is not how first dates are supposed to go."

Eden laughed softly and then sniffled, kissing the top of

130

my head. "No, in general circumstances, this would not be a good beginning."

I chuckled too and then sat up. Eden leaned forward and kissed my cheeks, rubbing her face against my own so that our tears mingled. She smiled against my mouth and then kissed me lightly. We kissed gently for a few minutes, me sucking her bottom lip between my own and nibbling at her mouth. It was slow and gentle and soothing to my soul.

After a few minutes of that, my blood started to heat to a point that wasn't going to be comfortable parked in Xander's truck in a public parking lot. So I pulled away and scooted back over to my side of the truck. I looked over at Eden who was wiping away the last of her tears.

"This is going to take some time before it feels like reality," I said. "It's going to take a while before I have a handle on my own damn emotions."

"You don't have to explain it to me, Calder."

I nodded, looking out the windshield. Of course she understood and it was a blessed relief. I'd always had Xander, who got it more than most people could. But he also hadn't lost the love of his life the day he lost everything else.

But now you have her back. The love of your life is sitting right next to you.

I reached over and grabbed her hand, that same tremulous joy I had felt at her mom's party filling my heart. "This seems like as good a time as any to make some bowling memories."

She laughed. "Will there be nachos?"

"Hell no, there won't be nachos."

She laughed again and we got out of the truck and walked into the bowling alley together. Fifteen minutes later, we had bowling shoes on and were directed to our own lane.

As I typed our information into the computer, Eden went about finding a bowling ball. When I finished, I stood, looking around for Eden. I didn't immediately spot her and my heart sped up, blood pumping faster. I swiveled my head everywhere, panic setting in. "Eden!" I called. Several people glanced at me curiously. I jumped up on one of the chairs to get a better view over the tops of people's heads and called Eden's name again a little louder.

A guy at the lane to my right said, "You missing a kid?"

"No, my…" My words trailed off as a blond head came into view, Eden turning the corner of a shelf of bowling balls and walking toward me. The smile on her face faltered when she saw me standing on the chair, probably looking panic-stricken. I hopped down and raced toward her, exhaling and pulling her to me, the bowling ball she held colliding with my stomach. I didn't care. I held her for a minute, allowing my heart rate to return to normal.

"Whoa," she whispered, "are you okay?"

"Yeah, sorry. It's just, I turned around and you weren't there, and—"

"I get it," she interrupted, giving me a sympathetic smile. "Sorry. I couldn't find a ball that I could even lift. I just went around the corner." She pressed her lips together momentarily. "It will get better for both of us. I know it will."

I nodded and we returned to our lane. God, I hoped it would get better. Would I ever stop immediately assuming the worst when she wasn't right where I expected her to be?

Eden sat down, and I noticed that the guy in the next lane was staring suspiciously at me. Yeah, I probably looked like a nutjob, panicking because my girlfriend turned a corner out of sight. Oh well, he didn't know a thing about what we'd been through.

"You're up," Eden said.

I picked up my ball and walked toward the lane and lined up my shot like I'd seen countless other people do as Xander and I had sat shoveling free nachos into our hungry bodies. If someone had told me then I'd be the one bowling, *with Eden*, a couple years later, I would have punched them in the face for making such a cruel joke.

I stepped forward and let the ball go. It glided down the lane, making a sharp turn at the end and knocking over the one pin to the far left. Well, one was better than zero. "Yes!" I said as I turned around and walked toward Eden.

"I don't think that's actually very good. You got one pin," she noted.

I gave her a wink, determined to make this a decent first date. "Yeah"—I leaned in and kissed her quickly on her smiling mouth—"but things can only go up from here."

"Or you could get a gutter ball next."

"Very pessimistic. I won't."

Her brows went up. "How can you be so sure?"

"Because I learn from my mistakes." Then I picked up the ball the machine spit out, strode up to the lane, and lined up my shot. Only this time, I started the ball all the way at the very right edge of the lane so that when it made the sharp turn at the end, it hit the center pin and they all went flying. *Spare!*

I heard Eden whoop behind me and turned around to her grinning and clapping. I laughed, and when I got to where she was sitting, I picked her up and spun her once and then kissed her hard, registering the music playing softly over the sound system. "Dance with me," I mumbled into her hair after I'd broken from her mouth.

She looked off behind me, obviously hearing the music

too. The lyrics sang of loss and something about all of the stars, which seemed apropos. "Since when do you know how to dance?" she asked teasingly. I opened my mouth to speak, but then closed it, not wanting to bring Madison up. Her face fell slightly and she said, "Oh," as her eyes darted away from mine.

I took my fingers and put them under her chin, turning her face back to mine. "I've never danced with *you*. I want to change that. It feels very important that we change that."

"I'll probably step all over your feet."

"That's okay," I said, taking her in my arms and pulling her close.

Our bodies started to sway to the music, the boisterous noise of the bowling alley fading away for me as the song seemed to rise in volume and it was only me and her, our bodies moving as one, her sweet softness pressed against me.

"Come home with me, Eden," I whispered into her hair.

She leaned back, her deep blue eyes looking up at me with love and tenderness as she nodded. Joy pulsed through my body. We continued dancing until the song ended and then got back to our game. We laughed and had fun through the next nine frames. Eden was even a pretty good bowler after she got the hang of it. Mostly though, I just enjoyed sitting back and watching her have fun. Other than that long-ago game of kick the can, I'd never had the privilege of watching Eden *play*. And I vowed right then and there, that I was going to give as much of this to her as I possibly could. It was going to be my life's goal to make up for everything she'd lost.

As we were getting ready to go and changing shoes, a little girl around three or four ran by, giggling and being chased by her mother who was laughing too, and calling,

"Get back here, you!" I smiled and looked over at Eden and was surprised by the look of sorrow on her face. *Oh.* She seemed to catch herself as her expression brightened and she looked down to adjust the shoe she was putting on.

"Eden," I said softly, sitting down next to her and taking her hand. "I know. They told me about the baby. Someone slipped me a note while I was in the cell in Acadia."

Tears sprung to her eyes and she released a whoosh of breath. "I wasn't going to say anything. I didn't want you to have to carry that too."

"My Morning Glory," I whispered. "I'm so sorry you endured that. It killed me to imagine what you must have gone through." I let out a breath, attempting to compose myself, to be strong for her. Truthfully though, I still felt rage at what had been taken from us. And conflicted despair at the fact that the people who had done the taking were already dead. "We'll remember that small life together, and someday when we're ready, we'll make another."

Her shoulders sagged. "Calder," she started, my name seeming to catch in her throat.

"What is it?" I asked, squeezing her hand.

Eden took a deep breath. "When I first came to Cincinnati, I had a lot of pain and Marissa took me to a doctor and…he told me that I have scarring from the miscarriage. Hector gave me some kind of tea and it…" She gave her head a shake. "The doctor didn't think there was much chance I could get pregnant ever again." Her anguished eyes met mine. "I can't have any more babies."

Her words hit me like a body blow. "No," I choked out.

"I'm sorry," she said. "I shouldn't have told you now. It's just—"

I pulled her against me and gripped the back of her head

with one hand. "We'll get a second opinion when we're ready, or we'll adopt, or"—I shook my head and kissed her temple—"whatever you want."

Eden gripped my shirt. "Okay."

We held each other for a few minutes longer before she sat back. "My sweet Morning Glory. You've been carrying that around all this time too?" I asked.

She released a shuddery breath. "I had made peace with it," she said very quietly. "Before…" She trailed off.

I moved a piece of hair off her cheek, suddenly understanding her reaction to the condom I'd worn the night before—or at least, the true depth of her emotions where that was concerned.

She looked away for a second and then back to my eyes. "This date is really all over the place, isn't it?" she asked on a thin laugh.

"That might just be us for a little while."

"Us," she said softly, a light coming into her eyes that hadn't been there a moment before.

"Yeah. Us," I repeated, smiling. I took her hand and pulled her to her feet. "Now let's get us home."

We drove to my apartment mostly in silence, the radio playing softly. I only lived about ten minutes away. When we entered my apartment, the city lights glowed outside and the entire place was bathed in soft light. I really did love this place, despite the fact that there was still no electricity. I loved the open feel of it, the view, but most of all, I took pride in the fact that I'd done the hard work to fix it up myself. The project had been a distraction and a form of therapy. I'd not only gained skills I hadn't had before, but I'd discovered what I liked and what I didn't—what made a space feel like my own. I'd picked out and installed the new hardwood floors,

I'd chosen the countertops I'd liked best and learned how to hang cabinets. Even though I didn't actually own it, it was the first thing that felt like mine.

Eden put her purse down and glanced at me shyly as though she wasn't quite sure what to do from here. A flash of her standing under moonlight staring at me in the same way skittered through my mind, bringing not grief as it had these past few years but a warm happiness and a sense of deep gratitude.

CHAPTER EIGHT
Eden

"I have something to show you," Calder said, taking my hand.

I looked at him curiously, but he just smiled and led me down the hall and then into a semismall bedroom, the only furniture a big bed against the far wall. "What am I looking at?" I asked.

"That," he said, pointing at the bed with the gray and white striped comforter and a few pillows. "I bought it for us today. All the bedding too." He walked over to it and pulled the comforter back to reveal light gray and purple flowers on the other side. "It's reversible," he said. "You can put it on whatever side you like better."

My heart flipped in my chest. *Sweet man.* "Calder," I said, joining him where he stood. "This is your house. You should pick what you like."

"I want it to be your house too," he said quietly. "I want my home to be your home, my bed to be your bed. I want your nighttime heat to be within arm's reach."

Those words. Oh. *Oh.* My knees felt suddenly weak and I gasped out a breath. "Our letters," I said.

He smiled so softly. "Please move in here. Live with me. Let me protect you. Not just for tonight but for always. We've spent enough time apart, Eden. Too much."

God, I loved him. But I felt uncertain too, at least on this front. "I want to. I do. I don't ever want to be apart from you again. It's just…you were living in another woman's house yesterday and I worry…I worry that us moving too quickly will be more a reaction out of desperation than rationale." I met his gaze. "I want to ensure that we start on solid ground. And it might be wise to take some time to…be sure about the way you feel," I finished.

"The way I feel? About you?"

I nodded. I felt vulnerable bringing it up again after he'd reassured me earlier that he still loved me. That he'd chosen me. But wasn't it smart to take it slow? To allow reality to settle?

"Then ask me," Calder said, his voice raspy. "Eden, just ask me. All you ever have to do is ask me. I will always tell you the truth."

Tears pricked my eyes. I could see the conviction in his expression and hear the intensity in his voice and both worked to put me at ease. "Do you still love me, Calder? Am I the only woman you want? Are you certain?"

"God, yes," he said before I'd even finished the last word. "There isn't a question in my mind, no doubt in my heart. I want you, and only you, then, now, forever."

I sucked in a shaky breath. "I feel the same way."

"I never stopped loving you. I never will. Ever."

My muscles relaxed and I wiped the tears from my eyes. "Do you think we're making a mistake rushing back into this too quickly? We've been through a lot and we've both changed in ways good and bad… Plus, we have issues."

He considered me for a moment. "It's because I cried on our first date, and then almost called security when you went to get a bowling ball, isn't it?"

I let out a wobbly laugh and then laughed harder when he gave me a lopsided grin. God, he was adorable—gorgeous—ridiculously beautiful. And I loved him so much. My gaze landed on the bed with the new bedding, a tag still hanging off the edge. He had bought it all as a gift to me, just today, not only as a place to sleep, but as a declaration that he wanted me in his life. That he wanted to wake to me each morning and close our eyes together every night.

"The thing is, we *are* both desperate…still hurting, probably needy." Calder paused. "No, *definitely* needy. I was dead yesterday, Eden. I was trying to live, I was. But now you're back, and I'm suddenly *alive*." His eyes filled with that wonder I'd seen off and on since that miraculous moment in the gallery when we'd first seen each other again. "I don't want to waste time 'figuring things out.' They'll be obstacles to face, but I want to do it together. You and me, side by side. I don't need time. I need you. You're all I've ever needed."

I opened my mouth to speak, but Calder cut me off. "And before you say anything, there's something you should know about this bed. It's not just an ordinary bed." He tipped his chin toward it. "No, this here is…uh…" He smiled suddenly as if something had just occurred to him. "The Bed of Healing. This bed here has the power to heal the hurt, the pain, and soothe the desperation inside of us. But we'll need to stay in it for quite a while, until we feel like we can leave each other's presence without experiencing a sick feeling of dread that the other person will disappear again. We'll need to stay in it until we've made up at least a little bit of the time we've lost. And once that's done, and we're both more levelheaded, then you can decide whether or not you'll move in with me."

I laughed softly, shaking my head. "The Bed of Healing? Really?"

Calder nodded again, his smile fading. "It's worth a try, isn't it?"

I glanced at the bed. "We definitely could use some healing."

"Are you saying I can take you to bed now?"

I nodded slowly and he brushed my bangs away from my eyes, his gaze warm. "You realize you might be here for quite some time, working through our...issues. Do you need to clear your schedule?"

"I don't have a schedule. But I should text my mom so she doesn't worry."

"Okay."

My gaze darted to his beautifully shaped lips and a shiver moved through me. The air around us seemed to thicken and charge. We had had sex the night before, but this was different. This was *going* to be different. We were going to take our time. We had a *bed*. *Our bed*. A thrill ran along my nerve endings, causing another shiver. "Be right back," I said.

I hurried out to my purse and quickly texted my mom. I felt like a little girl, checking in, but it was only polite, and I didn't ever want to cause her one more minute of pain than she'd already experienced over me in her lifetime. She deserved to know I was safe.

When I got back to Calder's room, I heard him in the

master bathroom. I sat down on the bed and waited, feeling suddenly very nervous and unsure.

Calder came out with no shirt on and rubbing a towel on his neck. My eyes moved slowly over his muscular chest and arms, down to his ridged stomach and lower, to that sparse trail of hair. I knew right where that led. I swallowed heavily, my body alert, alive, as I fidgeted with the edge of the comforter. The last time I had really looked at him naked, he had barely been a man. He was twenty-two now, and he had filled out in ways that made my stomach clench and a steady buzz begin between my legs.

"There's a candle in the bathroom if you need to use it," he said. "Sorry, I didn't get to the electricity today."

"Well, you were shopping for healing beds," I said softly, my gaze still trained on his chest. When I finally dragged my eyes to his, one side of his lips was quirked.

I let out an embarrassed exhale as I stood and then moved around him to the bathroom, scurrying faster when I felt the heat of his body so close to mine. *Get ahold of yourself, Eden. This is Calder. Not some stranger.* Only in some ways that was exactly what he was.

I closed the door to the bathroom and stood against it for a minute, taking deep breaths. A single candle was flickering on the counter, casting the bathroom in a dim glow, and I simply stood there for a moment watching the flame jump.

Calder was right; we didn't have to decide anything right now. Didn't we owe it to ourselves to try to work through the feeling of desperate neediness and surrealism that I, at least, hadn't been able to shake since I'd walked into that gallery? It'd only been a day since we'd found out we were both still alive, but was there really a good reason to force ourselves to stay apart? I wanted him, and he still wanted me.

Did it need to be more complicated than that? Wasn't that rational enough?

I used the bathroom and freshened up, using his toothpaste on my finger to brush my teeth, and then I blew out the candle, took a deep breath, and walked back into the bedroom.

Calder was sitting on the bed and the light in the room was flickering with candlelight now too, as he had closed the blinds and the light from the city outside was no longer shining in.

I walked toward him slowly, and when I got to where he was sitting, he pulled me closer, laying his head on my stomach. I ran my hands through his hair, acquainting myself with the feel of his longer strands. It was thick and silky and almost black in the candlelit room. Calder turned his face into my stomach and inhaled, running his hands up over my backside and then down again. He tipped his head and brought his hands around to the front and put them under my shirt, his warm palms grazing the sensitive skin of my rib cage. He lifted the hem slightly, his eyes meeting mine, his expression a mixture of relief and desire and *love*. I took the hem from his fingers and lifted my shirt the rest of the way and tossed it on the floor.

He gripped my waist and then brought one of his hands around to my back again, running his fingers up my spine, pressing gently on each vertebra as if every tiny part was further proof of my existence. Tenderness swelled in my heart and I drew in a quick breath.

If the night before had been about testing the sturdiness— the *reality* of our bodies—this night was about taking in the details, investigating each swell and ridge—the miracle of fingertips, and hip bones, and shoulder blades, the beauty of lips, the curve of an ear, the hollow at the base of a throat. We explored each place slowly and reverently, with hands and lips and tongues, until I was dizzy with desire and bursting with love and thankfulness.

He pressed his lips to mine firmly and I opened them for him so he could slide his tongue inside. We kissed slowly and deeply, finding our rhythm once again. *Oh God, I missed this.*

Blood pumped quickly through my veins and a throb of need beat between my legs. I pressed into Calder's heat and moaned into his mouth. He broke from me, looking slightly drugged, then reached around and unhooked my bra. It fell to the floor and Calder brought his hands to my breasts, my nipples already pebbled. I gasped when he brought his thumbs to them and circled the tender, aching buds. It felt heavenly and torturous and I tilted my head back as the throbbing in my core increased.

Suddenly Calder's heat moved away from me and I blearily watched as he kicked his shoes aside and pulled off his pants. He was wearing white briefs, the outline of his erection pressing against the thin cotton. I stared at the covered bulge. The look of the full, heavily strained material made my mouth go dry. "I like you in underwear," I said, and he chuckled softly.

I hooked my thumbs in the side of the fabric and pulled them down. He sprang free and I swallowed. I liked him out of underwear too.

"What's funny?" he whispered.

I shook my head. I hadn't even realized I'd laughed. "I just can't believe we're here, that you're real, that you wear underwear," I said.

"I don't have to wear underwear if you don't like it." His voice was gentle, filled with a warm humor as though he understood what I was saying and was teasing me just a little.

I laughed again but it sounded strangely distant. "No, I like you in underwear. That's not what—"

"I know, Eden." He leaned in and kissed me and I put my hands on his shoulders as I kicked off my shoes. After I'd broken from his mouth to pull off my jeans and my own underwear, we both stood before the other, completely naked.

"You're exquisite," Calder whispered. "More beautiful than in my dreams."

We got in bed together, our bodies meeting under the blankets. Our hands wandered as our tongues met and my fingers brushed down Calder's stomach, grazing over his tight, ridged muscles. They contracted under my touch and he groaned into my mouth. "Do you like that?" I asked. I needed to know. We'd only just begun to know each other intimately before we were torn apart and I desperately wanted to know how to bring him pleasure.

"Yes. God, yes. Your hands on me...it's making me crazy."

I explored every dip, going over the spots that made him press his head back into the pillow and groan. I loved the sounds he made and the way he bit his lip, his brow creasing as though he was focusing on not climaxing from my touch alone.

After a few minutes, he rolled and came on top of me and I laughed, a chuckle that turned into a sigh as his warm, bare skin pressed against mine, my softness giving way to the hard planes of his body.

He met my eyes as his hand moved downward until it hovered just over the spot where I pulsed with desire, needing him to touch me. When he hesitated, I pressed myself upward and I felt him smile against my mouth as he kissed me. "Tease," I whispered, lifting my lips from his, and then, "Oooh," as he dipped his finger inside me and used his thumb to massage the small bundle of tender nerves. "Calder," I gasped. "I can't...I—"

"I know." And if the strain in his voice was any indication, he did.

He used the head of his penis to circle against me, and we both moaned into each other's mouths. His chest was rubbing against my nipples and my body felt deliciously achy, and tingly, and beautifully needy. Because need *could* be a beautiful thing if you knew another person wanted very much to meet those needs. And what I needed right that moment was for him to be inside of me. It felt like life or death that I be connected to him in every way possible. I reached down to guide him to my opening, but he beat me to it, lining himself up and surging inside. The feeling was so immediately *full* and blissfully intense that I arched backward on a cry of pleasure.

Calder began to move very slowly, moaning out my name as I rubbed my hands up and down his body, relishing the feel of his warm skin, his *size*, his perfect maleness moving over and inside me. My body melted beneath his and my heartbeat pulsed between my legs where he was pressing in and out of me in the perfect rhythm. I gasped as bright-white pleasure pulsed through my core and caused my toes to curl as I gripped the sheet beneath me.

Oh God, oh God, oh God.

"Eden, Eden," Calder was moaning as his thrusts grew faster, more powerful. "I love you. Oh God, I love you so much." He pounded inside me for a few more strokes and then he froze, and his expression contorted in a look of overwhelming pleasure. I watched him fall apart, spellbound. His lips parted on a final groan as he circled his hips slowly and then opened his eyes.

"You were made for me," I said quietly, as I gazed up at his beloved face. I remembered thinking it the first time we were together, and I thought it now.

Calder smiled as he rolled to the side. "Yes," he said. "I was. And you were made for me."

We spent the rest of that night clinging to each other, running our hands over each other's bodies, reacquainting ourselves with and memorizing each part of the other, discovering the many ways in which we still fit together so perfectly.

We whispered the words of love and devotion that we still felt, reassured each other this was real and true, and that we'd never be separated again. Our souls clung to each other as much as our bodies did. And yes, there was healing.

At some point in the night, I heard Calder cry out in his sleep and realized we'd drifted apart in the bed. I scooted over to him and ran my hand over his hair, whispering his name softly. We'd blown the candle out, so the room was dark, but I could still see the tense expression on his face. His eyes flew open and he blinked around in confusion before his gaze landed on me and relief filled his expression. He blew out a long breath as he gathered me in his arms. "They live behind my eyes, Eden," he whispered. "Each one of them. I see them; I hear them; I feel their fear and their horror. I *feel* it. Every night."

"What makes it better?" I asked in the darkness.

He sighed and gripped his hair in his hand. "Sleeping on the floor helps sometimes. Maybe because that's how I slept as a child. It comforts me, I guess."

"Then let's move to the floor."

"I don't want you to sleep on the floor."

"I don't want you to hurt."

Calder squeezed me to him tighter. "You're here. I'll be okay because you're here. And tonight I won't make myself picture each of them, one by one. I won't torture myself."

"Why do you do that?" I asked. "You don't have to do that."

"All these years, I've felt like I deserved it. I've felt like, if I got to live, then it was my duty to keep hurting for them."

"And for me?" I asked softly.

He shook his head in the darkness. "No. It was different with you. With you, my greatest fear was that I would start forgetting you…the details of you. It tortured me. It *tortured* me," he rasped. He turned toward me, and his eyes moved over my face in the near darkness of the room.

"And so you painted me?"

"Yes, I painted you."

I leaned forward and kissed him hard on his beautiful mouth, overwhelmed with my love for him. "I love you, I love you," I chanted between kisses. "I know the goodness in you, Calder. I do, more than anyone. I know the tenderness of your heart, and I know all that was taken from you. I know the awful sorrow inside of you. I live it too. I know. I *know*. But I also believe we are going to be okay—we are going to love so hard and with so much intensity that it's going to melt away all the pain. And if now and again, the grief comes back to haunt us, then we'll come back here, to the Bed of Healing. And we'll spend as much time as we need just escaping from the world. That's our plan because I swear to you, my beautiful, sweet love, everyone deserves a love story that doesn't hurt."

Calder let out a loud exhale of breath and leaned his forehead against mine. "Even us?"

"Yes. I promise you. Even us."

And that's how we fell asleep, wrapped around each other, love filling the room, and Calder didn't wake up again until the next morning when I felt him pressing against me, his morning heat right within arm's reach.

———————

We spent three days in that bed. Three days telling each other about the time we'd spent apart, three days talking about our many fears and hurts and the things that were the hardest to move past. We created our own little world with nothing but bodies and hearts and whispers and truth.

We had both spent so much time grieving for each other that we hadn't taken the time to grieve for ourselves— for what we had endured that day, for the horrors we had seen, for the guilt we each carried. And so in that bed, we exorcised those demons still in our hearts by speaking of them and setting them free.

I kissed his legs, the scars still visible from the torture Hector had inflicted on him. I rubbed my lips over the larger scar on the side of his thigh where he had been shot. Hurt moved through me, but just as I'd promised all those years ago, so did pride.

Our innocence had been destroyed that terrible, terrible day. Our hope had been stolen. But neither of us had seen what the aftermath looked like for the other person. And there was grief in the discovery just as sure as there was pride in the evidence of our survival. A part of me rejoiced and a part of me mourned, and I thought that was as it should be.

I moved up his body and we both forgot about scars

and hurts and felt only pleasure—only the meeting of our bodies—and all the ways in which we were still very much whole and very much alive.

We only got up to use the bathroom, brush our teeth, and for me to text my mom and Molly to let them know I was still with Calder. But even after those few minutes, a small feeling of fear and loss would descend and I'd practically run back to Calder. Almost every time, he would be out of bed and on his way to me too. We weren't ready just yet. To me, being with him in a place that was warm and safe and private felt like a miracle. And who would be eager to leave the scene of a miracle?

We grabbed what food Calder had in his kitchen and ate it in bed—bread with peanut butter, raisins, half a bag of corn chips. We made do. On the second day, Calder said he was going to go out and get us some real food, but after getting dressed and kissing me goodbye and walking out of the bedroom, I started feeling anxious and so I got up to tell him not to go. I met him at the doorway to the bedroom, coming back. He wasn't ready to leave yet either. He grabbed a can of peaches from the kitchen, opened it, and brought it to bed. We undressed and fed each other peaches with our fingers, sticky syrup dripping on our skin. Calder grinned wickedly and dribbled more of it on my nipples and licked every bit off until I was writhing and moaning and begging him for more than that. When we were both fed and satisfied, I asked jokingly, "How much sex do you think you can have?" Because there had been a lot, and Calder was not a small man; my own body was deliciously sore and achy.

Calder turned toward me, his cheeks still flushed from the workout of minutes before, looking beautifully happy.

"Well, I'm young and healthy, and I'm desperately in love with the woman in my bed. *So, a lot.*"

I laughed.

The Bed of Healing felt holy—as if, in it, we had been reborn somehow. And every second was precious to two people who knew the next breath was never guaranteed.

"Eden," Calder asked. "You said you've been studying religions. Why?" He was looking at me, as if my answer mattered very much to him. In this way, Calder hadn't changed. I wondered how many had possibly fallen a little in love with him over the years, because his quiet intensity and unwavering ability to listen was probably one of his finest attributes. Rare in a boy, and possibly even rarer in a man.

I thought about his question. "I guess…I guess I just want to figure out what feels right to me, you know? Not what feels right to anyone else, but to *me*. What kind of *god* feels right to me."

"And what have you figured out?"

"I don't know yet. I'm still working on it. All I know is that just like love, God shouldn't hurt." I sighed. "That's really all I've figured out so far."

He frowned up at the ceiling. "I'm not working on it," he said. "I have no desire to worship a god or gods who looked down and watched what happened in Acadia without intervening. They did nothing to help."

I'd thought the very same thought a million times over. "They brought the rain," I finally said.

Calder was quiet for a minute. "If they did, then they also watched Hailey's four little boys die a terror-filled death they didn't deserve. They watched thirty-seven children under the age of ten as their small lungs filled up with water and they flailed and asked the gods why they weren't helping them. They were far more innocent than me. The gods ignored *their* cries." He looked over at me. "The littlest one of Hailey's boys, he still sucked his thumb, Eden. He still sucked his thumb. How can I believe in any power that would allow that to happen? I can't."

"I don't know. I don't understand it either."

After a minute of each of us lost in our own thoughts, I said, "I will tell you this though. In those last moments, in the midst of the screaming and the terror, I heard mothers comforting their children. I heard words of love drifting to me through the walls." I paused, remembering, hearing the whispers in my mind. "In those last moments, yes, there was horror and there was fear. But there was also love. As unimaginable as it is, Calder, there was love in that room. And maybe…maybe that's where God was."

Calder remained silent, but he pulled me to him and held me tightly.

On the third morning, we woke up and Calder wrapped himself around me like he did every morning. He hadn't woken up from a nightmare in two nights now and he looked happy and rested and beautifully messy.

"Mmm," he murmured, pressing his nose against the back of my neck. "You smell good." His voice was deliciously gravelly. I loved his morning voice.

I laughed softly. "I'm sure I *don't*."

He shook his head, rubbing his nose against my shoulder. "You do. You smell like my woman."

"We should really take a shower," I whispered. Although in truthfulness, I loved the way he smelled too, even though he was sweaty and dirty and unshowered. I could have stuck my nose in his armpit and inhaled happily. It was one of those very human things that was sort of sexy and sort of gross at the same time.

Calder was quiet for a minute. "I guess. Are we going to get out of the Bed of Healing?"

"Do you feel healed?"

He kissed my shoulder blade, rubbing his lips against it, taking time to consider my question. "I think I do, yeah. Enough to function somewhat normally anyway. How about you?"

I nodded and pulled his arm around me tighter. "I think I do too."

Calder sighed. "I'm going to miss this bed."

I grinned and looked back over my shoulder at him. "Well, we're still going to *sleep* in it. We're just not going to *live* in it anymore."

He groaned. "I liked living in it."

"Me too."

"So does that mean you'll move in with me?" he asked.

"Yes," I said. "I'll move in with you."

"Thank you," he said, and I heard the smile in his voice.

We snuggled for a little while longer, Calder hardening against my backside. I was sore, but I didn't care. We needed this one last time before we got up and faced the real world again. I wiggled my bottom against him and he sucked in a breath, bringing his hand around to massage me right where I needed it. He made love to me slowly, thrusting into me leisurely from behind while he touched me with his hand. Beams of sunlight filtered in around the shade, casting the whole room in a pale-yellow, magical glow, and Calder's heartbeat surrounded me, against my back and deep inside. We fell over the edge together—me crying out and Calder shuddering behind me—as he circled his hips slowly and gave my shoulder a gentle nip.

"Anything you want," he whispered, kissing the place where his teeth had just been. "If it exists in this world, it's yours."

"Hmm," I hummed. "Anything? Well, there's this painting in a gallery in Paris of a girl with a mysterious smile. I fancy it."

He smiled against my skin. "You fancy it?"

"Mmm," I murmured.

"I fancy *you*," he whispered. "I fancy you a whole lot."

I laughed softly, and he slipped out of me as I turned in his arms and snuggled into his chest.

"I'd like to string some stars together and hang them right above this bed," I said.

"I'll build a ladder," he told me. "I'll climb up and I'll lasso a few for you."

I laughed and then we both startled as a knock sounded loudly at his front door, the sound echoing through his mostly empty apartment.

"Should we answer?" I whispered.

"No," Calder groaned.

"I thought we were getting up. Maybe this will be a good way to force us out of bed."

Calder chuckled but then the pounding started up again. "What the hell?" he said, getting up and grabbing some jeans.

I sat up and pulled the sheet up against me as Calder left the room. Then I got up and went to use the bathroom and quickly brush my teeth.

I dressed quickly and then pulled the sheet and comforter up on the bed when I heard male voices outside the bedroom and went out to see what was going on.

When I walked out to the large living area, Calder was standing with his arms crossed against his bare chest and Xander was leaning against the counter, raking his hand through his hair. His eyes were red-rimmed and he looked like he hadn't slept a wink.

"Hey, Xander," I said haltingly.

He gave me a fleeting smile. "Hey, E."

I joined Calder who put his arm around me. Xander smiled at us. "I knew you two would work it all out."

"What's wrong?" I asked, ignoring his comment and focusing on him. He looked terrible.

He blew out a breath. "I'm sorry," he said. "I didn't come here to interrupt this reunion. Shit. You guys don't need this. You deserve—"

"Xander," Calder said. "Whatever I have—"

"I have half. I know," he finished.

Calder looked at me. "You know what Xander needs, right?"

I widened my eyes. "You can't be serious."

"I am. This appears to be a desperate situation."

I glanced at Xander. "It does appear…at least semidesperate."

"There's only one sure fix."

I sighed. "The Bed of Healing."

"I'm afraid so."

Calder let go of me, and I grabbed Xander's arm and pulled him along behind us to the bedroom.

"Whoa! Where are you taking me? This sounds… creepy."

"To the Bed of Healing," Calder said as we entered the room.

"I don't think—"

"Don't think. Just get in." I pulled Xander and he stumbled and fell onto the bed. Calder and I plopped down on either side of him, and we lay there on top of the comforter staring up at the ceiling.

I giggled and Xander turned his head to Calder and then to me, finally staring back up at the ceiling. "I'm not having sex with either one of you," he said, starting to sit up. Calder brought his arm straight down on Xander's chest and Xander fell back down with an *oof.* "Okay, maybe Eden, but definitely not you, *Storm,*" he added.

"Don't even let your mind go there," Calder instructed, an edge to his voice.

I laughed.

"I thought this was the Bed of Healing. Already I sense anger here," Xander said.

Calder chuckled and threw a leg over Xander's leg. "No anger," he said. "Only healing. And quit it with the Storm business. You know I couldn't put my real name out there. Storm is a cool name."

Xander laughed. "It sounds like a stripper."

I couldn't help giggling, and after a short pause, Calder laughed too.

We all lay there silently for a minute. It *was* a really comfortable bed. I took Xander's hand in mine and squeezed it.

"The Bed of Healing smells like sex and…*peaches,*" Xander said, wrinkling his nose.

"The Bed of Healing smells just like a bed of healing should," Calder said.

"Dude, when was the last time you showered?" Xander asked.

"Three days ago," Calder answered, sounding proud.

"Yeah, I can tell." Xander scooted closer to me and I gave another short laugh and then turned his way.

"Seriously, Xander, what's wrong?"

He took his hand from mine and dragged it over his dark five-o'clock shadow. "There's this girl," he said.

Calder laughed. I sat up slightly, frowning over at him. "Sorry," he mumbled. "It's just that every story of woe and tragedy throughout history starts out with those exact same three words: 'There's this girl.'" Then he groaned dramatically and threw his hand up over his eyes.

I wanted to disagree but maybe he was right.

"Does she have you all twisted inside out?" Calder asked as he lowered his arm.

"Hell yes," Xander said.

Calder sighed. "Yeah."

"What's the problem here, Xander?" I asked. "You're in love. Does she not love you back or what?"

"*That's* the problem. I think she might."

"Why is that a problem? That's great."

Xander grimaced. "The problem is that I might have totally screwed it up. I'm not ready to love anyone."

"Oh, Xander." I moved closer to him and threw my leg over the top of Calder's.

"No one will ever get it except for you two," he said. "No one understands me. So if I do let myself get closer to this girl, how should I explain the fact that I can only fall asleep on the floor?" he asked. "Or wait, how about this— when she asks me to tell her about my family, I'll say, 'Oh them? Yeah, did you hear about that cult? Acadia? Right, well they were there—they drowned; my mom, my dad, my pregnant sister, dead, all of them. Deal with that. Good luck because I still can't. Oh and these scars on my back? Yeah, that was from the time I was beaten with a whip like a damn dog. You wanna catch a movie tonight?"'

"Xander," I said. "Maybe no one will get it to the extent that we do, but someone will want to hear about what you experienced because they'll want to know you—all of you. The good and the bad. Other people have been through terrible things too. Or if they haven't, they have the compassion to understand people who have been. Give her a chance."

He let out a sigh and continued to stare up at the ceiling. "I still hear his voice in my head," he said. "Like, all the damn time. It's like he *haunts* me."

I grabbed his hand and squeezed it. "I know. I hear it too," I admitted.

Calder cleared his throat and said, "Me too."

We were quiet for a minute. I listened to them breathing right next to me, gratitude filling my heart at their presence alone. We'd not only escaped Acadia with our lives, but we had each other. The miraculous joy of that almost left me breathless. "So, okay, here we are," I said. "Three messed-up people who experienced an awful trauma, but we're alive. I know we have things to work through. But we get a second chance. All those other people who died that day don't get that." I paused, taking in a gulp of air as I pictured the innocent children who'd been robbed of the lives they'd been meant to live. "And so, I don't know"—I lifted up on one elbow and faced the boys—"I for one am going to grab it. If this is the one life we have to live, *if this is it*, then I'm not going to live it being miserable. *Especially* now that I have you two back. What do you say? We'll try our best? Together?"

Calder's smile was soft as he met my eyes. Xander paused but finally murmured, "Yeah."

158

"Agreed," Calder said, reaching across Xander and taking my hand. I smiled at both of them and then laid my head on Xander's chest and wrapped my arm around him and Calder. Calder laid his head on Xander's chest next to mine and wrapped his arm around both of us too. Xander started laughing as we all hugged in the somewhat ridiculously, but still aptly, named Bed of Healing, and there was always healing in laughter and so that bed did its job once again—at least for that moment.

"First step, Xander, is you go to this girl and you tell her where you came from. Share your heart with her if you think she's worthy of that," I said.

Xander sighed. "Okay. I'll do it."

Calder and I rolled onto our backs. "And as for me," I said, "I'm going to claim my name." I paused. "It was stolen from me and I'm going to take it back." Not today, maybe, but I vowed to claim what was mine—what had been taken from me by evil.

"Morning Glory," I heard Calder murmur.

"As for you, Calder Raynes," Xander said, "no more taking your life in your hands. Not only because you found Eden, or because you don't want to leave me alone, but because you recognize that your life is valuable."

Calder paused but then said, "I promise."

"And also, Calder," Xander went on, "if we're all really going to heal, you need to come clean about your strange Coca-Cola hoarding habit. I know you hide it all over your apartment."

"Okay," Calder said slowly, dragging the word out and glancing over at me. "But I don't even drink it."

"Yeah, so, that doesn't actually make it less weird."

I laughed, and after a minute, Calder did too. "All right. It's just this thing I have—"

"Yeah, we're both well aware of all your 'things,'" Xander said, a grin bursting forth. I laughed harder and so did Calder.

"Okay, you two, seriously, time to shower." Xander said when we'd gotten hold of our laughter.

"You're one to talk. You look like something the cat dragged in."

"Fair enough," Xander said.

Calder and I sat up. "Okay, but before showers, let's go get some food. Eden and I haven't eaten properly in three days."

We all got out of bed and Xander ran a hand through his messy hair. "How about you two go get some food while I clean up?" I suggested.

"Are you sure you'll be okay here for half an hour or so?" Calder asked.

I nodded. "Yeah, I'll be fine," I told Calder on a smile. And I felt fine. Stronger. More in control emotionally. Calder smiled back though he appeared slightly unsure. I walked over to him and wrapped my arms around his waist and pulled him close. He squeezed me back and kissed the top of my head, and then he and Xander left the room, closing the door behind them.

Fifteen minutes later, I was showered and feeling like a new person. I was standing in front of the mirror with a towel wrapped around me, brushing the snarls out of my hair, since Calder didn't have any conditioner in his shower when I heard a loud knock on the door.

Had Calder forgotten his key? Or maybe they just had too many take-out bags in their hands to reach for it.

I hurried out of the room and down the hall. "Hold on,"

I called. I swung the door open and Madison was standing there. My smile faded and my cheeks heated as I realized I was just in a towel.

Madison's face blanched. "Oh," she said.

I backed up and pulled the towel more tightly around me. "Sorry," I muttered, "I thought you were Calder."

She glanced away. "So he's not here?"

I shook my head. "He and Xander went out to get food."

She stood staring at me, and I shifted from one foot to the other, still holding my towel in place with one hand and the door with the other. "Um, do you want to come in?" I asked. "He should be home any minute."

Madison frowned but walked in past me, and I shut the door behind her. Well, this was awful. I knew better than anyone how difficult it was not to love Calder. I could understand how hard this must be for her. After all, I had felt that same devastation when I'd realized he had a girlfriend at the gallery.

"Um..."

Madison turned toward me. "I know, this is weird, right?" She gave her head a slight shake. "I won't make it weirder. I just came over to drop off the few things Calder had at my place and to ask him what I should do about the money he earned from his show. He doesn't have a checking account. You probably know that. I planned to pay him in cash, but that was before he sold every painting in one night."

I nodded. Of course he didn't have a checking account. He didn't have any ID. I didn't either. *Yet*. But I'd already vowed to change that.

"You could write the check out to me," I said softly.

Madison seemed to consider that and then shrugged her shoulders. She really was very, very pretty. She had expressive green eyes and dark silky hair that hung straight to her shoulders. She was wearing a tight red skirt with a crisp white blouse and her makeup was perfect. I pulled my towel tightly around me, feeling small and plain, my wet hair sticking to the sides of my face. "I guess I could do that," she finally said.

She set her purse down on Calder's kitchen counter and began rummaging through it.

"My last name is Everson," I told her.

Madison looked up in surprise. "Eden Everson? Seriously? You were the missing girl all over the news when I was just a kid. There were posters of you everywhere around town. It was the first time I learned what a 'missing kid' was."

I swallowed. "Yes, that was me. That *is* me."

"Wow," she said after a short pause. "Why hasn't it been on the news that you're back?"

"We haven't gone to the police yet," I said. "If you could keep it quiet until we do—"

"I won't say anything. I haven't said anything about Calder getting out of Acadia. That's yours to do with what you will. I mean, it's your life."

"Thank you," I said quietly.

She looked down at the checkbook and pen she'd set on the counter, and silently filled the check out as I waited. When she was done, she pushed the check aside and put the checkbook and pen back in her purse, swinging it over her shoulder and turning to me. "Well, that's that. There's a business card under the check. It's a gallery downtown that's interested in him. Clearly, us doing business together isn't a great idea"—her eyes cast downward—"for me at least."

"I'm sorry," I said lamely. "I'm really so grateful to you for being his friend." Her lips twitched into a frown as if barely containing her pain, and I immediately regretted the choice of the word *friend*.

"And for teaching him a few new bedroom tricks?" She laughed coldly. I flinched. Madison grimaced and looked away. "I'm sorry. I said that to be a bitch."

I blew out a breath. "I know this is a really terrible situation for you. I'm sorry for your pain."

"Jesus, you're sweet too," she said. "Of course you would be." She seemed to consider her next words. "Eden, here's the thing: I hoped for more with Calder. I won't lie. This hurts—a lot." She paused. "But I guess if I look back, I can see I pushed him into a relationship with me. We *should* have been just friends. That's what I should have offered him because that's really what he needed. But, Calder...well, you know who Calder is and, Jesus, what he *looks* like." She shrugged. "I wanted him. I thought about myself, not him. And I hope I don't hurt you by saying this, but I should have known when he got up to go *paint* after every time we were...*together* that it was because he felt guilty and needed to be with *you* in some way because of it. I see that now. And it sucks. He wasn't ready to move on. I wish I had realized that at the time, I really do."

I shook my head. "It had been three years. Everyone thought I was dead for God's sake. Encouraging him to move on wasn't the wrong thing to do."

She considered me for a second. "It *was* though. With Calder, it was. I have a feeling he could have lived to be ninety-nine and still not have gotten over you. Treasure that."

I turned my head as she walked past me, some delicate-smelling, flowery perfume wafting by.

When she got to the door, she turned her body halfway toward me but didn't meet my eyes. "You should go look in his studio. I haven't seen what's in there, but I think you should." Then the door closed quietly behind her.

I stood there for a minute, just staring at the closed door. Then I turned and walked to the only door I hadn't been through in his apartment. *It must be his studio.* I took a deep breath and opened it.

CHAPTER NINE
Calder

Xander and I entered my apartment, kicked the door shut behind us, and set the take-out bags on the counter.

There was a check sitting there from Madison's gallery, made out to Eden. My breath caught not only with the knowledge that Madison had been here while I was gone, but also at the amount the check was written out for. Could that be right? *Holy shit.*

"Eden?" I called. I was greeted only with silence. I began heading toward the bedroom. I wondered where she was, but that same terror that had gripped me in the bowling alley when she was out of my sight for three minutes didn't grip me now, which was a positive sign.

However, I *was* just slightly worried Madison had said something that would have upset her. Madison wasn't a mean person, but I'd also never seen her in a situation like this one.

I turned down the hallway and saw that my studio door was open. My heart jolted. *Oh no, Eden.* I let out a shaky breath as I stepped into the doorway. Eden was standing stock-still in the middle of the room, wrapped in a white towel, her head moving slowly in every direction, taking in the paintings surrounding her, some sitting propped against the walls, some hung *on* the walls, some resting on easels. There were hundreds of them. And they were all of her... and the small beginning of a new life I had imagined to be our daughter, the girl next to her on the canvas with the dark hair and blue eyes, the one who had been stolen right from the safety of Eden's womb. As it turned out, the only one she'd ever carry. I swallowed, feeling tense, not sure how she'd react to what she was looking at. I'd painted these never imagining she'd see them.

"She'd be about two and a half now," I said very quietly.

Eden must have heard us enter the apartment because she didn't jolt at the sound of my voice behind her.

"She?" she asked.

"I...I always imagined it was a girl. I don't know why. I just did. I do."

She turned toward me and a tear slipped down her cheek, but she smiled softly and wiped it away. "Me too, actually. I believed you were with her. I pictured you together—it soothed me."

She continued to look around, not just at the pictures of her and who I imagined would have been our daughter, but Eden as a young girl and through the years. The one of her playing kick the can, a look of fierce joy on her face as she slid to a halt, reaching one foot toward the can of safety, a bigger kid fast on her heels. The one of her sitting at the front of the temple, one long strand of hair between her fingers as her eyes gazed upward, a small dreamy smile on her face. The one of her eyes meeting mine, a flush on her cheeks, a morning glory clutched in her hand, the one she'd just picked up from beneath her chair.

"I was going to show you..." I trailed off. I moved into the room and she walked over to a painting of her hands as I remembered them. My greatest fear had been that I would begin to forget the details of her. And so I painted them—not just the moments we'd shared but *her*. Each part of her, like snapshots from my mind. Creating pictures of Eden brought me the only real serenity I'd experienced since I lost her.

"I wondered why my face wasn't in any of the paintings hung up in the gallery," she murmured.

"I couldn't share all of you. I wasn't ready."

She approached a painting of her face, turned to the sun, a secretive smile just beginning to blossom. She ran her finger over her own cheek, down lower to the small swell of her pregnant belly as it might have looked had she continued to carry our child. Her finger stalled and she pulled it back, her expression sorrowful even in profile.

"I just...I didn't have any photographs. I feared the world might just...forget you," I said. "It was my way of keeping you alive, keeping *her* alive," I finished. "Please say something, Eden."

She faced me, tears shimmering in her eyes and clinging to her lashes. She walked slowly to me, twin tears rolling down her cheeks. "Thank you," she said simply, wrapping her arms around me and pulling me close.

"For what?" I asked as I nuzzled into her hair.

"For loving me so much. For keeping me alive when I wasn't."

I released a gust of breath. "You don't ever have to thank me for that. It's just what I was made to do."

167

She sniffled against my shirt and then tipped her chin as she gazed at me. "Me too," she said.

"Morning Glory." I smiled and brought my hands up, running them through her still-damp hair. I glanced around at the paintings, thinking about what her mom had said at the party about not having photographs of Eden through the years. "Do you think your mom would want a few of these... from when you were younger? Or do you think they'd make her sad for what she missed?" And that each scene was from Acadia.

"I think she'd like them," she said. "I think she'd treasure them."

"Okay, then, I'll give her a few. We'll need to go and get your things anyway. Do you think she'll be all right with you moving in here?"

"Probably not, no. But I'll be right across town. We'll work it out. She wants me to be happy."

I heard Xander's footsteps and then turned to find him standing in the doorway. "I see you came across his Eden shrine," Xander said. "I told him this was strange and scary." But despite his words, his smile was kind.

"Shut up, Xander," I said.

Eden laughed softly. "It's the most amazing thing I'll ever see in my entire life."

I let go of Eden and retrieved a small canvas from the back of the room. I brought it to Xander and handed it to him. "For the next 'Throwback Thursday,'" I said.

Xander's eyes widened as he took a step back and let out a small disbelieving laugh. "Holy shit," he said.

Eden walked over to him and peered at the canvas he was staring at. It was a picture of him as a kid, ten years old or so, standing on top of this rock we used to play on near our cabins. He was laughing—probably at his own joke, knowing him.

"It's…" He trailed off, appearing overcome with emotion.

"See, I have a very small Xander shrine too," I said as I patted his shoulder. "Now you don't have to be jealous."

He met my eyes. "Thank you, brother."

We left my studio, and after Eden put some clothes on, she met us in my kitchen, where we ate straight out of the take-out containers. And damn if that wasn't the best meal of my entire life.

Xander's mood seemed to have brightened when he left a little while later. I hoped he'd find the courage to give the girl a chance. If Xander loved her, she must be someone special. And if anyone deserved to be loved in return, it was Xander. He was one of the most selfless people I knew. But that was his story, and in the end, we were the only ones who could decide the part we were going to play in our own.

I showered and shaved the three-day growth off my face and then changed into fresh clothes. When I emerged from the bathroom, I saw that Eden had stripped the sheets off the bed. If there were ever any sheets that needed to be changed, those were them. I chuckled softly to myself as I walked to the kitchen where Eden was standing at the counter, her hair in a knot on top of her head as she looked down at her phone with a worried frown on her face. "What is it?" I asked.

She looked up at me and smiled, but it quickly dipped again. "My mom. I didn't mention this, but her messages have been increasingly frantic." She sighed. "She's overprotective. I guess I can't blame her, and I've tried to be understanding, but… Anyway, I should get back and reassure her. Do you want to come with me? Or do you have to work? Your roofing?"

"No, I took some time off so I could focus on the show." I ran my hand through my semidamp hair. "Now." I inclined my head toward the check still sitting on the side of the counter. "I guess I don't have to continue roofing for at least a little while."

"Or ever," she said, moving in close and setting her hands on my hips as she tilted her head back to meet my eyes. "Calder, clearly your work is sought after. Set up another show if you want to. Madison left a business card under the check. And surely there are galleries all over the city who would want your work, *Storm's* work." Her eyes brightened, dancing with mischief. "However, *I* get the stripteases." She grinned as if she couldn't help it and I laughed, my heart skipping a beat at the sudden beauty of her happiness. "Seriously, Calder, I'm so proud of you," she said.

I squinted one eye. "Remember when I used to draw in dirt with a stick?"

"Yeah, I do." Her smile was soft. "If ever anyone was meant to do something, you were meant to create art. You make people feel things with your gift. If that's not a true calling, I don't know what is."

"Thank you." I kissed her forehead. "Okay, I'll call a couple galleries. But today…today, we go over to your mom's house and tell her our plans. And then we go to the grocery store and stock up on food for *our* home—at least things that don't need to be refrigerated." I smiled and pushed a piece of her bangs to the side of her forehead. "And after that, I'll start working on the electric so we can live in the light and eat refrigerated food." At the picture in my head of us doing such normal tasks, joy flooded through me. "Maybe tomorrow we can go to a furniture store and pick some stuff out. Do you think your mom would help us cash that check?"

"Yeah, I think so." Her eyes shifted. "Calder?" She bit her lip and paused.

"What, Morning Glory?"

"We're going to need to go to the police. Us, all of us." For a moment I was confused. "I know *you* do, Eden. To get your name back, I know you do. But not me. Not Xander. We don't have to."

She gave her head a shake. "Don't you think your name is important too?" she asked. "Don't you want your own name back? You deserve to have an identity, Calder. I mean, Madison understood about you not having any ID—she was willing to do whatever she did to bypass that because you two—" She took a deep breath, apparently deciding not to voice the rest of that thought. "But not everyone is going to be willing to set that aside. What if you got pulled over driving without a license? You'd be forced to tell your story. Let's do this on our own terms. Let's do this together."

I pressed my lips together. We'd discussed reclaiming our lives with courage and gratitude, and I was committed to trying my best. But I didn't know if I was ready to take every step all at once. However, I also admitted the truth in what she was saying. I knew that most of the reason we hadn't been reunited sooner was because none of us had been willing to go to the police. But still, the thought of it made me dizzy with anxiety. "What if they try to separate us somehow?" I asked. "What if we did something wrong by not going to them immediately? I don't know all the laws. They could put us in jail or something." Clive Richter's face loomed large in my mind, the memory of sitting in the back of his police car as he returned us to Acadia causing my guts to clench.

Eden shook her head. "I don't think so, Calder. And my mom has a good relationship with the Cincinnati police department after all these years. There are people she trusts there. There are people I think we can trust too."

"Clive Richter—" I started.

"I know. I know. But all these years...all these years and he's gotten away with what he did that day. He's always claimed he lived there, in Acadia, but that he was working the day of the flood and didn't have any part in any of it. He says he wasn't even there. But we know that's not true. He lied, and there must be a reason for that. Maybe he's the one who broke the law."

I turned away from her. Apart from Hector, Clive Richter was one of the first men I learned to despise. I hadn't known distrust and animosity prior to that first time he put his spineless hands on me. And him using his badge to terrify, belittle, and humiliate Xander, Eden, and me had decimated my trust in the police. My hand went unconsciously to the scar on my thigh, ugly and raised under my jeans. I needed so badly to be able to protect Eden this time. The thought of putting ourselves in the hands of the police filled me with fear. I understood that people trusted the police in general, that the police were there to help, but my heart screamed something different, my blood pressure skyrocketing each time I passed one on the street. "Can we just talk about how we'd go about it?" I asked. "Can we figure it out beforehand and consider all the possible outcomes?"

"Of course," she said. "There's no rush. We'll talk about

it with my mom, and then with each other and with Xander. We'll come to a decision together, all right?"

I released a long breath. "Yeah."

"All right." Eden tilted her head and smiled. "We're going to be okay, you know that, right?"

I smiled back despite the simmering anxiety at simply having uttered the name Clive Richter. Because Eden was in front of me, real and whole and *here*. "Yeah, I know," I said, mostly believing it. I took her in my arms and kissed her deeply, losing myself in the sweet taste of her.

"Careful or we're going to end up back in the Bed of Healing," she said between kisses.

"That's the idea."

We kissed and laughed for a few more minutes, finally managing to pull away from each other. Eden waited while I collected two small canvases of Eden as a preteen from my studio and wrapped them in brown construction paper. "Ready?" I asked when I was done with the task.

"Yup," she said and grabbed her purse.

I locked the door behind us and we took the elevator down to the lobby. I'd never liked elevators; I'd never liked small spaces in general. Not after Acadia. But I was also eager to get Eden back home and pack up her stuff so we could start our life together.

We opened the door to the street and, suddenly, all hell broke loose.

A large crowd surged forward and I dropped the paintings and grabbed Eden, my head swiveling in every direction as we stumbled backward.

"There they are!" I heard yelled. "Eden Everson!" someone called. "Why haven't you told police you're back? Were you really at Acadia during the mass suicide?"

"Get back!" I yelled, my voice bursting out of me before I could even form a coherent thought. Two men pushed forward, smashing the canvases under their feet. I swung my fists, the world turning red around me, pulsing with blood and panic.

"Calder Raynes! Storm!" someone else called. "Is it true that you're from Acadia, too? How'd you both make it out? Is it Eden in all your paintings?"

I pushed my way through the throngs of people, hardly able to make sense of their shouted words, holding Eden tightly around her shoulders, both of our heads bent. My heart galloped, adrenaline pumping. I swung one arm in front of me, pushing anyone out of the way who didn't move on their own. The shouts only got louder.

"Get the fuck away from her!" I yelled when a man tried to yank on Eden's arm. When he refused to unhand her, I let go of Eden briefly and moved toward him, swinging at him and connecting with his face, blood flying into the air around us. I let out a loud yell, kicking at him as he hit the ground. I heard Eden scream and the world around me blurred, the sounds suddenly coming from underwater.

I felt something inside me snap, and suddenly, my fists were flying and I distantly felt pain exploding across my knuckles, but I didn't care. *Eden screaming. Blood on her clothes. Men pulling her away from me. Eden screaming. I can't get to her. I can't protect her. Eden screaming. Blood on her clothes. Men pulling her away from me. Eden screaming. I can't get to her. I can't protect her.*

When I came back to myself, the crowd had moved back and I was hunched over Eden on the sidewalk, heavy breaths of exertion rasping from my lungs. I looked around wildly to identify any more threats and saw several men with blood on their faces and two still sprawled on the ground. I sprang to my feet, bringing Eden with me and pulling her in tightly to my chest as my head continued to whip in every direction. There were words coming from my mouth and as I gripped my pounding head, I realized they were, "Never again, never again, never again."

"Calder? Calder?" Eden's voice. Her soft, angelic voice. I gasped, my vision clearing. Eden was crying softly against me. I ran my hands up and down her body, tilting her head up so I could rake my eyes over all her features, assessing whether she was hurt.

"I'm okay, Calder," she said and I could hear the tears in her voice. "I'm fine. I'm okay. I promise." She reached out tentatively as if trying to calm a wild animal. "I'm okay. You protected me. I'm okay."

I let out a gasp of breath and then wrapped her in my arms, soothing myself with the feel of her body against me. *Safe. Protected.* I became aware that the crowd of people I now recognized as journalists, and several others who had gathered on the street, were all gaping at me, some with cameras turned in our direction.

I let out another haggard breath as I heard a car come to a stop behind me. "Calder. Eden. Get in the car," I heard called, and I turned around and saw the girl who had been with Eden at the gallery the week before. Molly, I thought her name was Molly.

I opened the back door and practically shoved Eden inside before getting in behind her. The car lurched into drive and sped away. Outside the car windows, the day grew dark, storm clouds moving quickly across the sky.

I pulled Eden right up next to me and attempted to get myself back under control, breathing in and out slowly, wrapping my hand around her wrist so I could feel the steady beat of her pulse right beneath my fingertips.

CHAPTER TEN
Calder

We had driven in silence, Molly glancing repeatedly in the rearview mirror at us, a worried expression on her face. Eden had simply let me hold her, her head resting against my chest.

I couldn't be sure, but I thought Molly had driven around for a while before going to Eden's mom's house, perhaps giving us both time to settle down and collect ourselves. My fists were bloody and I still felt shell-shocked.

Once the car stopped and we got out, I held on tightly to Eden as we walked to the house, shooting looks over our shoulders to make sure we hadn't been followed by any of those newspeople. How in the hell had they found out about us?

Eden's mom came rushing out when we were almost to the door. "Oh my goodness! It's all over the news. Come inside. I'm so glad I sent Molly for you when I did." She hurried us in and then took one look behind her before shutting the door and locking it.

"Carolyn, Calder needs a first-aid kit for his knuckles," Molly said.

Carolyn put her hands up to her cheeks when she took in my bruised and bloody hands. "Oh no, oh no. Of course," she said, rushing over to Eden and running her eyes down her body twice before squeezing her shoulders and rushing out of the room.

Eden and I sank down onto the sofa and I put my hands palm down on my lap so I wouldn't bleed on all the nice furniture.

Molly left the room, saying something about iced tea, and when she was gone, I turned to Eden. "I'm so sorry," I muttered, putting my forehead to hers. "It was like I was back there for a minute. I…freaked. Damn, I'm sorry."

Eden brought her hand to my cheek. "I understand. And truly, Calder, they were like a bunch of vultures. They practically attacked us. Anyone would have freaked."

"Maybe. But I can only imagine what that news footage looks like. I must look crazed." *Like Hector at the end.* A shiver snaked down my spine.

"We won't watch," she said with the glimmer of a smile. She kissed me softly right as Molly came back into the room with a tray of glasses filled with iced tea.

I took the one she offered and drank deeply. Eden sipped at hers, and Molly set the tray down on the coffee table and took the chair across from where we sat on the sofa.

"So who the hell told the news about you guys?" Molly asked.

I glanced at Eden. "I don't know. Madison?"

Eden cast her eyes to the side. "I guess it could have been, but I don't know. I talked to her this morning and she specifically said she wouldn't do that. She seemed sincere."

I nodded. I didn't think Madison would either. She'd always been trustworthy from my experience. Still, people did things they might not ordinarily do when they were hurt, and I'd hurt her. I took a sip of iced tea. "How'd you know to come pick us up?" I asked Molly.

"I didn't," she answered. "Carolyn sent me." She raised her hands. "I swear though, I was just going to take a selfie with Eden to prove she was alive and then leave." She lowered her voice. "She's been a little crazy since Eden's been with you, as if she was kidnapped again or something. I've been trying to help her keep a rational perspective." She raised her brows as if she wasn't sure how effective she'd been. *Damn.* I couldn't help wondering if Carolyn tipped off the police. But…Eden's mom wouldn't do that to her, would she?

"As for who told the media, I guess it could have been any of a hundred people," Molly went on. "That party… we asked the guests not to say anything, but the bartender could have heard just enough and put it together. Or the string trio. Who knows? We weren't exactly running a stealth operation." She paused. "Now that I consider it, I'm actually more surprised it took *this* long for the media to come knocking at our door."

I surprised myself by chuckling. *True enough.* I already liked Eden's cousin. She was thoughtful and personable and she seemed to care a lot about Eden.

"You're right," Eden said. "And really, does it even matter?" She looked up at me. "I just wish it had happened on *our* time frame."

"It's all right," I said quietly. "It's probably for the best. You can claim your name now and that will open so many doors." I moved my own fear aside as best as I could. There was nothing I could do now but wait to see what would happen. I looked down at my bruised knuckles, the blood already dry and caked.

Carolyn came back into the room with a first-aid kit and looked questioningly at Eden. Eden nodded and took the kit from her and moved to kneel in front of me. As she dabbed alcohol on my knuckles, the biting sting served to bring me fully into the present. While Eden bandaged my hands, Carolyn told us she had spoken to one of the detectives on Eden's case while she was upstairs and that the police were on their way over. They had called her when they saw the news footage on TV.

"Will that look bad for us?" Eden asked her mom.

"I don't think so. The detective seemed understanding about why we had taken our time. I think the way the journalists attacked you both is proof enough that we had good reason to keep to ourselves for a little while." She frowned, her gaze lingering on me. After what Molly had told us, I didn't blame her for looking at me like that. I had taken Eden away from her for three days after telling her I'd bring her daughter right back, and then I went mad-dog crazy and beat people in the street who posed a threat to us. Or what I'd considered a threat at the time. I tried to think back and could barely remember the details other than I felt like Eden's safety was at risk. Her mom now probably thought I was sketchy at best, despite the fact that I thought I'd made a good impression on her at her garden party.

"I'm really sorry for...everything," I murmured to Carolyn.

"I know," she said. "I can see that you are. And I'm sorry that happened to you too. If only you'd brought Eden back sooner." An accusatory look passed over her face and I felt even guiltier. Then again, Eden and I had needed that time together so desperately. How could I even begin to explain that to her mother of all people? Carolyn took a deep breath, looking away from me. "The good news is that the police are going to put a couple officers here on detail, so no one bothers us or gets to the front door without us knowing. You're safe here, with me." I hoped she was talking about both of us, but she was only looking at Eden.

I stretched my neck from side to side. Now that the adrenaline was subsiding, my muscles felt stiff and sore. All I wanted was to take Eden home with me and start some sort of a life together, have her to myself, be able to *protect* her myself, prove that I was worthy of that.

Carolyn stood. "Eden, I'm going to make you a fluffer-nutter sandwich. They were always your favorite, and if any situation calls for comfort food, this one does." She rushed out of the room calling behind her, "No crusts, of course."

Molly brought her hand to her temple as if she suddenly had a very bad headache while Eden looked at the place Carolyn had just been in confusion. I assumed, like me, she had no idea what a fluffernutter sandwich was.

The doorbell rang and the next five hours were spent being interviewed by the police as Eden and I told our stories, individually, together, over and over until they were just words and there was no emotion behind the scenes I continued to paint. People came in and out, some in uniforms, some in street clothes; the officers all held the same incredulous look on their faces when they heard our story. At first I was fearful, wary, but as the day wore on, I became numb and desensitized.

The police seemed stunned by most of the events of the day of the flood, especially by the roles Clive Richter played, both in bringing us back to Acadia, in standing by while

Hector tortured us and tried to murder me, and in then shooting me in the leg. I didn't know what would happen to him, if anything, and despite the many people who listened to our story with compassion in their eyes, I couldn't help the fact that my stomach roiled when I considered Clive would now know we were alive. Or perhaps he'd seen the news coverage and he already did.

I kept my eyes focused on Eden when I could and looked her way as often as possible. I watched her talk to a young-looking detective in a suit and she seemed to feel comfortable with him, even laughing softly several times as he jotted down notes. He looked at her with a sort of reverence in his eyes. My stomach twisted in jealousy and I had to remind myself to relax. We were out in the big community now, *the world*. Lots of men were going to look at Eden and try to make her laugh. It didn't mean they were going to try to steal her away and lock her in a room so they could marry her. We'd come from an extreme circumstance that had nothing to do with the way things worked in normal society. It was a good reminder for me to check my reactions often because they were likely to be based on my own fears rather than current reality.

I had called Xander once the police arrived, and a couple hours later, he rang the bell and began being questioned by the police as well.

I hadn't been prepared for this day, and despite my nervousness, a small part of me also felt relieved. It wasn't hanging over our heads anymore. And it didn't seem that us not coming forward sooner was an issue anyone was going to press. And maybe Eden was right, maybe now I'd be able to find out my own last name too. Surely someone out there knew who I was. Was it possible someone like Eden's mother cared that I had been missing all these years? Guilt knotted in my stomach when I considered the fact that I could have put someone out of their misery much earlier than this. But I hadn't been ready, and that was the simple fact of the matter.

Finally, as the sun began to set outside the windows, we said goodbye to Xander, and then a little while later, the police started to gather their things and leave Carolyn's house too. Eden came around behind me and leaned over my chair, wrapping her arms around my shoulders and kissing my neck. "We did it, Butterscotch," she whispered. *Butterscotch*. How long had it been since I'd heard Eden call me Butterscotch? I closed my eyes and welcomed her physical and emotional comfort. Her strength, her resilience, they had given me courage before and they gave me resolve now. We did it. *We*. I wasn't sure if I could have coped with this day without her, but together, we could; I could.

I looked over my shoulder at her and smiled. "Yeah, we did."

"And now," she whispered in my ear, "I'm going to cook you dinner, and later, you're going to sneak into my small pink twin-sized bed." She kissed my ear. "My mom made up the guest room for you, but we'll work around that."

"What does your mom think we've been doing for three days?" I whispered.

"I'm sure she's trying not to think about it," she said, standing and coming around in front of me. "You might have noticed that she's sort of in denial about me being a woman. She can't help but regard me as a little girl, I think." She chewed at her lip. "I'm trying to be respectful of that. But there's no way you're going to be under the same roof as me and not be in my bed for at least part of the night." She sat on my lap and wrapped her arms around my neck.

182

I leaned forward and kissed her. Living at her mom's house—even temporarily—wasn't ideal, but we were together. We were safe.

A woman cleared her throat and I looked up to see Carolyn standing in the doorway. I dropped my arms and Eden stood up and went over to hug her.

"You did so well," Carolyn said when Eden had pulled away. She came into the room and sat down on the chair across from me. "There is going to be news coverage about this ad nauseam, just like there was after Acadia...just like there was after your father..." She trailed off, but then took a deep breath and continued. "The phone isn't going to stop ringing, and you're going to be hounded when you leave the house. We all just have to be prepared. It will stop eventually, but not for some time. Are you going to be okay with this?"

"It's not ideal," I said. "But, we'll have to make the best of it."

Eden nodded, coming to stand next to me and reaching for my hand. I grasped it, squeezing it three times unconsciously. And suddenly, a peace filled my heart, some inexplicable feeling I had trouble naming. *I love you.*

"Yes," Eden said, meeting my eyes. "We'll make the best of it." She looked at Carolyn. "Mom, obviously we don't want to watch all the news coverage, but is there a way someone can watch enough to give us any information on Clive Richter, or if someone comes forward about Calder?"

"Of course. I'll make sure that happens. So this is a no-TV zone for now. And we hole up for the next few weeks and wait until the worst of it has died down."

With that plan in place, we all went into the kitchen and Eden insisted I sit down at the table by the window while she cooked for me. I watched her move around the kitchen, somehow, unbelievably falling even more in love with her. I'd never had the pleasure of seeing Eden do something as normal as boil pasta and toss a salad together and it was almost magical to me, as ridiculous as that might have sounded to someone else. I watched as she interacted with Carolyn and Molly too, laughing and listening intently to what they had to say. She was so damn *good*, so kind and filled with light. It was what Hector had seen in her all those years ago, surely. And yes, he had exploited it for his own sick and twisted fantasy, but he hadn't been wrong in his recognition of it in the first place. It was the quality that had attracted both of us to her. But I swore on everything I loved in the world that I would make her light shine even more brightly and never, ever diminish it like he had.

She smiled over at me and I smiled back. Since I'd been outside of Acadia, I'd noticed how few people held that same genuine gentleness of spirit that Eden exuded. And how was it that *this* girl, my girl, of all people, had managed to retain that quality? After everything she'd been through, the soul-stealing trauma, how had she hung on to that part of herself? Sometimes I felt like falling down on my knees in front of her in worship. She was so unbelievably beautiful in every possible way. Still. After all this time, and after everything, *still*. Only now, she not only held a gentle beauty, but that quiet strength I'd always seen in her was even more apparent.

We sat down to eat dinner and Eden's loving eyes watched me as I ate the food she'd cooked, and it seemed to bring her joy and make her shine brighter, so I ate three helpings even though I was full after two.

Later that night, I snuck out of the guest room and into Eden's room and climbed into her small pink twin-sized bed.

I pulled Eden into my chest and her hand wandered to my briefs and I sucked in a breath, instantly hard. But when I moved over her, the bed squeaked so loudly that I froze. If I took her as hard and vigorously as my body was screaming at me to do, the whole neighborhood would be woken up. I had to wonder if Carolyn had switched out the mattress while we were brushing our teeth.

Eden's wide eyes met mine in the semidarkness of the room and her face contorted in laughter as she brought her hand to her mouth so as not to make any noise. I grinned down at her, holding back my laughter too.

After we'd collected ourselves, we moved down to the floor. "We're always having to sneak around," I whispered against her lips.

"This is different," she whispered back.

"I know." I still didn't like it though.

I made love to her on the floor of her bedroom like we were two sneaky teenagers, a blanket beneath us. Although we had to be quiet and it wasn't a bed of our own like I would have preferred, we were together and that was enough. She put her hand to my cheek and gazed into my eyes lovingly as our bodies joined, and I found the deep peace I always did when I was connected to Eden.

We both fell over the edge of bliss together, breathing against each other's mouths in order to be as quiet as possible. I put my face into her neck as I slowly came down, and her hands ran over my back, kneading the muscles there.

I rolled to the side so I wasn't crushing her and we lay like that for a little while, me nuzzling into her, and her stroking my skin.

"I wanted our baby so badly," she said after a little while.

I could only imagine that each time I came inside her, a

part of her would acknowledge I wouldn't get her pregnant, that it wasn't possible anymore. My heart twisted and I leaned up on my arm. Her face was filled with sadness. "I know. I did too," I said.

"I had found peace as far as not being able to have any more." She paused and I waited for her to go on. "I had thought to myself that there was almost something...*right* about the fact that *your* baby was the only one I'd ever carry, even if I didn't get to keep it." She was quiet again. "But now, I have you back and it's like I'm grieving it all over again."

I pushed her hair aside. "I understand. I'd do anything to change it, Morning Glory." I leaned down and kissed her. "And like I said, we will have kids if you want them. Somehow. We'll adopt. Whatever you want. Anything. I'll do anything to give you everything you want from this life."

She let out a small sniffle. "I know you will."

We lay holding each other for a little while, me staring at the back of her closet door, wondering at all the information she had pinned up on the other side, the research that had served to make her feel active in her life, rather than passive. "Tell me more about what you were researching about Hector," I said.

Eden snuggled against my body. "I started looking into Hector because I just figured, who knows more about the religion he created than me? Us? The news always seemed so perplexed about it all, and I felt like, if I wasn't ready to contact them, then it was at least my duty to look into what I could based on our lived experience."

I was silent, running my fingers up and down the smooth skin of her arm. "Did you mention any of what you were looking into to the police today?"

"No, because I don't have any answers yet, but I thought if I kept going, I might."

"Like what?"

"Like who he really was. Where he came from."

"How were you trying to determine that?"

She leaned up slightly so she could look at me. Her eyes were wide like they always were when she latched on to a topic that interested her. *I love you so much, Morning Glory.* "Well, the more I researched the lessons the Holy Book taught, some of our rituals, the way Acadia was organized, the names for things there, I discovered that a lot of it was based on Greek society, Greek religion, Greek myths. It all fit, almost every bit of it." Her voice sounded more animated. "Not everything, but a lot of it."

Greek? That confused me. "What else?"

"Well, Hector's name—which we know now wasn't really his name. Isn't that sort of a strange name for a blond, blue-eyed man?"

"I don't know. I guess." There were a few Hispanic men named Hector who worked on the construction site with Xander and I. Of course, I always cringed when I heard someone call out their name.

"And his sons—Jason, Phineus, Simon, and Myles." Her voice cracked slightly on the last name and she laid her head back down on my chest. I held her tighter. She still carried grief in her heart for those innocent boys she had known much better than I had. The ones she'd loved.

"What about the names?" I whispered, leaning down to kiss her head.

"They're all names from Greek history or Greek mythology. One is a god, one a hero, one a sea spirit... I can't remember the other one. I have it on the back of my door."

I thought about that for a minute. "Okay, so Hector was obsessed with Greek history for some reason? So much so that he created a religion and a society out of it? Or used it as some sort of inspiration. What does that mean?"

"I don't know. I think it might have started in Indiana though."

I blinked. "Why Indiana?"

"Because I think that's where he took me when he stole me from my parents. He kept me somewhere for almost two years before I came to Acadia. I have this brief flash of memory, of waking up in a car for just a split second and seeing a sign that said something about the Crossroads of America. I always remembered that, but I had no idea what it meant. I looked it up—I *Googled* it," she said, nodding her head as if she was agreeing with the proper use of a new term. I smiled. "That's what the welcome sign to Indiana says. Very shortly after I saw the sign, we arrived at the house I was in with him for the next couple of years. That's where my memory starts fading again."

Talking about the specifics of her kidnapping made my blood feel like it had dropped a couple of degrees. "What did he do to you there? In that house?"

"Nothing like what you might be thinking. He…made me read the Holy Book a lot. He talked to me about my role…constantly. It's foggy. I was grieving for my parents. I thought they'd died. I was alone…*a lot*. I wasn't allowed to go outside very often. It's all very…blurry."

"He brainwashed you."

She seemed to think about that for a minute. "Maybe."

"Only it didn't work very well, my strong Morning Glory."

"No, it didn't. But on some topics, it *did*. And I couldn't remember so much…"

"Why do you think it started in Indiana? Acadia was already functioning. Why would he bring you somewhere else? Potentially his home?"

"I don't know. Maybe that's where he felt safest. Maybe he had things to wrap up in whatever life he was living before Acadia. Who knows?"

"Were you…considering going there, Eden?"

She paused. "I had considered it, yes. As a future possibility, something to work towards. It seemed daunting, though. How would I get there?" She sighed. "I just thought, you know, I had a whole lifetime to fill, and I needed something to fill it with."

My heart dipped. I related to that thought. That feeling. *This life feels so damn long.* "Morning Glory," I murmured, kissing her head, "you found a way to live, to survive. I'm so proud of you. But now we can let all that go. Hector's dead. The police know about Acadia, they know our story, and it's all in their hands now."

"Hmm," she hummed, not sounding totally convinced.

I turned her toward me in the dark. "Eden, there's no point to that line of research anymore."

"What about finding out if you were really born somewhere other than Acadia like you suspect?"

"We've done what we can for now. As we lie here, millions of people across the world are hearing our story and learning about me. If I did come from somewhere else, then surely, someone reported me missing once upon a time. Surely someone knows me. And if so, they'll come forward to claim me like your mother claimed you."

"Yes," she agreed. "They will."

"And so we wait to find out. We wait to find out who I am."

"No, Calder. We already know who you are." She gazed up at me. "We wait to find out where you came from. There's a big difference."

She was right. If my identity remained a mystery, I still knew who I was: *Eden's*. "I love you," I said, pulling her in to my chest.

"I love you too."

We snuck to the bathroom and cleaned up and then got back in her squeaky bed. When the first light of dawn was streaming into her room, I snuck back into my own.

CHAPTER ELEVEN
Eden

A beautiful blond filled the screen, microphone in hand. "This is Sara Celi of Fox Nineteen, Cincinnati, live from the home of Calder Raynes and Eden Everson. A new development has occurred in the reopened investigation of the Acadia sect where a hundred ninety-eight people tragically died in one of the largest mass murder/suicides in history. Tricia, back to you for the rest of the story."

After briefly going back to the anchor in the studio who introduced the Fox affiliate in Arizona, the screen focused on a young brunette woman holding a microphone, her hair blowing slightly in the breeze. "Michelle Mathis here, just outside Goodwin Police Headquarters, where Officer Clive Richter, former Acadia council member, has been arrested for drug trafficking and money laundering. His ex-partner, Officer Michael Owens, has been given immunity, and as Chief Bard told me, he has been very cooperative. The chief was also able to tell me that in light of information Calder Raynes and Eden Everson have given, Clive Richter is now also a suspect in the attempted murder of Calder Raynes. We'll continue to bring you coverage as we receive new information."

Calder and I sat side by side on the couch, holding hands and watching the footage. "Turn it off," he finally said when we'd seen the same shot played over what seemed like a hundred times.

I clicked the TV off and Calder sat staring straight ahead, a look on his face that I couldn't read. "Are you okay?" he asked flatly.

I nodded, trying to figure out what I felt exactly. For three years I had felt such paralyzing fear whenever I thought of Clive Richter, or even the police in general. But now, seeing him being led away in handcuffs, appearing small and weak, the only emotions coursing through my body were relief and a certain sense of triumph.

"Are *you* okay?" I asked Calder, glancing at the detective, who was sitting on the chair across from the couch. He had shown up at my mom's house to let us know in advance there would be breaking news about Clive Richter. Apparently, finding out Calder and I were alive prompted Clive's ex-partner to seek immunity and bring to light crimes he knew Clive was and had been involved in.

Calder kept staring ahead for a minute and then he gave a barely perceptible nod before standing up. "I'm going to get a glass of water. Do you want one?"

"Yes, please."

"Detective?"

"Sure. Thanks, Calder."

I watched Calder worriedly as he left the room. Initially, hearing there was news about Clive had rattled me too. But for Calder, I could only imagine that seeing

Clive's face had brought up the rage and helplessness of that final day, despite the good news that Clive would very likely pay for his crimes, or at least a few of them. I wasn't surprised in the least that Clive had been involved in a number of other illegal activities. If you were willing to turn your back on murder, was there anything you weren't capable of? I just hoped there would be enough evidence to convict him for the crimes he'd committed against Calder and me too. But for now, all we could do was wait and see. I turned my attention to Detective Lowe and took a deep breath.

"How are you feeling?" he asked.

"Fine, I think…it's just…so strange seeing him again."

"I can imagine." He stood up and came to sit on the couch next to me. "Hey, Eden, you're doing really great under the circumstances. I can't even imagine how difficult this is, and you're holding up so well. I hope that doesn't sound patronizing. But I see a lot of people in difficult situations and I just wanted you to know that I'm really impressed by your poise and your courage."

I smiled, thankful for his words. "Thank you, Detec—" I looked up as Calder moved into my vision. His jaw was hard and he put the two glasses of water down on the coffee table hard enough that a little bit of water sloshed over onto the wood. I looked up at him and he flinched slightly as if with embarrassment. "Sorry, I'll go get a napkin," he muttered.

When he left the room, the detective said, "This is just as hard on Calder, I'm sure. Take care of each other."

"We will. I appreciate that." I walked him to the door and stood against it for a minute after I'd closed it behind him. I wasn't sure what to think about this new development.

I made my way to the kitchen where Calder was standing

with his hands braced on the counter. "Hey," I said, coming up behind him and hugging his waist.

"Hey," he said softly, turning in my arms. He brought his arms around me and I laid my cheek against his chest.

"Everything's going to be okay," I murmured.

"Yeah," he said and paused. "Just seeing Clive's face…"

"I know."

We stood like that for a few minutes, taking comfort in each other.

"What do you think he thought?" Calder asked. "When he heard we're still alive? What do you think went through his mind?"

I looked up at him. "I don't even want to try to get into his mind. I can only imagine it's a really ugly place to be."

Calder let out an agreeable chuff, leaning his chin on my head.

After that, the media amped up their efforts to get to us—for right then, it was safest and most convenient to be at my mom's house. So a couple days after we'd arrived, the police drove us to Calder's apartment so he could pack a small bag and grab what he needed for an extended stay.

When we all got to the top of the stairs, one of the policemen said suddenly, "Stand back," and drew his gun. I drew in a surprised breath and Calder's arm shot out in front of me, pushing me back and positioning his body in front of mine. *What is going on?*

The officers hurried past us and one of them nudged Calder's door open with his foot. It was then that I understood. Calder's door was slightly ajar. My heart sank. I knew we had closed and locked it when we left a couple days before. I peeked around Calder as the door swung open and gasped, horrified, when I saw the destruction.

Calder let out a choked groan as the officers went in, their guns drawn. Calder grabbed my hand and moved me to the side of the door as we heard the officers searching the apartment. After about five minutes, they came out. "I'm really sorry," one of the officers said. "Prepare yourself. It's bad in there."

Calder held on to my hand as we both entered the apartment. I put my hand over my mouth to stop myself from sobbing. All the kitchen cabinets had been torn from the walls, and the beautiful flooring was gouged and looked like a jackhammer had been taken to it. The counter was smashed and all the light fixtures had been torn down. Oh God, oh no. *Why?* Calder had done all the work on this place himself. I looked at him and he seemed shocked, his expression blank, but his jaw set.

My eyes moved from him to the words written in black paint across what had been clean, white walls: *Satan Worshippers*, *Acadia Devils Die*, and *Evil Lives Here.*

I choked out a horrified sob. My gaze flew to Calder's, and before his eyes met mine, I swore I saw deep shame move over his expression as he read the words. Hector had called him evil too. Satan's spawn. Somewhere inside, did he still wonder if that was true? Was it a wound that gaped open sometimes, like now? *Oh, Calder.*

Calder pulled me through the destruction that was the open-space living and kitchen area down the hall to his studio. My shoulders shook in silent sobs when I saw what had been done to his priceless work. Every painting was smashed and destroyed—completely obliterated. Bile rose in my throat and I choked it down. The same graffiti was all over the walls of his studio too, but when I looked at Calder, he wasn't staring at that. His gaze hung on a ruined painting of me, smashed on the floor. "Calder," I whispered, "I'm so sorry." My voice broke on the last word.

Calder stared straight ahead for a minute, clenching and unclenching his fists, and then he reached for me, gathering me to his chest. We stood there for a few minutes, clutching each other as tears coursed down my cheeks and wet the front of his shirt.

"It's okay," Calder said, running his hand over my hair. "Those paintings were my longing for you, Eden. I have the real *you* now. I don't need them." But his voice seemed distant and I had this strange sense that though he was holding me, he wasn't really here at all.

"But it was your work. Your beautiful, beautiful work."

"I can make more. And now I have you right in front of me, so every detail will be right and perfect." His words were calming, but the lack of emotion in his voice scared me.

I turned my face in to his T-shirt and cried a little more as he held me. "I'm sorry. I should be holding you right now."

"You are," he said.

I sniffled out a small sad laugh when I realized that indeed I was—*and tightly*.

We walked to his bedroom and I looked around unbelievingly at more graffiti and the clothes that were cut and flung all over the room. And in the middle of it all, the sheets had been stripped off our Bed of Healing and the mattress was slashed everywhere. I felt as if it were *me* that had been slashed right down the middle. I felt violated and sick. *Who would do this and why?* Calder's hand gripped mine so tightly it was almost painful. His whole body was tense as we turned and left the room and returned to where the two officers were waiting. "There's nothing here to pack," Calder said as we walked past them.

"We'll write up a report when we get back to Mrs. Collins's house," one of them said behind us.

The police created a barrier from reporters as we got back in the cruiser parked out front. Calder stared out the window as we drove. "That was the first place that was ever my own," he murmured. "I wanted to keep you safe there."

My heart constricted painfully. I pictured the small two-room cabin he'd grown up in…and then the blanket on the floor in the laundry room where Hector made him sleep. He had never had a place of his own, a home to take pride in, a safe haven to enjoy peace and privacy. And he had wanted to make it ours.

I didn't have any words. I simply moved over on the seat and held him again.

The weeks dragged by. Calder didn't talk a lot about what had been done to his apartment. But I could tell it had affected him deeply—not just the destruction of his *things*, his *space*, but the fact that there were people that hated us for being any part at all of Acadia. Both of us were even more leery of the media and of making any attempt to go out of the house. When he wasn't with me, Calder spent most of his time out by the pool. I couldn't help seeing the similarities of when I had looked out my window at the main lodge and saw the shadow of a boy sitting out on a small front porch. The house was bigger this time, but just like then, he was looking for his own space—and not finding it.

As the days passed, I could tell Calder was getting more and more antsy to get out of my mom's house, and what had felt like a refuge for a little while was now beginning to feel like a prison. We did try to go out one day when the yard was empty and we thought we could escape unseen, but as soon as we stepped outside, car doors opened and closed down the street and reporters ran toward us shouting questions. I felt Calder tense beside me and I dragged him back inside.

Xander visited whenever he wasn't working, and my mom and Molly fluttered around us, trying to make sure we were doing okay and that we were entertained.

It seemed that a competition had formed between my mom and Calder for my time, though, especially on my mom's end. I did my best to split myself between them. But I was only one person. And we were all trapped together in one house.

The media was making Xander's life inconvenient, but they weren't hounding him to the degree they were hounding us. The triple news story of my kidnapping and return, Calder and I having been at Acadia the day of the flood, *and* our love story turned the media into vultures. I didn't understand it. We were just two scared people who had survived something horrible and life-altering. Didn't they care that they were only making it worse?

The police still came and went, stopping by to clarify something or to give us information they thought we'd appreciate having, such as the fact that all of Clive's assets had been frozen in light of the money laundering charges. He wouldn't be able to make bond—he'd be in jail until his trial. Somehow I doubted he had any friends who were willing to help him out.

It was obvious my mom had a special affinity for Detective Lowe, the young, handsome detective I felt most comfortable talking to as well. One day after he'd been by with some questions, my mom came into the kitchen where I was making popcorn for a movie Calder and I planned on watching.

"Eden," my mom said, grabbing a bowl from the cabinet next to her and handing it to me. "Bobby is so handsome, isn't he?"

I paused. "Bobby?"

"Oh." She laughed. "Detective Lowe."

"Uh, yeah, he is, Mom."

She smiled happily, leaning on the counter and taking in a deep breath. "I think he likes you," she said.

I halted in opening the bag of popcorn and stared back at her. "I'm with someone, Mom, in case you might have forgotten? Calder? He lives in your house here with us?"

My mom laughed uncomfortably. "Well, of course, I'd never forget Calder. How could I?" She pressed her lips together as if in annoyance, but then her expression gentled. "I just hope you notice how attractive other men find you. You've never experienced any of that." She patted my hand. "I know I'm meddling, Eden, I do. It's just…I never got to be involved in giving you any motherly advice when it came to dating or…" Pain washed over her face, but I pulled my hand from beneath hers. "I just think it's always good for a woman to recognize all her options. Calder is such a nice boy and so very handsome, obviously, but, you know, you don't have to feel guilty if you think about experiencing a man who could possibly give you more security, someone who doesn't constantly remind you of the terrible past. I swear to you, I'm only saying this out of love."

Then why doesn't it feel loving? I opened my mouth to say something to her, I wasn't even sure exactly what, when I heard movement behind me. I turned to see Calder standing in the doorway, a look of hurt plastered all over his face.

"Calder—" I started, glancing between him and my mom, who was avoiding his gaze.

"The movie's starting," he said, turning and leaving the room.

I gave my mom a death glare. She shrugged but had the grace to look embarrassed.

"Hey," I said when I got to the living room, where he was waiting for me on the couch. "I'm not making excuses for her, but you know my mom is just kind of controlling with me because she's fearful of losing me again, right?" God, I *was* making excuses for her. I felt deeply frustrated—with the situation, with myself. I wasn't sure what I should do.

"Yeah," Calder said, not meeting my eyes. "This is just a tough situation. It'll pass."

I nodded, but he still looked hurt. Surely he knew I'd only ever love him? He had to know he meant everything to me. I moved in and snuggled with him on the couch for the rest of the afternoon, ignoring my mom but not knowing if that would make things better or worse.

CHAPTER TWELVE
Eden

A couple days later, I awoke bright and early, despite the fact that I had barely slept the night before. I was worried about Calder. We spent all our time together, and yet I felt like he was withdrawing from me. And for the first time since we'd arrived at my mom's house, he hadn't come to my room. The thunderstorm that had practically rocked the house all night hadn't helped matters.

When I went downstairs, I heard a male voice in the kitchen and walked in to see Xander sitting at the kitchen table with Molly.

"Hey," I said to both of them.

"Hey," Xander said, standing up and giving me a hug.

"Morning." Molly smiled.

"What are you doing here so early?" I asked Xander. I poured myself a cup of coffee and joined them at the table.

"I work this morning," he said. "I just wanted to stop in and check on Calder. And I was hoping you'd be up first so we could talk."

"Calder's still sleeping," I said, pouring some half-and-half that was sitting on the table into my cup. "Are you worried about him?"

"A little. He called me last night. It sounded like he's having a rough time."

I paused, my cup halfway to my lips. My shoulders sagged and I set my cup down. "This is just so hard. I never expected things to be this way. I wasn't at all prepared for this situation, especially so soon after reuniting with Calder." I paused. "He's not handling it well."

Xander sighed. "I can't say I blame him. He's trapped again, pent-up, feeling worthless."

"Yes, I know. I want so much to help him. Any ideas?"

"You could get away from here for a while."

"Oh God," Molly interrupted. "Carolyn would freak."

I groaned and put my face in my hands. When I looked up, I said, "I know she would. But she doesn't want to share me with him either. And she still wants me to be twelve…or six…or sometimes I don't even know. It changes by the day, and because of it, I'm having an identity crisis."

Molly looked sympathetic. "I don't blame you. I see it too." She paused. "They both lived without you for a long, long time."

"I know. Where is she anyway?" My mom was usually an early riser and I didn't want her to walk in on us talking about her.

"She left early with her friend Marla. I insisted she get out of this house and go to an antique fair that's a couple hours away, and Marla helped me convince her. I think it will be good for her. She's holed herself up in this house too."

"Thanks for suggesting that to her, Molly." God, what would I *do* without Molly?

"I do what I can. I figured having Calder alone in a quiet house wouldn't go unappreciated." She shot me a wink and stood up. That was for sure. I smiled at her gratefully. "I've gotta get to class. Xander, nice seeing you."

Xander and I called our goodbyes to her as she left the room and then Xander eyed me. "Other than the stuff with your mom, how are *you* doing?"

I sighed. "I want to tell you I'm great, because how could I not be great with you two back in my life?" I paused. "On one hand, I feel like I'm living a dream, and on the other hand, I feel frustrated I'm not able to enjoy the gift I've been given. I feel constantly conflicted." I furrowed my brow. "Does that sound ungrateful?"

"No, not at all. Just true. And I get it. It's a lot to handle."

I nodded. "And then there's my mom. I love her and I want so badly to have a good relationship with her, and I keep reminding myself that she is not Hector." I grimaced. Despite my irritation, comparing anyone to Hector wasn't fair. Even saying his name out loud made my body tense. "She loves me, I know that. But the way she treats Calder makes me want to scream. It's like he's back in the dogs' quarters at the main lodge." I paused, biting my lip, feeling heartbreak at the memory alone. "But I don't know if it would help or make matters worse if I gave her some kind of ultimatum. Shape up or we're moving in with Xander."

Xander laughed. "Whoa. No Beds of Healing at my apartment. No peaches either." He raised his hands and grinned.

I laughed and it felt good. "You should rethink that."

"Absolutely not. Also, no pool and, more importantly, no police protection."

"Ugh. I'd forgo amenities and security for some

freedom." But in truth, I knew feeling safe was important, and if it wasn't at least mostly guaranteed, Calder would end up feeling even more anxious and our presence might put Xander at risk too. I wrapped my hands around the warm coffee mug in front of me, seeking the small comfort. "Let's talk about you, Xander," I said, happy to change the subject. "Tell me how you're doing. What's going on with the girl?" I'd asked for an update a few times since the day he'd mentioned her, but he'd been somewhat evasive, and I figured they were still working things out. Or I hoped so anyway. I wanted so much to see Xander happy.

Xander ran his hand through his hair, appearing suddenly bashful and boyish. I brightened. That was a good sign. "She's good. Really good," he said.

"Yeah?" I prompted with a grin.

"Yeah. She's been so supportive during this whole unexpected situation. Her name is Nikki by the way."

I leaned forward. "We get a name? This *is* good," I teased, wondering at the girl that had stolen Xander's heart—*such a beautiful heart*. She was a lucky, lucky girl. "When do we get to meet her?"

He smiled. "Soon. I just want to introduce her to you two once some of this craziness blows over, you know? It'd be nice if we could all go out without a horde of people with cameras chasing us."

I gave him a chuckle, filled with little amusement. Yeah, I knew, and I didn't blame him.

Xander studied me for a minute. "I'm so damn happy to have you back, Eden." He looked down, playing with the edge of the napkin under his coffee cup. "It's been hard, you know? I'd do anything for Calder, and I know he'd do anything for me, but…all this time, I didn't want to burden him with so many things." He rubbed the back of his neck. "I was more capable of moving forward in the last few years than he was. But now...we've got our team back and things just feel... right. Like we're *all* going to be stronger because of it."

Tears sprung to my eyes. *We've got our team back.* I grasped his hand across the table. I felt stronger too. I had the two people back who I could be completely *myself* with. I had a home now because of my mom, but my *true* home—my heart—had always belonged to Calder, obviously, but certainly Xander as well.

Xander smiled. "As far as the hard stuff...we've been through worse than this, right?"

I conceded the point with a small breathy laugh. "I guess that'd be the understatement of the decade."

He laughed too, and we looked up as Calder came into the room, looking tired but as beautiful as ever.

"Hey, brother," Xander greeted.

"Morning," Calder croaked, sitting down at the table. He looked over at me, the expression on his face full of regret. "Sorry."

I figured he was apologizing for not coming to my room, but I didn't say anything, just gave him a nod and a smile. I stood up and poured him a cup of coffee and set it in front of him and kissed his cheek before sitting back down.

"I actually have to be going," Xander said, glancing at the clock on my mom's wall and standing up. "I just wanted to check in on you and Eden," he said, his eyes on Calder.

"I appreciate that. I'll text you later?"

"Yeah." Xander smiled and winked at me, looking less worried than he had just twenty minutes before. "By the way, Throwback Thursday was a big success." He grinned. "I got about a thousand likes."

Calder laughed softly. "It *was* an incredible painting."

"It's the subject that makes that painting great. God, I was even good-looking at ten."

Calder walked Xander to the door as I laughed after them and then he came back and took his seat. "Sorry again," he said, reaching for my hand across the table. "I went to bed while you were watching that movie with your mom last night and I didn't wake up until this morning. I promised we'd never sleep apart one single night again." His gaze slid away. "I just…I felt like I was going to melt down…so many things swirling through my brain. Sleep seemed like the best option."

"I understand. I know this is hard, but I want to be able to help."

He let go of my hand and sat back. "I know you do. I know that. And that means everything to me. Truthfully, I don't know if there's anything either one of us can do right now."

I got up from the table and went over to him and sat down on his lap and pulled his head in to my chest, stroking his hair. "It'll all be okay."

"When?" he asked.

"That's the part I don't know."

We sat in silence for a few minutes.

"Madison called me yesterday," he said.

I froze. I hadn't expected that. "Oh?"

"Yeah, she called to let us both know it was her assistant that leaked the news about you, and about us. She confided in him and…anyway, it doesn't even really matter. Like Molly said, it was bound to get out sooner or later. I just wish it had been on our terms, on our time line. Madison feels badly. She wanted me to apologize to you."

I nodded, continuing stroking his hair. "You're right, what's done is done. I don't blame Madison." Although inside, just thinking about Madison still brought a sharp pang of jealousy. But I needed to move past that.

Calder leaned his forehead on mine just as the doorbell rang.

We both went to answer it, and when I swung the door open, Detective Lowe was standing there with two other officers. "Eden, hi," he said, his eyes sweeping down my body. I was still only dressed in a short bathrobe. I pulled it more tightly around me. Detective Lowe seemed to catch himself and cleared his throat.

"Uh, come in," I said.

He did and I looked over at Calder, who was frowning at the detective.

"Sorry to bother you two days in a row, but we just have a couple questions for Eden about Clive."

"Oh," I said, "okay. Let me just go pull on some clothes and I'll be right back."

Calder followed me upstairs. "I'm gonna get in the shower," he said, his face still tense.

"Hey, you okay?" I asked.

Calder spun around, talking in a loud whisper. "I hate the way that guy looks at you," he said. "God, maybe he should just move in here too. He's here enough." He grimaced and the officer's voices drifted up the stairs. "Sorry. That was uncalled for. Go answer their questions," he said more gently, turning toward the bathroom. I sighed but went to get dressed. I'd answer their questions and get them out of here.

An hour later, when the detective and officers left, I heard splashing sounds coming from the pool outside and looked out the back window to see Calder doing laps in the pool.

I went upstairs and changed into my swimsuit. When I walked out the side door onto the patio, Calder was out of the pool and sitting on one of the deck chairs next to the stone bar. Water was cascading down his bare, smooth, muscled chest in little rivulets and his hair was pushed back away from his face in wet spikes. God, he was ridiculously gorgeous. And there was something especially beautiful about him when he was wet. I'd thought it before and I thought it now—it was as if water was his own personal element and he wore it better than anyone else on the face of the earth. It transformed him in some elusive way I couldn't even define. "Hey, handsome. I thought you were getting in the shower."

"I changed my mind." His eyes swept up and down my bikini-clad body and I blushed despite the fact that this man had seen me as naked as the day I was born a hundred times over and from every angle imaginable. It was difficult to shake the modesty that had been so ingrained in me or the shame I'd been taught to feel when I was showing an "indecent" amount of skin. I was intent on shaking that though, especially with the man who loved me.

I sat down on his lap and ran my thumbs over his chiseled cheekbones and down his strong, masculine jaw, rough with a day's worth of dark stubble. I leaned forward and kissed his lips. "You taste sweet," I said.

His lashes lowered as though he was embarrassed. "I had some Coca-Cola," he said, mumbling as if that were some sort of crime.

"Mmm." I kissed him again.

"What'd the detective want?" he asked when I leaned back, his gaze trained somewhere over my shoulder.

I studied him as I ran a fingertip over his dark eyebrows,

one by one. "Just more questions about Clive's role in the council—what I experienced of him in the main lodge," I answered. "You don't have to dislike Detective Lowe. He's actually very nice. And he's on our side."

Despite my attempt at reassurance, Calder's jaw tightened subtly. "I just worry," he started, his gaze moving away again. "Sometimes I think maybe you wonder...or maybe you *will* wonder—"

"Then ask me," I said softly. "All you ever have to do is ask me."

He met my gaze and there was a world of vulnerability in his eyes. *Oh, Calder.* "Do you ever wonder what it'd be like to be with another man? A man you could start fresh with? A man who could give you more than me? A man who's *better* than me?"

"No. No man can give me more than you. No man is better than you," I said without hesitation.

He released a breath and his smile was crooked and full of hope. My heart lurched as the flash of him as a little boy looking up at me after I'd put a butterscotch candy in his hand blinked brightly in my mind, and all the love and tenderness I felt for him filled my chest so full I ached with it.

His smile dropped. "I don't even have a name, Eden. No one's come forward to claim me. No one ever even reported me missing."

"Oh, Calder," I said. "Is that why?" He'd seemed so quiet lately, lost in his own head, and he'd leave the room each time the police came by, and now I knew why. The news they were bringing was never about him. "There must be an explanation," I said.

He shrugged.

"And regardless, the police said they'd help you and Xander get the necessary paperwork to get IDs."

"I know, and that's good news, but it won't really be me. I guess…I guess once I allowed myself to hope that my real people were out there and would come forward, I started realizing that if they don't, then I'll always be the person Hector created. If I'm Calder Raynes, I'll always be a slave, a *water bearer*."

I wasn't sure what to feel about that. I had loved him then, and I loved him now. His name—any title someone else gave him—would never, ever change that. It didn't alter who he was under his skin. And we didn't even know for sure that he had been abducted anyway. "Calder," I started hesitantly, "is it possible that Hector was just talking gibberish? At the end you have to admit, he was out of his mind."

"Maybe, but Mother Willa—"

"We can't put a whole lot of stock in what she said either."

Calder pulled his bottom lip between his teeth and sucked on it for a minute. "Okay. But my family, Eden, you have to admit, I didn't look anything like any of them, not in coloring, not in features."

I squinted, trying to picture his mom and dad. I couldn't create a clear picture of their faces in my mind. But I remembered making note of the fact that he didn't look like his family many times in Temple as I watched him interacting with them. "That's not definitive proof of anything either though," I finally said.

Pain altered his features momentarily. And I understood why he'd latched onto the idea that the people who'd raised him weren't his real parents. He didn't want to believe his own mom and dad could have ever done what they did to him at the end. He was looking for hope. He was picturing someone else out there who loved him and would fight to the death for him, unlike the woman who'd stood by as he'd been brutalized, or the man who'd followed the unthinkable directive to burn him alive. I smoothed my thumbs over his cheekbones again, staring into his anguished eyes. "I love you, Butterscotch," I said, feeling the emotion of the statement well up in my throat.

He offered me a small lift of his lips. "I love you too." He paused. "This whole situation is turning me into someone I don't like. I feel like we're trapped, caged again for the second time in our lives and it's making me want to crawl out of my own skin." His lips set. "I can't work; I can't take care of you. I haven't painted. I can't even wake up in the same bed as you. And now I don't even have a home to take you back to once all this clears."

"We'll find a new home together."

"I know." He sighed. "I just feel…stripped bare, I guess."

I studied him for another minute, my eyes drinking in the striking male beauty of his face, the depth of emotion and sensitivity behind his eyes. I'd never get tired of looking at him. Loving him would never cease being my greatest pleasure in life. "I've always liked you stripped bare," I said, giving him a cheeky smile and trying to get him to smile back. It worked. "You've always been most beautiful when you're stripped bare," I said, meaning that in every single way. "You, *just you*, with nothing else, no name, no job, no house, no money, nothing. Stripped bare. *You* will always be enough for me. You will always be my dream come true. You will always be my destiny."

Calder leaned forward and kissed my lips. "I *will* give you more though."

"I know," I whispered, giving him another quick kiss and pulling away. "Want to get in the water with me?"

"Yeah, okay."

"No one's here. We could be naughty and really strip bare." I inclined my head toward all the trees blocking the pool from anyone's sight. "No one can see us."

Calder chuckled and immediately began removing his swim trunks.

When we were both naked and submersed in the heated water of the large pool, I wrapped my arms around his neck and we bobbed like that for a little while, me sighing at the delicious feel of the water tickling my shoulders and Calder's hard, wet, bare body right up against mine.

"Right now, I can imagine we're in the water at our spring," he said, smiling. "I can imagine it's just us and the stars."

I nuzzled into his neck, kissing him softly there. I felt him stir against my belly, and as if my body was answering, I felt an immediate tingling between my thighs. "This is even better," I whispered. "We're free. It's definitely still not ideal, but we're here, we're together."

Calder turned us around in the water and I laughed, leaning my head back and smiling up at the overcast sky above.

"Sometimes I miss it," he said. "Is that insane?"

I lifted my head and looked in his eyes, moving a piece of dark hair off his forehead. I shook my head slowly. "No. We both knew ourselves there. Even if we didn't like it, we knew who we were. We knew what we wanted. Out here"—I brought one hand from around his neck and waved it to the side of us—"it's not always clear. It's confusing and scary sometimes."

"You always get it," he said. "You always get *me*. It's a fucking relief."

Calder's use of a swear word sent a jolt of surprise through me that ended between my legs. I raised a brow. "The big society is rubbing off on you. Now you're using dirty words?"

He grinned wickedly and spun us around again. "Only with you. I only get dirty with you." He leaned in and ran his tongue up my neck and I moaned. "Let's get dirty."

A thrill shot through my body and that pulsing throb intensified between my legs. It was somewhat shameful how little Calder needed to do before I was practically panting for him. But hadn't it always been the case? I figured it always would be.

Calder gazed at me, his eyes moving over my face. "You're painfully beautiful," he whispered.

I breathed out a small laugh. "It's not supposed to be painful."

"It is." He pushed my bangs to the side. "Yours is the type of beauty that makes a man want to fight wars and demolish villages full of other men who might dare to look at you."

I laughed softly, my heart skipping a beat. "No demolishing necessary. I'm yours. I've been yours since the beginning of time."

Calder's eyes flared, and I leaned forward and kissed his lips gently. He walked us over to the wall of the shallow end of the pool and sat me on the edge, at the perfect height so that our faces met as he rested his hands on the tile next to my hips. He leaned into me and took my mouth, moving in between my thighs, so I could wrap my legs around his hips.

He broke from our kiss and gazed at me with heated

eyes. The internal throb pounded now as my breaths grew quicker. Calder's gaze moved to my pebbled nipples and his eyes drooped very slightly. *That look... Oh God, that look.* "Please," I murmured, bringing my hands up to his head and pulling him forward. I needed his mouth on my breasts right that second. He obliged, and when his warm, wet mouth closed over one nipple, I moaned loudly. It felt so good. I always felt like I was at risk of climaxing just from what Calder did with his mouth on my nipples. It was bliss. With one hand braced behind me, I used my other hand to hold the breast Calder was licking and sucking and watched him as he pleasured me that way. The sight of him along with the delicious feel of his mouth was almost my undoing. "Calder, I need you inside of me. Now." He smiled against my skin and then glanced up at me with heated eyes before he moved to my other nipple. I panted out in time with his tongue flicks, pressing into his erection, which was right at my core.

"I'll never stop wanting you," I said, my voice barely a whisper. Calder's mouth paused for just a brief second, but then his tongue lashed out again, harder this time. I gasped, my body pressing into his more forcefully.

He reached down and took his erection in his hand. I watched him stroke himself a couple times, my breath catching in my throat.

"Scoot forward a little," he said, sounding strained, that beautiful gravelly voice making me shiver.

I swallowed and did as he asked, moving from side to side until I was at the very edge of the pool. I brought one fingertip to a vein that started at his abdomen and ran downward, imagining the blood pulsing to his shaft below. The erotic thought stole my breath.

Calder let out a strained groan, his eyes unfocused as he lined the tip of his erection up with my entrance. I groaned out too, half in frustration, half in relief.

Our gazes held as he pushed into me inch by slow inch. I wanted to close my eyes and relish the sensation of his body filling mine, but I couldn't look away. There was something dark and deep and powerful in the way he was watching me.

He pushed in until our bodies connected, and I gasped and he moaned, his eyes falling shut and his lips parting. I wrapped my legs around his hips as he began to move slowly, so excruciatingly slowly. He wrapped his arms around me and brought his mouth to my ear, tickling it with his breath and causing my body to unconsciously buck into him. The sensations he was causing were almost too much. I wanted to tell him to slow down and speed up. I wanted to ask for peace and beg for torment. He made me weak and strong and my thoughts were spinning, spinning, spinning...

"The things you do to me, Eden," he grated, his voice low and raspy.

The things I do to him?

I raked my fingernails over his back, incapable of words as he started another slow slide out.

"I love you so much it makes my guts ache." He slid in slowly, pressing firmly against the part of me that felt swollen and achy with need. Sparks of pleasure burst through my body and my legs tightened around his hips. "I want to fuck you and worship you." He slid out and I made a gurgled sound of loss in my throat, excitement making the surroundings blur. It was only him. He was the only part of my world in focus. He pushed in again more quickly, brushing his thumbs over my nipples and causing sparkles of pleasure to dance around the perimeter of my foggy vision. "I want to worship you while I fuck you. I want to fuck you until you feel how much I worship you." He slid out and then pushed in, in several quick thrusts, bumping his pelvis against my body in a delicious tease that was too much and not enough at all. "I hate it and I love it because I know it will never change. It's been this way from the moment I laid eyes on you and it'll be this way until the day I die."

"Calder, Calder." I grasped at him. There was so much I wanted to say, but none of it would organize itself in my brain. He was holding me hostage on the edge of orgasm and it was glorious and torturous. I was rendered completely useless when it came to any words other than his name.

"I'm tormented by you, and I'm the luckiest man in the world," he rasped, finally, finally moving faster, bumping the juncture between my thighs at the absolutely wonderful speed I needed it. I panted to his rhythm, my fingernails scraping down his back.

"I want everyone on earth to know you're mine. And I"—he took two quick thrusts—"can't even marry you because I don't have a name."

My mind scrambled and my body tightened as pleasure exploded through me, causing me to cry out his name again and again. Calder pumped into me fast and hard twice more and then pressed into me, groaning his own climax into my neck.

I came back down woozily as he breathed harshly against my skin, circling his hips very slowly to draw out his pleasure.

When he finally pulled back and raised his face to mine, his expression was both pained and blissful.

I took his face in my hands and kissed his lips softly. "You want to marry me?" I whispered.

"God, yes."

I smiled against his lips and brought my arms around his neck as joy bloomed in my chest. "Then let's figure this out, because if there is one thing I am absolutely sure about in this world, it's that I want to be married to you."

Calder kissed my lips again, smiling against my mouth as he pulled his body from mine. He was silent for a minute as his eyes moved over my face. "I've been thinking, Eden." He paused, running his hand through his hair.

"What?" I probed, putting my fingers on his chin and tilting his face back to mine.

"What would you say about taking a road trip to Indiana?"

I blinked. "Road trip?" Xander's words from that morning came back to me. *You could get away from here for a while.* And suddenly, it seemed like the best possible idea. "Yes," I said. "But are you sure about Indiana?" *The place I remembered living with Hector before Acadia. Or so I thought.*

"Yeah. It gets us away, but it also provides a purpose. We could see if you recognize anything from there. Maybe it's a long shot but…at least it's close by, and we'll be able to walk around without being hounded, to be together, to sleep in a bed that doesn't announce my every move to your mother." He smiled, but then went serious again. "To get some freedom."

It *would* be a wonderful relief not to worry about who was outside our door for at least a short while. And maybe by the time we returned, things would have died down. "Yes," I said again.

Calder looked relieved. "Thank you."

"No, this is for both of us. Xander mentioned us getting away this morning too."

He nodded. "We need it. Do we have to tell the police?"

"I don't think so. They didn't say we couldn't leave town." I shrugged. "I mean, we could anyway, just to be considerate, I guess, but I don't think we're required to. And I don't necessarily want them to know where we're going."

"You already told them about recognizing the Indiana sign though."

"I know, but I don't want them to think we're going on some vigilante information-gathering mission. Chances are good that nothing at all will come of it anyway."

"And that's okay. It just seemed like it made sense as far as a location."

"It does." I smiled. "Now, go gather my bathing suit before my mom comes home and finds me undressed."

Calder's eyes widened and he turned immediately and dove into the water as I laughed. He swam to the other side of the pool, where my suit sat discarded on the edge.

I grinned and then squinted upward as the sun broke through the clouds, casting the gloomy day in unexpected light. It felt appropriate, because while before it had seemed as though a cloud was over us, very suddenly everything looked brighter.

_____

Later in bed, cocooned in Calder's warm arms and drifting toward sleep, he suddenly said, "That day, Hector kept calling me Satan's spawn. He said it over and over. What do you think he meant by that?"

I opened my eyes in the darkened room and shivered, even though I was far from cold. "I don't know," I said. "There's no telling what was going through his sick brain." But as I drifted toward sleep again, the thought that ran through my mind was: *Maybe you don't want to know.*

CHAPTER THIRTEEN
Calder

Once Eden and I decided to take the trip to Indiana, my mood improved immensely. I had felt trapped, confined, and worthless for almost a month. And I had been trying so hard to snap myself out of it. After all, I had Eden back. If someone had told me two months before that Eden would be back in my arms, I would have happily agreed to live in a dark cave with her for the rest of my existence. And now, here I was edgy and frustrated. I felt ashamed of myself. But the simple truth was, I longed to take care of her. I longed to feel like the man she deserved. I wanted so desperately to give her things, to work for her, to provide a home for us, *marry her*. And I couldn't exactly do any of that from the guest room in her mom's house, especially considering how unwelcome her mom made me feel.

All of that, in addition to my apartment and my belongings being destroyed and then seeing Clive on television, had brought on a deep despair. I hadn't expected the very sight of his weaselly face to plummet me into a spiral of anger and feelings of defeat. But it had. Despite Clive Richter's small stature, he had always held a place of authority and power over me. Physically, I had always been stronger. But emotionally, or rather power-wise, he had controlled me, and in some sense, that was still true.

We definitely needed to get away.

The day after we decided to take a trip to Indiana and before we could plan a thing, the FBI showed up at Carolyn's door. My heart jolted and my breath came short when Molly came out to the patio where Eden and I were sitting to tell us. We exchanged fearful glances, and followed Molly inside, where a heavyset man with dark hair and a tall bald man, both wearing suits, waited.

"Hello," the heavyset man said, not smiling. "I'm FBI Agent Rivera." He nodded to his right. "This is Agent Glenn. You must be Calder Raynes?" he asked, offering me his hand.

I nodded and shook both their hands. "Please, call me Calder. And this is Eden," I said as Eden came up right behind me and then shook their hands too.

"Nice to meet you both," Agent Rivera said. "We need you to come down to the local FBI field office where we can interview you. Is now okay?"

My hands were suddenly clammy, but I reached out for Eden's anyway. I had no idea what this meant. When I gripped her hand in mine, she looked over at me, a small crease between her eyebrows.

"Now?" I asked. I'd been dying to get out of this house, and suddenly, I had this strange instinct to barricade myself inside. The last time we'd gotten in a police vehicle, things had not ended well. "Can I ask what it's about?"

"There's no need to be alarmed. We're responsible for

numerous missing children's cases, and we need to close yours out. Plus, we'd like to discuss a few other things that I'd rather address when we get to our office."

That last part worried me, but I nodded. What other choice did we have? *This is not like last time. This is not like last time.* The last time we'd been in a police car for reasons we didn't entirely understand, we'd been coerced, tricked—and we'd been led straight to hell. *This is different.*

Carolyn came rushing into the room still wearing gardening gloves and introduced herself to the detectives. "Does my daughter need a lawyer?" Carolyn asked, her eyes darting between them and Eden. I noted that she hadn't mentioned me.

"If she feels more comfortable having her lawyer present, he can meet us at the field office," Agent Rivera said.

"Mom," Eden said, "they just want to close out our case." Despite the reassurance to her mom, she shot me a nervous glance.

"I'll have my lawyer meet you at the office. It'll make me feel better. It's the smart thing to do," Carolyn said.

"Do you want to call a lawyer too, Calder?" Agent Rivera asked.

I shook my head. I wouldn't even have any idea who to call.

My nerves spiked again as we were escorted to Carolyn's driveway, where a police car waited. *This is not the same, this is not the same*, I kept repeating. Just the sight of the police cruiser alone made my fight-or-flight instinct kick in, and I squeezed Eden's hand as she gripped me back. Whether she was scared too, or whether she was holding me so tightly because she knew I needed it, I wasn't sure. I thought I had let go of some of my fear of the police after sitting through the questioning about Acadia recently. But in that moment, anxiety assaulted me because I didn't understand what was happening. Once again, I felt like everyone except me had the upper hand.

We sat huddled together in the back of the cruiser as the officer in front drove us to the downtown field office, the agents following behind. When we arrived, we were hurried in a back door and brought into a small room with nothing more than a table, two chairs, a TV in the corner, and another table with a coffee maker on it.

I scooted my chair closer to Eden's and held her hand under the table. "Are you okay?" I asked, looking at her and forcing myself to calm down for her sake.

"Yes, I'm okay. Are you?"

"I will be," I said, forcing a small smile.

A moment later, Agent Glenn walked into the room, a woman following behind. "Calder. Eden. This is Agent Malloy. She'll be interviewing Eden."

I frowned and glanced at Eden. "I thought we'd be interviewed together."

"It's easier if we interview you separately," Agent Glenn said. "And it will go a lot more quickly too. Plus, Eden's lawyer just arrived."

Eden leaned over and kissed my cheek, squeezing my arm. "It'll be fine. I'll see you right outside, okay?"

I let out a harsh exhale. "Okay." I turned to Agent Malloy. "She'll be close by?"

"Yup, right next door. It shouldn't take long." I nodded, and the agent escorted Eden out the door.

Agent Glenn sat down at the table. "Calder, I appreciate you being willing to give us an additional statement. We're glad to be able to close a case that so many of our agents were involved in back when Eden was abducted." He looked at me very directly. "We haven't found any evidence that you were taken from a different family, but I know that you've indicated you believe that to be the case."

I cleared my throat. "I do, but I don't have any concrete evidence. Mostly comments from others who are no longer able to shed any light on what they said to me. Truthfully, Agent Glenn, half the time I don't know what to think."

He nodded. "Please, call me Floyd. And I know; we're having trouble digging up information too. There are no records of those who lived at Acadia, other than the ones Hector kept on the council members. As you already know, it's been three years, but we still haven't identified so many of the adults, and identifying the children who were born there poses even more of an impossibility. As far as society knows, they never even existed."

My heart dropped. I felt responsible for that. "Maybe if I would have come forward years ago…"

"You wouldn't have been asked to attempt to identify the bodies. They weren't recognizable, I'm sorry to say. The list you gave to the police of all the children you remembered, their ages and descriptions, was very helpful. And between you and Eden, you accounted for all of them. We can at least give some of them names now." He studied me for a minute and then stood up and went to the TV in the corner and pressed a few buttons, bringing a remote control back to the table with him. "We don't have the most advanced technology here." He shot me a wry smile. "But I'm going to record this interview. Is that all right with you?"

"Uh, sure." I brought my hands together on the table in front of me.

223

"Would you like a cup of coffee or some water before we start?"

"No. Thank you."

He turned to the TV and pressed a button on the remote and then turned back to me.

"Will you state your name, please?"

"Calder Raynes."

"Thank you, Calder. I know you've given a statement to the local police about what happened at Acadia beginning several weeks before and leading up to the murder/suicides that took place there. Will you please take us through those steps, beginning with Officer Richter and Officer Owens locating you and taking you back to Acadia?"

I took a deep breath and went through the details again, beginning with being coerced into Clive's police car, being returned to Acadia, living in that small dim cell alone for two weeks. I left out my emotions, recounting those weeks as if I were describing a movie I'd once watched.

The agent asked several questions here and there so that I added details or cleared something up for him. When I got to the end of the story, and although I'd only gone through the facts, I felt like I'd run a marathon. I was exhausted. I rubbed my palms on my thighs as the agent picked up the remote and clicked off the video recorder.

"That was good. Thank you, Calder." His expression was neutral. "The other reason we wanted to talk with you is because we've been investigating the case against Clive Richter for a little while now. As you know, it was you two coming forward that encouraged his ex-partner, Officer Mike Owens, to seek immunity and offer his testimony. Without that, we wouldn't have the case that we do as far as the drug trafficking and money laundering." He shook his head. "When it comes to dirty cops, he takes the cake."

I let out a breath. "So he'll go away for a long time?"

"For those crimes, I'd bet on yes. However, now that Officer Owens is providing testimony against Officer Clive Richter that supports your account of him being at Acadia the day of the flood, Officer Richter is alleging you planned and carried out the deaths at Acadia that day."

My mouth fell open, my blood chilling. "What?" I croaked. My worst fears were being realized. Visions of being carted away to prison as Eden screamed and reached her arms out for me assaulted my brain. *Calm down, Calder. Get a grip.* My fists clenched and unclenched on my thighs. The very, very worst had happened to me before. I couldn't make myself believe it wouldn't happen again in a whole new way. I knew the way life worked.

"Officer Richter is claiming he picked Eden up per Hector's request—believing her to be an underage runaway—and that you came along willingly back to Acadia," Agent Glenn said. "He claims that on the way there, you were spouting off about killing everyone and leaving with Eden, so it would look like you two were dead along with everyone else."

"That's a lie!"

Agent Glenn nodded, his lips coming together for a second. "He says you kicked over the water system once it started raining. He didn't understand at the time what that would result in, but he ascertains that since you built it, you did. He says he left, but once everyone took shelter in the cellar, you must have locked the door behind all those people and left with Eden like you threatened."

Cold dread shot through my system, and yet, I was also

sweating. "I did kick over that system," I said. "I told the police. That's true. I did. I didn't mean for anyone to get hurt." A silent scream rose in my chest. Was I going to be culpable for the crime now? Would they believe Clive? "Am I being charged with something here? Do I need a lawyer?"

The agent leaned forward and put his hand on my shoulder. "No, we are not charging you with anything. Let me make this clear, son. I've personally met Clive Richter. I've interviewed him. I've assisted in the investigation of the crimes he was involved in—not even half of which have been reported on the news. Between you and me, and I have a feeling you'd agree wholeheartedly, Clive Richter is not only a dirty cop but he's a lying, conniving, manipulative opportunist. Not only do we not believe his assertions, but Officer Owens is corroborating *your* story, not his." He studied me for a minute before continuing. "We haven't released this to the news yet, but we exhumed Hector's body and we found the key. He locked those people in; we know that. Eden's and your stories add up and we believe we can finally close out this case." He paused as I digested his words, my breath evening.

"However," Agent Glenn continued, "it's unlikely that we'll be able to prosecute Clive Richter for the crimes against you and Eden. There simply isn't enough evidence after three years. It's Eden's and your word against his. I'm sorry for that." His expression told me that he truly was.

I swallowed heavily and brought my hand to my chest, my heart rate slowing as I took in one breath and then another. "He shot me," I said.

"I know. And if only you'd saved the bullet, this would be a whole different story."

I blinked. "Saved the bullet?"

"Yes, each bullet is specific to a gun. If we had the bullet, we could match it to Clive's duty weapon. That would be the piece of evidence that would make it easy to charge him with the crimes against you."

"I did keep the bullet, Agent. It's still in my leg."

His eyes widened. He paused for a beat and then a slow smile spread over his face. "Well, this changes everything."

My shoulders lowered. Kristi's friend had said that, with the placement of the bullet in my leg, it would be safer just to leave it where it had lodged. Which was lucky considering he didn't have any operating capabilities anyway.

"Are you willing to undergo a small operation?" the agent asked.

"If it means charging Clive Richter, hell yes."

Agent Glenn smiled again. "Well, all right, then." He shook his head in disbelief.

I watched him as he wrote something down, the smile still on his face. He looked kind, trustworthy. *He is on our side. We have someone on our side.*

He set the pen aside. "You'll probably have to testify against Clive in court."

"Will you be there?"

"Yeah, son, I'll be there."

I nodded. "Then, happily," I said.

He tilted his head, studying me. "I come across a lot of cases in my job, Calder. What you and Eden went through…" He shook his head. "It's hard to imagine. And I can count on one hand the number of missing kids I've seen returned in my twenty years as an agent." Something moved behind his eyes, sorrow perhaps. He looked at me pointedly. "Treasure the second chance you've been given. Be proud of yourself. You don't hold responsibility for any of it—not one piece. You were victims. But don't live like victims. Live like survivors. I hope you'll take my words to heart."

I thought I moved my head up and down, but I couldn't be sure. "Thank you, Floyd," I said, gratitude overwhelming me and making my voice sound choked.

He nodded once, and as I stood up, he offered me his hand and I shook it. "I'm proud to shake your hand," he said. He smiled and then turned and walked toward the door. I followed, feeling numb, overwhelmed. Grateful. Relieved.

Outside the door, Eden was waiting for me. I gathered her in my arms and hugged her. "Ready to go?"

"Yeah."

We got back in the police car waiting for us outside and were driven back to Eden's mom's house. I held Eden's hand loosely in mine, thinking about Clive Richter and Agent Glenn, thinking about how there were good and bad people everywhere, and that somehow today, I had let go of the last piece of the fear I'd been carrying around for so long. It might take a little longer for guilt to lose its malicious hold on my mind, but what Agent Glenn had said would help that too, I imagined. It was time—time to move forward. Without fear, without guilt, but with my Morning Glory. I leaned back on the seat and exhaled a breath I felt like I'd been holding for three long years.

CHAPTER FOURTEEN
Calder

After the meeting with FBI Agents Glenn and Malloy, another weight lifted. Later that day, Eden waited for me in a private room while I underwent a thirty-minute surgery that resulted in a small bullet being extracted from my thigh. I had always hated that ugly scar—a physical reminder of the worst day of my life. But suddenly, what had been unsightly to me before now looked like victory.

I felt like I was actually using the full capacity of my lungs to breathe again. And now Eden and I could finally get our plans underway. I woke up early the next morning filled with energy and purpose.

Yes, it might take a little time for charges to be brought against Clive for his crimes against us, and yes, we'd have to testify eventually, but the win for us was that we weren't afraid of him anymore. Freedom came in many forms—we had finally been set free from fear.

And so we began planning our trip.

Eden disagreed when I told her I thought I needed to

be the one to tell her mom we were leaving for a while, but she gave in anyway. I had tried to be understanding when it came to her mom—Carolyn had been without Eden for so long. I had told her I knew what that felt like, and obviously I did, better than anyone. And so I could appreciate her wanting to make up for lost time. But dealing with her neediness twenty-four hours a day was exhausting—and I had to believe that was true for not only me and Eden, but for Carolyn as well. I was going to be in her daughter's life for a long time, so it was necessary that we come to some sort of peace or at least an understanding.

And so with that in mind, I joined Carolyn, who was sitting on the patio with Molly, the next morning. "Good morning." I smiled and took a seat as they greeted me back.

"There's a full pot of coffee in the kitchen," Carolyn said.

"I'll get a cup in a minute." I ran my hand through my hair. "I actually wanted to talk to you."

Carolyn arched a brow, and Molly paused in taking a sip of her coffee. "Should I leave you two alone?" she asked.

"No, it's okay. You should know this too, uh…" I took a deep breath. "Eden and I are going to take a road trip and get away from here for a little while."

Carolyn blinked and Molly smiled. "Oh no, no," Carolyn said, shaking her head.

"I think you know better than anyone how difficult this has been for Eden and me," I said. "Not just as a couple, but individually. It's been difficult for all of us." I glanced at Molly and she gave me a small encouraging nod. "We just thought that getting away for a short time would ease the pressure on everyone and would give us a chance to have some time together after being apart for so long."

Carolyn's lips set in a thin line. "And what about me?

She was stolen from me. What about the time I need with my daughter?" She shook her head adamantly. "No, you won't take her away from me."

"I don't want to take Eden away from you," I powered on. I'd known this wasn't going to be easy. "Carolyn, Eden has longed for you all of her life. I know that better than anyone and I would never do anything to get in the way of your relationship with her. I know you have a lot of catching up to do too, a lot of lost time to make up for." I paused. "I was even hoping maybe you and I could..." I trailed off, feeling frustrated and at a loss for words, trying to ask for something I didn't know how to name. Acceptance? Family? Carolyn's cold glare wasn't helping me grasp the phrasing I hoped would help soften her heart.

An awkward silence ensued. *I should have rehearsed this.*

Suddenly Molly threw her arms up and let them come back down heavily on the table in front of her. Carolyn and I both startled, our gazes whipping her way. "Jesus, Carolyn! Here he is sitting here asking you to be a mom to him too. In case you forgot, he lost everyone he loved." She leaned forward. "You have an opportunity here not just to mother *me*, who has no mother anymore, but Eden *and* Calder... and Xander too, for that matter! You could have a bounty of people who need mothering right at your feet, people who would soak it up like sponges. And instead you're choosing to act in a way that will eventually do nothing except push us away. I'm sorry, but I can't be quiet about this for one minute longer. Look at yourself!"

Carolyn stared at her with wide hurt eyes. Molly lowered her voice. "You yourself described how you looked the other way and buried your head in the sand regarding what happened with Uncle Bennett, and then with Hector." Her expression filled with sympathy. "Don't do it again, Carolyn. Please don't be oblivious to what's going on around you. Your daughter is a woman. I'm sorry you didn't get to watch that happen. But you can't turn her back into a little girl by cutting crusts off her bread and brushing her hair before bed every night, by denying that she fell in love with someone when you weren't there. You can be a part of it *now*." She sat back in her chair. "Eden, she has this…quiet *strength* about her. She's been patient with you because she loves you, but she won't be patient forever. If you don't see that, then you're not seeing your daughter for who she is and you're going to lose her just when you found her again. And Calder"—she looked over at me—"Calder is sitting in front of you asking you to love him too."

I stared at Molly for a minute, shocked and grateful and maybe just a little embarrassed. But Molly was right. I hadn't actually acknowledged for some time how much I missed my mother's love, hadn't spoken of it with Eden yet. Despite the deep, aching feeling of betrayal at the end, *I missed my mother.* It was confusing and it hurt like hell. Did I want Eden's mom to love me as a son or as her daughter's boyfriend? Whichever it was, my heart was so thankful for Molly's comment, and for all she'd said. "Molly…thank you," I said to her, hoping she could see the sincerity in my eyes.

Carolyn remained silent, staring down at the table. I waited hopefully for her to respond. Instead, she stood up—her chair scraping over the stone patio—turned her back on us, and walked through the french doors and shut them behind her.

My shoulders drooped. I looked at Molly, whose expression was pained. "I meant every word I said to her. I just hope it did some good," she said.

"I appreciate it, Molly. Either way, I appreciate all the ways you've been so supportive of Eden and of me."

Molly smiled sadly. "You've both been through so much. If anyone deserves to find their place in this world, Calder, you two do. I hope I've helped."

"You have," I said, meaning it with my whole heart. Now I could only hope Carolyn would come around too.

Carolyn spent the rest of the day in her room. Despite the fact that we didn't have her blessing, Eden and I decided that we'd still go on our trip. It wasn't going to start off with quite the same support we had hoped for, but it was necessary for us and we were going to go anyway.

Late that afternoon, when I was in the kitchen getting a glass of water, I turned around to see Carolyn enter the room. I was surprised to see her with her hair pulled back and no makeup on. I'd never seen her not looking perfectly done up, regardless of the time of day. Her eyes were rimmed in red as if she'd been crying, but she offered me a sad smile. "Can we talk?" she asked.

I nodded and then joined her at the table, where we both sat down. I regarded her warily, not knowing where this was going to go.

"Calder," she started, and then paused. "I owe you an apology."

I let out a slow breath.

"I owe Eden an apology too."

"Thank you, Carolyn, I—"

"No, wait," she said. "Let me just say this and then you can say what you need to say to me. I can imagine you'd like to get some things off your chest too." She looked down, studying her fingernails. "I've been up in my room thinking so much about Eden's father, Bennett, today. I…I've been thinking about the ways I wish I had been more for him when he needed me." She shook her head. "Molly was right to point out that even though I'd acknowledged I buried my head in the sand then, I wasn't admitting that I'm doing it now too."

She was quiet for a moment as I waited. I could see she needed to organize her thoughts. "I have her back, and yet I'm so filled with grief over the moments I missed. I wanted so badly to experience the ways I lost out on mothering her, and that included being there to guide and experience her falling in love with someone." She gave a small shrug. "That's what I owe you the biggest apology for. I could see that day at the garden party how much you loved and adored her…how deeply your hearts are entwined, and yet"—she took a big shaky breath—"I tried to push her toward another man."

She clasped her hands together on the table. "I'm jealous of how deeply you love each other, how deeply you *know* each other. I'm jealous you got all those years and I didn't. Even though I know it's irrational, and I see now how it's affected my behavior and made me act so selfishly." She met my eyes, tears shining in hers. "Please yell at me. Tell me how awful I've been."

"I don't want to yell at you. I understand." I pictured myself standing on a chair in the bowling alley, panicked because Eden stepped out of my line of sight for a few minutes. It had to be the same way for her mom too. "There's no handbook for Eden's and my situation, and there's no handbook for yours either." I paused. "What I hope you know is that what Molly said about Eden having a quiet strength…nothing is more true. I love that so much about her. And that strength came from *you*. Eden was able to hold on to that quality because she never let go of her belief in love. You gave that to her. She drew on all the love you gave her in the first years of her life and she never let go. It kept her alive. All those years, you *were* with her because your love was still in her heart. Your love gave her the bravery to be who she is."

Tears spilled from Carolyn's eyes and coursed down her cheeks. "Thank you," she said. "And I'm sorry, I'm so sorry. I never considered that you need a mother too. I'm here for you." She reached her hand across the table, and I took it, smiling as relief moved through me like a cool breeze.

"I'm going to try to stop treating her like a little girl and see her for who she is," she said. "I'm going to try my very best. I'm going to focus on what I *have*, not what I missed."

"I know Eden will be thankful for that." I paused. "Just so you know though, there's no reason to stop making those fluffernutter sandwiches." They were damn good.

Carolyn laughed and wiped her tears and that's when Eden walked into the room. She stopped and took us both in and a huge smile broke out over her beautiful face, making her look radiant with happiness, as she rushed forward and draped one arm over my shoulders and reached one over Carolyn's. She leaned in and kissed my cheek and then leaned over and kissed Carolyn's. We laughed and something inside me felt *right* in the same way that a certain mix of colors and lines on the canvas came together to create the exact picture I'd envisioned in my mind.

Later, up in Eden's room, we opened her laptop and began planning the specifics of our trip.

We looked through a couple Indiana tourist sites and each one recommended the same resort again and again—French Lick Springs Hotel. We couldn't resist choosing the one place we found that had the word "springs" in it. It seemed too perfect a choice as a getaway for us. We had gone to another spring to get away once upon a time too. Plus, it was only a three-hour drive. We wouldn't have to risk too much by being on the road for very long. Neither one of us had a license, although Molly had agreed to loan us her car.

"Carolyn said we'd need to open up an account in your name to cash the check from my showing so I can finance our trip," I said as Eden entered in the information on the computer in order to book our room.

Her brow creased. "I have another account in my name too, that Felix left for me." She looked up at me. "We can access that too, now that I have a birth certificate."

"Okay, but I'm paying for this trip. I insist."

She gave me a soft smile. "Okay. Still, Felix left me that money because he wanted me to have it. It wouldn't be right to leave it there."

I nodded, thanking Felix in my head each time his name came up. I would be forever in his debt for taking care of my girl when I hadn't been able to.

The next day, we both accompanied Carolyn to the bank where Eden's mouth fell open when we learned that Felix had left several hundred thousand dollars for her. When we got home, she dropped down on the couch, her face in her hands, choking out sobs. I pulled her close and held her as she cried. I could hardly believe it either. What an incredible, generous man. *Thank you, Felix.*

And so it came to be that Eden and I were driving out of Ohio in Molly's car just as the sky began to dim. We had successfully snuck out through the back bushes while Xander made his first statement to the press in front of Carolyn's house. It was the perfect diversion.

As the miles flew by, my shoulders began to relax, and I felt like my muscles were fully unclenching for the first time in a little over a month. Eden shot me a flirty smile and winked, putting her feet up on the dashboard. My heart flipped and I almost laughed at myself. Would I ever stop being a lovesick schoolboy around her?

Her smile faded and she squeezed my hand. "How are you feeling?"

"Better. I already feel freer." I looked at the road in front of us.

"Yeah," she agreed. "Everything feels more hopeful when you're free. Who knows that better than us?"

I nodded, glancing at the speedometer to make sure I was going the speed limit. I wasn't going to risk that freedom for anything.

"Do you think the media will look for us?" she asked.

"They won't know we're gone. We haven't been outside your mom's house in a month, so they'll think we're still holed up. And even if they did know we left, by the time they know to look for us, we'll have Molly's car parked in a parking garage somewhere. The news plays the same fuzzy pictures of us coming out of my building again and again. The only other one they have of you is from when you were a kid. I don't think anyone will recognize us, especially if I put a ball cap on and you put your hair up."

We were quiet in our thoughts for a few miles, just watching the scenery go by, my mind roaming. "You know what I keep thinking about, Eden?" I asked. "You know what I've wondered about off and on all these years?"

"Hmm?" She looked at me and leaned her head back on the seat.

"Me kicking over that water system was just chance—a random, unplanned act that ended up flooding the cellar."

"Yeah," she said softly.

"Yeah. So how did Hector know? All those years, how did he know that there would be a flood on *that day*, under an eclipse? If he didn't *plan* it, how did he predict it?"

I glanced at Eden and she was studying me quietly, her brow furrowed. "I don't know," she finally said. "Do you think...I mean, is it possible Hector had some kind of psychic gift and that he...?" She sighed, looking frustrated before continuing. "Oh, I don't know...thought it was the voices of the gods speaking to him?"

"Psychic gift? Do you believe in that?"

"I'm not sure. But I'm willing to entertain it." She turned more fully toward me, getting that bright look in her eye that made my chest feel tight—my open-minded knowledge seeker. "And if he did have a"—she waved her hands around—"precognition? I don't know. I'll have to look it up, but maybe he misinterpreted the visions or the voices or whatever as some sort of message from the gods, because along with being psychic, he was also a little crazy." She frowned. "Is that...? Does that sound totally off the wall?"

"I have no idea. Yeah, it does sound a little off the wall, but that doesn't mean it is, you know? I don't have a better explanation. Unless he planned to kick over my system or do something else to cause a flood, and I just coincidentally happened to do it for him."

"Or that all the factors came together in just the right way. Coincidence all around—the rain, the eclipse..." She bit her lip, not looking convinced by that explanation. "I guess we'll never truly know."

"No, we won't. And somehow, I guess, that has to be okay."

"Yeah, that's the hard part. I still can't believe they exhumed his body."

We were quiet for another minute before Eden turned to me again. "You know what else I wonder about?"

"Hmm?"

"Well, Hector always proclaimed that the foretelling said I would become his only legal wife. But at our marriage, I never signed anything. And I didn't even know my last name at that point. He couldn't have made it legal. Could he?"

I thought about that. "I don't know a lot about the laws of marriage, but no, I can't see how he could have made it legal considering the fact that you were a missing kid." I paused. "One of the council members was a judge in Arizona though. Could he have planned a way to forge documents?" Something came to me. "Or maybe it was just a way *not* to have to marry Miriam or Hailey. He was using a false name. He couldn't really marry anyone. Maybe he used the gods' foretellings as a way around things that just wouldn't fit in with his lies."

"So many lies," she whispered. "It's so hard to differentiate sometimes."

I grabbed her hand. "We know what's true and what's not, Morning Glory." I paused. "It sounds like something between a feeling and a whisper. Remember?"

Eden gave me a smile and squeezed my hand.

After a minute, I said, "On a more casual note"—I grinned over at her—"guess who I caught making out on the side of the house when I went around to the garage to get your mom's suitcases?"

Eden's mouth opened and she stared at me for a minute before her eyes widened. "Bentley and Molly?"

I frowned. "How'd you know?"

"I knew it! I had a feeling. Did they see you?"

"No, I ducked back around the house. I felt like a Peeping Tom. I've only met the guy once."

She laughed, but then her face went serious. "Wait, are you sure he wasn't taking advantage of her?"

I glanced at her, smirking. "I'm sure, unless a woman being accosted sometimes wraps her legs around her attacker's hips and says, 'Yes, yes, Bentley, don't stop.'"

She threw her head back and laughed. My heart soared. Just being silly with her, talking about casual things, felt like a small miracle. In one sense, I wanted that feeling to lessen, and in another sense, I hoped it'd never go away.

After a minute, Eden mused, "There are stories to be told everywhere, aren't there?" She leaned back, looking happy about that.

We arrived in French Lick, Indiana, at about eight o'clock that evening and followed the directions we'd written down to the resort where we had reservations under Molly's name, along with her identification.

"Oh wow," Eden whispered when we pulled through the gates and drove up a long winding road toward West Baden Springs Hotel, just up the road from the French Lick Hotel and Casino.

Even though it was dark, I could see the grounds were landscaped perfection, featuring shaped shrubbery and flowering bushes, and an abundance of huge ancient trees.

We were silent as the hotel came into view, a massive historical resort painted a soft yellow, with a circular building in the center featuring a colossal glass dome. All the tourist sites we'd looked at said the building was fashioned after the most luxurious spas in Europe. I'd never been to Europe, but I could agree with the luxurious part.

I pulled into a lot just down the hill and parked in the corner, next to some tall shrubs. We got out and I retrieved our bags from the trunk and took out a baseball cap and stuck it on my head. Eden got some kind of hair band out of her purse and put her long blond hair up in a tight bun at the back of her head. Then we walked hand in hand the short distance to the hotel.

"Oh," we both said when we'd stepped through the main doors. I looked over at Eden and we both laughed softly. From the inside, the dome was even more breathtaking. We walked through the large atrium with our heads swiveling in every direction. There were hotel room balconies surrounding the perimeter of the dome with wrought-iron gates to make them look old-fashioned. The huge open room had sitting areas sprinkled everywhere, a bar, and a couple shops on opposite sides. I'd never seen anything like it. I felt like we were in another world altogether or at least another country. *Away.* This was exactly what we needed.

I sat on a small couch in the lobby area and pretended to look through a brochure as Eden went to the front desk to check in. A few minutes later, she was coming my way, grinning with a key card in her hand. We held hands as we went up the elevator to our room and I couldn't help the smile that took over my face and the emotion that welled up in my chest as the feeling of freedom increased.

We followed the signs to our room, and when I spotted a Coca-Cola machine down a hallway, I pulled Eden with me, dropping our bags, taking out a couple dollars, and purchasing two cans. I handed one to her and then popped open the other one and leaned against the wall as I downed the whole entire thing in long swallows, the sweet fizziness filling my mouth, the taste that I still associated with forbidden joy. When I lowered the can, I saw that Eden was watching me with a big grin on her face. She laughed and then leaned forward and kissed me quickly on the mouth. "Good?" she asked.

I tipped the can back to get the last drops. "So good," I said.

Two minutes later, we were safely locked inside our hotel room.

CHAPTER FIFTEEN
Calder

"It says here there's a museum in town that tells the history of the hotel," Eden said, taking a bite of buttered toast with jelly with one hand and holding the brochure with the other.

I leaned back in my chair, sipping my coffee and letting my eyes roam over her. "Whatever you want to do," I said, "I'm game." I cocked one brow. "We could just stay in bed for a couple days."

She grinned but didn't look up at me. "Haven't you gotten enough of me yet?" she asked, still reading the brochure.

"Never."

She finally brought her eyes to mine. "We did that once before, remember? It was…sticky."

"It was wonderful."

Her expression grew tender. "It was. And necessary. But this week I want to get out and walk around with you, feel the sunshine on my face."

I smiled. "Then get your perfect little butt in the shower."

She headed to the bathroom, shooting me a flirty look over her shoulder. "Aren't you going to join me?"

I didn't need to be asked twice. I was up and out of my chair before she could take another step. Her laughter rang out as I came up behind her and scooped her up so we could get in the shower as quickly as possible. We left the bathroom door open and didn't try to be quiet. Not sneaking around felt so damn good.

An hour later, we were dressed and strolling hand in hand through the shops in the lobby. Eden had her bangs brushed back, held by a wide, pale pink scarf tied in a knot at the back of her neck and sunglasses on that took up half of her face. People still glanced her way, but I realized it was only because, even mostly covered, she was stunning, and not because anyone recognized her.

I had the same baseball cap on, but not much else in the way of a disguise. It seemed like enough. No one looked twice at me.

The weather was cool and crisp and we'd both brought jackets, but on that particular day, the sun was shining and it was warm enough to stroll to the casino a little ways away and eat lunch on the porch of a local restaurant.

My body relaxed and so did my soul, finding peace and serenity in just *being* with Eden, enjoying our freedom. It'd taken all this time, and we finally had a small measure of it. Despite everything we'd lost, despite all the ways in which we'd *both* been stripped bare, we had each other and we could finally celebrate that. I could finally start letting myself believe that life held promise—for me, for her, *for us*.

That entire week, we relaxed. We walked around enjoying the small-town sites, we picked through tourist shops surprising each other with small trinkets we thought the other would like, we made love whenever we wanted to, and we woke up every morning tangled in each other. It was heaven. Eden went to the spa once, and we swam in the large picturesque indoor pool. As we lounged at the side, Eden pulled out a book and I squinted over at the cover.

"*His Rockin' Heart?*" I asked.

Eden giggled, placing the book down on her stomach and looking over at me, her cheeks taking on a pink tinge. "It might sound like a silly title, but it's so good. Over these last few years, I've read a lot, but I couldn't bring myself to read romance books." Her expression took on a brief hint of sadness. "I just couldn't. It hurt too much. That one I read at Kristi's, it was the last time I remember having *hope*." She paused for so long, I wondered if she'd go on. "But now"— she laid her head back on the lounger and bit her lip—"I can, and I enjoyed that first one. *A lot.*"

I thought back to that day at Kristi's apartment, to the sweet look of hope on Eden's face...our last truly happy moment before we were dragged back to hell. Looking at the same gentle, hopeful expression on her face now caused gratitude to slam into my heart with such sudden force, I almost jolted. Somehow...*somehow*, we had found our way back. And I never, ever wanted that look to disappear from her beautiful face. My lip quirked. "Oh, I remember that book," I said. "It was a masterpiece."

Eden laughed. "Actually, I looked it up before I bought this one because I thought I'd buy more from the same author if possible, and all the reviews said it was a really bad book." She brought her voice to a dramatic whisper on the last three words.

"Fools! I'm in total disagreement. Whatever the highest rating is, that's what *I* give that work of art."

"Five stars." She grinned.

"Five life-changing, *extremely* satisfied stars," I said, adding a dreamy tone to my voice.

Eden laughed. "We'll have to hope this one measures up, then." She smiled flirtatiously at me again and went back to reading.

Later, we strolled the grounds and talked about where we saw our life going. I would call a couple galleries when we got back and Eden would pick up her piano lessons. We'd buy a new Bed of Healing and we'd hire someone to clean up and repair my trashed apartment so I could hand it back over to the guy who'd rented it to me. Then we'd find a new one in a better part of town, one we both picked out together. I'd buy the most high-tech alarm system on the market. And I'd marry my girl. I didn't mention that part to her again, but in my mind, it was my first priority when we returned. I wouldn't be able to afford a very fancy ring right away, but I didn't think Eden would mind.

We texted Xander, Carolyn, and Molly frequently, updating them on what we were doing, and attached lots of pictures.

On the fifth day we were there, Molly sent Eden a text that sounded important and so Eden called her back. I was lying back on the bed, flipping through the movies. We'd gone horseback riding earlier that day, and so we were both tired and sore and looking forward to relaxing for the evening.

"Hey, Molly," I heard Eden say.

She listened for a minute, and when I saw her face drain of color, I sat up, watching her.

"Okay," she said quietly. "Thank you for letting us know... No, I know... Yes, I'm fine. We're fine." Eden glanced over at me and then away. "Okay. I love you too. Bye, Molly." She hung up and stood staring straight ahead for a minute.

"Eden?" I asked, fear creeping into my voice. "You're scaring me. What's wrong?"

"Clive Richter was murdered in jail this morning. The police just came over to tell us. Molly told them we were staying with a friend for a couple days. She told them she'd call us." Her voice sounded flat and alarm speared through me.

"How?"

Eden's eyes met mine. "Stabbed."

I blinked at her, absorbing the news, trying to figure out if I was upset about it. "Do they know why?"

Eden came to sit down on the bed next to me. She shook her head. "She said they didn't even have a suspect. He was in jail with people he'd arrested though. Knowing Clive's personality, he made enemies all over the place."

I couldn't disagree with that. Clive was the type of man who got off on making people's lives miserable, especially when he held the upper hand. I thought about the time I'd physically overpowered him at the main lodge before I'd known he was a police officer. I knew now he was the type of cop who needed a gun to show any strength. And he hadn't had either the upper hand or a gun in jail. Still, was I disappointed he'd never serve time for his crimes? Was I disappointed he'd never be officially charged with the crimes against Eden and me? Flashes of him pulling up in his police car, throwing Eden and me in the back...watching as Hector started the fire at my feet...beating Xander... "Good," I finally said.

Eden searched my face for several beats and then she leaned in and wrapped her arms around me, pulling me close. She knew exactly what I was thinking, just like she always did. And she forgave me. I released a breath and pulled her against me.

"There won't be a trial now," she said when we'd let go of each other. "We know that for sure."

"Good," I repeated, realizing that although I'd have gone to the trial and faced him without fear, it was another way we'd been set free. "I don't know if he deserved to die, Eden. I guess it's not my job to determine that, although if I had had the chance to kill him that day, I would have. But he was guilty, and he was an evil man, there's no doubt in my mind there. So I don't have a problem with what happened to him. And maybe we don't get justice in the court system, but the justice we get by being free of him? That's enough."

She nodded. "For me too."

We took a long hot shower together, and when we got out, we saw that a light but steady rain was falling outside. We got under the covers and watched movies for the rest of the evening. Inside, I felt okay, but I still held on to Eden tightly that night. And in the morning, we stayed in bed well past eleven.

"Let's go to that museum today," Eden suggested as we were getting dressed. "It's really the only thing we haven't done."

"Okay," I agreed. "Should we think about going back to Cincinnati?"

"Maybe just a couple more days? I'm not ready to leave just yet."

I released a breath. "Me neither."

Outside, the air smelled fresh, and I inhaled deeply. The rain had washed everything clean and somehow the world seemed brighter.

We strolled downtown to the small building that held the French Lick West Baden Museum and waited as the guide finished with another tour. We were the only two in the next group, and I held Eden's hand as we walked through the building, the tour guide expounding on all the artifacts.

As we stood and looked at a poster of an advertisement from a company that sold the spring water as an elixir back in the 1800s, our tour guide explained, "Pluto Water is what made the French Lick resort famous. It was sold as a health remedy for chronic ailments of the stomach, liver, kidneys, you name it. It was declared that these waters had miraculous powers to cure everything from asthma to alcoholism to venereal disease." He chuckled. "Guesthouses were built around the springs so people could drink and soak in the Pluto Water."

Eden tilted her head. "Why was it called Pluto Water?" she asked.

"Oh, it was named for the god of the underworld because the waters came from underground and were dark, like the mythical River Styx."

I glanced at Eden, who was wearing a small frown, and then back at the poster. *Rest for the weary, Cure for the ill,* I read. "Did the stuff really work?" I asked the tour guide.

"Well, they tested the water at some point and found it was full of two things"—he looked back at us as he continued through the museum—"salt and traces of lithium."

"Lithium?" I asked as he stopped at another display.

"Yup, they use it now as a mood stabilizer for mental health issues. Of course you'd have to drink quite a bit of the water to get those effects, but a little bit of it could sure put you in a good mood, and the salt would clear you out real fast so that some of your ailments probably would feel better.

Temporarily at least." He continued on, my heart suddenly racing. I looked over at Eden and I could see by the expression on her face that she was thinking the same thing I was.

"Sir," I interrupted, "these springs, are there other ones? I mean, in other parts of the country? Is it possible?"

"Oh, I suppose it's possible. I don't personally know of any others but could be."

I nodded, and we continued through, my mind spinning in a hundred directions. When we finally thanked the guide and stepped back out onto the large front porch of the museum, Eden whispered, "Hector, he was here, wasn't he?"

"I think so," I said, looking around as if I would suddenly see him walking toward us on the sidewalk. I shivered despite the fall sunshine.

"Did he find a spring that had the same elements?" she asked.

"That or he added them, if that's even possible. I don't know. What I'm pretty damn sure of? Pluto Water"—I met her eyes—"it was the same as our holy water."

CHAPTER SIXTEEN
Calder

We walked back to the hotel and then Eden left for the appointment she had for a massage at the spa while I returned to our room. I was still attempting to process the information about the spring water and what I believed was a very likely connection to Acadia, but knew I was missing some vital piece that might make the link clearer. Was it possible it was just a coincidence? What connected Hector to this specific place in Indiana other than the fact that Eden was convinced Hector had brought her to this state after he abducted her from Ohio? I supposed it would make sense that the first council member he would try to recruit—Eden's father—would be within driving distance. And it would be more likely that Hector would have heard Eden's father's story since it was practically local. Still…those were a lot of maybes.

I lay back on the bed, my mind insisting on going over Hector's potential connection to Indiana, and now, this place in particular. There was Pluto Water's name—a Greek connection—just like all the other Greek connections Eden had discovered in our religion and so many other parts of Acadia. But what did it mean? Was it possible Hector had simply been traveling through this part of the country and had liked the idea of the spring and its uses and sought something similar in Arizona? I let out a frustrated breath. There were too many possibilities to count and my brainstorming felt useless.

I shot Xander a quick text about the natural elements in the water we'd discovered here and asked him to let me know what he thought. He texted back and told me he wanted to look a few things up but that he was working and would get back to me later.

Before I knew it, I'd fallen asleep and Eden was running her fingers through my hair gently. I opened my eyes and gazed up at her beautiful face, smiling sleepily. But my smile quickly faded and I sat up when I saw the worried look on her face. "Hey. Are you okay? How was your massage?"

"What? Oh, it was good. Nice." She stood up and headed toward the bathroom. "I'm going to shower all this lotion off and then we can go to dinner?" she called behind her, closing the bathroom door.

I frowned. She seemed off. "Yeah, okay," I called to the closed door.

We took the shuttle bus provided by the resort, to a restaurant that the front desk recommended. The atmosphere was romantic and the food excellent, and we held hands throughout our meal, but Eden seemed distracted. When I asked her about it, though, she just said the massage earlier must have fogged up her brain. And then she'd appeased me with a warm smile and a squeeze of my hand.

We went back to the hotel early and Eden got in bed

and took out her book, so I switched on a TV show and had fallen asleep before it even ended.

I was woken up by Eden's hand dipping below the waistband of my briefs.

"I finished my book," she said in my ear. "Were you asleep?"

"No," I lied.

She slid her hand downward and squeezed me gently. I groaned again. She dipped her hand lower and cupped my balls in her palm. "Oh God, Eden."

I rolled over and took her face in my hands, kissing her mouth deeply until those sweet little moans I loved so much came up her throat.

"Tell me about your book," I whispered when I'd broken free from her mouth. I smiled against her neck before I feathered my lips over it lightly and she arched her body into mine.

"Hmm," she hummed as I pulled her tank top up and over her head. My mouth immediately went for her sweet pink nipple. I knew she loved it and so did I. As I sucked and teased the stiff peak, she ran her fingers through my hair.

"Hendrix Cooper, drug-addicted, alcoholic manwhore and lead singer of Devout Wenches, has a one-night stand with who he thinks, in his inebriated state, is a crazed groupie."

I brought my head up. "Devout Wenches?"

Eden made a frustrated sound in her throat and grabbed my head, pushing it back toward her breast. I grinned and resumed what I'd been doing.

"What he doesn't realize until later is that it was actually his assistant, Polly Honeycutt, a poor southern girl whose whole family died when a tornado came ripping through

253

their small trailer park. She was forced to find the first job she could and, of course, fell secretly in love with the damaged but lovable bad boy."

"Damaged?" I scoffed, moving to her other breast and kissing it once, lightly. "He sounds more like a complete mess."

Eden moaned as I sucked her nipple into my mouth, and then flicked it with my tongue. She wrapped her legs around my hips and ground up against my hardness. I made a strangled sound in my throat. God, she felt good. I moved my hips in slow circles against her to the rhythm of my mouth. For several minutes the only sounds in the room were our soft moans.

"Aren't we all, in our own way?"

"Huh?"

"Messes?"

I paused in my exploration of the sweet dip right between her breasts as I tried to pick up the string of our conversation. *Hendrix. A total mess. Aren't we all? Right.*

"True enough," I agreed, kneeling up so that I could remove her bottoms.

As I began to bring her shorts and underwear down her legs, she said, "Anyway, he had his reasons. He had been abused by the headmaster at the boarding school where his parents cast him off because they couldn't be bothered by their own child, and although he cried out for help for years, no one ever came to his rescue." She shook her head, deep sorrow moving through her expression. I paused in confusion. Was I supposed to comfort her regarding the tragic childhood of a fake rock star, or persist in getting her naked? Thankfully, Eden kicked off her bottoms and sat up, bringing her mouth to mine.

We kissed in that position until I was throbbing so hard that I couldn't stand another minute. "Eden," I begged.

She blinked, her eyes shiny and half-closed. Then she pushed me down on the bed and removed my underwear quickly.

She got on top of me and held my erection in her hand as she lowered herself down on it. I gasped at the tight, wet grip of her.

Eden closed her eyes and started rocking very slowly. "It was a long road for them," she said, her eyes still closed. "Hendrix had to commit to rehab and then fire his manager, Naomi Garnet, who was constantly trying to get in his pants and ruin things for him and Polly in shrewd and ruthless ways." She began moving faster, and I felt like I might pass out with pleasure, my skin erupting in goose bumps as my nerve endings quivered. I reached up and took her small perfect breasts in my hands and ran my thumbs over her nipples until she threw her head back and started moving in earnest.

I felt my orgasm swirling through me, my balls drawing up tightly against my body. And then all at once, it hit and I growled as I bucked my hips up into her. Eden gasped and then fell forward, panting out her own climax. My brain felt hazy and bright at the same time, the stars that had burst in my mind, dripping through my limbs. *Holy hell.*

I brought my arms up around her, breathing in her sweet scent and loving her so intensely, it made my heart dip and then rise, seeming to hang suspended for a brief moment before it settled back into place.

"Polly," she said in a voice just above a whisper, "you deserve a man who is going to love you in ways that make you feel like the angel you are. I'm going to try my bloody best to be that man, but right now, I'm not. And I love you far too much to offer anything less. But maybe you'll…wait for me, Polly. Believe in me. Be my reason to fight."

I looked to the side as if the fictional person she was speaking to might be standing there.

"I'm sorry, Hendrix," she whispered. "I can't." I felt the wetness of a tear fall onto my shoulder as I waited again.

"She can't?"

Eden shook her head against my shoulder. "She can't."

"She can't be Hendrix's reason to fight? *Why?*"

"I don't know. That was the end."

"What the hell?" That seemed outrageous.

"It's a cliffhanger," she explained. "We'll find out what happens in three months."

Three *months?* "You bet your ass we will," I said with perhaps a little more hostility than was necessary.

Eden started laughing and I slipped out of her with the movement. She cupped her hands on my cheeks and rested her forehead against mine. "I'm pregnant," she whispered.

I froze. She watched me closely, which wasn't hard to do considering her eyes were less than an inch from mine. I pulled back slightly and gaped at her. "I… What? I thought… you said…"

She dropped her hands, moving off me and falling back on her pillow. I turned toward her. "I know. I'm shocked too. The doctor said it'd be highly unlikely I'd ever conceive without assistance. I don't know what to say. I feel like I tricked you or something."

"Eden," I said gently, my heart finally stuttering back to life. I brought one hand to her stomach, a feeling of…awe coming over me. There was a baby in there? A tiny life? I met her eyes, my lips curving into a wondrous smile.

She sat up slightly, supporting herself with her elbows. "Are you...are you happy?"

I was shocked. I had no idea if I felt ready to parent a baby. But I knew how much Eden had ached at the loss of our first baby, how much we *both* had ached. And then thinking she'd never be able to have another child, that it was yet something else that had been stolen from her—from us. But it wasn't. Of all the losses we'd had to accept, that wasn't one. Relief swept through me, followed quickly by joy. "Yeah, I'm happy," I said. "Are you?"

Tears filled her eyes and she nodded. I pulled her close and just breathed with her for a few minutes as the reality settled over me. "How far?" I asked.

"About five weeks, I guess. I don't know. I bought a test at the drugstore we stopped in today and took it in the bathroom down at the spa."

"Did we make this baby in the Bed of Healing?"

Eden let out a soggy laugh. "I think we did."

I let the news sink in more deeply. I was going to be a father. "It feels right. It feels like a second chance."

Eden nodded and sniffled again.

A part of me felt inadequate...I still didn't have a name, an identity, let alone the ability to support them. But I knew one thing. "I'm going to protect you, both of you," I said. "I won't let anything happen to you." Whatever I had to do to keep that vow, that's what I'd do.

Eden leaned back and studied my face, her eyes troubled. "I know you will," she said. "Never for one second will I ever doubt that."

We fell asleep in each other's arms—a small new life nestled between us in the safety of Eden's body.

In the darkness of night, Eden shook me awake. "You're

dreaming, Butterscotch," she said softly. "You're dreaming of them."

I let out a harsh breath, trying to get my racing heartbeat under control. I brought my hand up to my hair and gripped it. A pit of deep dread had opened inside me. "Yes," I gasped.

"You haven't had a nightmare in a long time," she said, laying her head on my chest and wrapping her arm around my middle.

"I know," I said, starting to relax, that gaping hole filling in just a little.

"Is it because of the baby?"

"I... Maybe." I pulled her closer. "But only because I want to keep you both safe."

"You will keep us safe. I trust you, Calder. I have no doubts."

For the first time in a very long time, I said a prayer to the God of Mercy—even though he had failed me once. I wanted so desperately not to let her down.

The next day was chillier than the one before and so Eden put on a big sweater and I layered two long-sleeve shirts before heading out to breakfast. The air was crisp, but the sky was cloudless and blue overhead, and there was that faint smell of burning leaves in the air that I had learned to associate with fall since being in the outside world. And in a location that had more distinct seasons than Arizona.

I held Eden's warm hand in mine and we lingered over our food. The dread of the nightmare released its grasp in the bright light of day and I was feeling hopeful. It had to be normal that I would have a few bad dreams, that the nightmares would come back temporarily. Eden had given me some life-changing news and it had rocked me, and naturally it brought up memories of the first time we'd created a life and how cruelly that life had been taken from us.

"We should think about leaving today or tomorrow," I said. Eden had her hair pulled back from her face and her sunglasses were resting on top of her head. Her thick black sweater came all the way up to her chin and the dark knit right up against her cheek highlighted how flawless her skin was. Or maybe she was just glowing. "I think you should go to the doctor as quickly as possible to make sure everything's all right."

Eden's eyes met mine and she nodded.

"As soon as we get back, I'm going to ask the police to help me get a social security number like they're doing for Xander. I can't wait any longer for someone to come forward. It likely won't ever happen, and I have a life to build for us." Marrying her was even more important than ever to me now. I wondered distantly how Carolyn was going to take this news.

"Okay," Eden said.

I watched her pick at her food, and after a few minutes, she said, "I have an idea."

"Uh-oh," I joked, one side of my mouth quirking up.

"Ha ha. But seriously, I know we haven't had much opportunity to talk about that water thing from yesterday, and maybe it's a coincidence. But I can't help but wonder if Hector not only passed through here, but... Oh, I don't even know." She pursed her lips. "I thought maybe we could go to the local library and just look up a few things."

"What kind of things?"

Her expression became pensive and she chewed on her bottom lip. "I don't know. But I think it's worth a try.

If nothing comes up, nothing comes up. But we're the only ones who know about this possible connection to French Lick, Indiana. The police aren't going to look into a hunch about spring water and lithium. If we don't try, no one else will. And who knows if we'll ever be back here?"

"My little knowledge seeker," I said on a smile.

"That's your fault." She winked. "What do you think?"

I crossed my arms in front of my chest. It suddenly felt chillier. "Yeah. Okay."

My phone dinged and I looked at the text:

Xander: Dude, I looked up Pluto Water. Sounds like our holy water. ???
Me: I know. We think so too. Not sure what to make of it. Looking into a few things. Will let you know.
Xander: Okay. You all right?
Me: Better than ever. You good?
Xander: Yeah
Me: Talk soon
Xander: Later

We asked the waiter about the nearest library, which turned out to be within walking distance, and then gathered our things.

Less than ten minutes later, we were walking through the doors of the public library.

"What are we hoping to find here?" I asked in a hushed tone as Eden looked around.

"I'm not sure. Like I said, maybe nothing. I thought we'd look back at some newspapers from the time when Hector took me from Cincinnati and brought me to Indiana, maybe even someplace close to here."

I frowned, thinking this might very well be a wild goose chase, but followed her when she headed toward a librarian unloading a cart of books.

Thirty minutes later, the librarian had us set up at a computer station and we were looking through back copies of the local paper on their database. The librarian had explained that back copies of other papers could sometimes be found online, but they were such a small town, the newspapers were only catalogued there. Eden sat and scrolled through the top stories as I sat beside her, just watching. I was happy enough just to stare at her as she researched. Plus, the quiet was nice as I considered all the things we'd need to do when we got back to Cincinnati.

After a while, Eden huffed out a breath and turned to me, a small embarrassed smile on her face. "I don't even know what I'm doing or what I'm looking for. I'm wasting our vacation."

I leaned back in my chair, taking in her disappointed expression. "Okay, wait, let's go over the time line. That one you had on the back of your door? Do you have it memorized?"

"Sadly, yes. Why?"

I leaned forward and put my elbows on my thighs. "So, we're looking at articles that came out about the time you were abducted. But"—I considered things for a minute—"Acadia was formed years before that. Wouldn't it be safer to assume if something happened that, I don't know, *inspired* Hector to form Acadia, that that event would have happened right before?"

"You might be on to something there," she said, her eyes

brightening. "So, from what we know from the police and when the land was purchased, Acadia was formed a year before you were born, whether you were born there or not." She glanced at me quickly. "So maybe we should look back at articles from the few months prior to that?" There was the glint of excitement in her expression, and despite the dark topic, I couldn't help but to feel like it was a bit of an adventure too.

"Sounds like a good idea."

Eden looked forward at the computer again, concentrating, and I sat back in my chair while she scrolled.

As she focused on what she was doing, I glanced around the library, people-watching for a few minutes. There was a young couple at one of the computers arguing in whispered voices. There was a mom picking out bright-colored cardboard books with her toddler. My eyes lingered on the child, who was excitedly reaching for the books his mom handed him. I could hardly believe we'd have one of those little people soon. I wondered if we'd have a boy or a girl... who he or she would look like.

When I glanced back at Eden, she was leaned in to the screen, focusing intently on something. She turned her head toward me, her face drained of color. "Hector's real name was Thomas Greer."

I jolted back and then instinctively stood and moved my body to protect Eden as if Hector would somehow materialize because of what she had just said. "How do you know?" I demanded, attempting to keep my voice low.

"This." Her voice was a mere squeak as she pointed at the news article on the screen.

I leaned in and looked over her shoulder. My eyes scrolled quickly through the article and then I went back and read it more slowly, my heart racing.

There was a picture of what was very clearly a younger Hector at the top of the page, with short-cropped hair and wearing a dress shirt and tie. The title of the article said, *"History Professor's Family Murdered in Robbery."*

"Oh God," Eden breathed. She brought her fingers up to her lips as we both read on.

The family of Indiana University Southeast's Greek history professor, Thomas Greer, was found murdered early Sunday morning. Professor Greer returned home from a conference to discover his wife, Alice, and five-year-old daughter, Danae, stabbed to death in their home. Police don't have any suspects at this time but are speculating it was a home invasion robbery. A source at the police department says the Greer home could have been targeted because Thomas's wife, previously Alice Lockwood, was the heiress to an Australian mining fortune and the thieves most likely anticipated the presence of money and jewelry. The family had planned to accompany Thomas Greer on his trip, but his daughter became ill at the last minute and tragically, now, they remained behind.

We scrolled forward, our eyes glued to the screen. We came upon a few short articles, but no more information was offered. After a couple months, the case had grown stagnant. The police didn't have any suspects and Thomas had a foolproof alibi. He'd been at the conference the entire weekend and presented several times.

My mind raced. An Australian mining fortune. Well, that answered the question of where Hector's money came from.

I watched as Eden did a search for Greer's name, but no more articles came up.

"Look at this," Eden said quietly, pointing her finger to the bottom of a short article. I looked closer and read aloud. "Alice Greer (née Lockwood), and Danae Greer will be laid to rest this Saturday at Our Lady of Mercy cemetery."

"No, this part," Eden said, moving her finger down.

I read quickly through "survived by" names, most with Alice's maiden name, and then stopped when I got to her mother-in-law's name: Willa Greer.

"*Willa*...she was his mother," I murmured, picturing crystal-blue ageless eyes.

Go to the far-left corner. It's the only place where you'll live! And somewhere in my barely lucid mind, those words had come back to me. And because of it, I had lived.

"Yes," she said, "and look at this."

I squinted at the screen again, to another article where they had taken a statement from Willa Greer. She was standing in front of her business, a fortune-telling shop in downtown French Lick, right next to another small tourist store. *"Madam Willa, Past, Present, Future Told. Come Inside."* I swallowed hard, not completely understanding what it meant. Another sign on her shop window declared "Holistic medicine sold here—treat ailments of all varieties."

There is room for me here. Here I'm useful.

I snapped back to the present as Eden clicked Print with a shaking hand, stood up quietly, and grabbed the article copies as they emerged from the printer. She folded the papers and shoved them in her purse, then shut everything down and pulled me out of the library.

When we stepped outside into the crisp fall air, we both sucked in gulps of breath. I leaned back against a column in front of the building and wrapped my arms around her and hugged her close. "Hey," I said against her hair. "You have to stay calm. You've got a little life inside of you."

"I know," she whispered against my chest. "It's just a shock. Seeing him...hearing about his past. I don't even know what to feel. Oh my God, Calder, we found him."

"We did. And I don't know how to feel either."

She looked up at me. "None of...none of what happened to his family makes it okay what he did."

I shook my head, staring out at the mostly empty parking lot in front of me. "No, it doesn't. In fact, it might make it worse—making victims out of others, exploiting people's pain, taking you from your parents when he knew what it felt like to lose a little girl, causing your miscarriage." My hand splayed out on her stomach.

Eden was quiet for a minute. "Did he"—she bit her lip—"just go crazy after what happened to his family, or...?"

"I don't know. Maybe the police can look into it when we give them his name."

She shivered against me and I pulled her closer. "Yeah, maybe." When she looked up at me again, she asked, "Should we call them from here and tell them what we found?"

I chewed at the inside of my cheek. "We're heading back tomorrow. Let's let them know when we get back. The very last thing I want is for a bunch of media to show up while we're still here. It's the very thing we needed to get *away* from."

"True," Eden said. "Hector...*Thomas* is dead anyway. I guess it's nothing that can't wait another day. We need to call Xander, though. He needs to know about this."

"Let's bring all this to him tomorrow too. That way we'll be able to show him all the articles. Plus, we should be there in person to drop this bomb on him."

Eden nodded. "Yeah, you're right." We stood there for a few more minutes, holding each other. I glanced down at Eden's purse, half of Willa Greer's face showing on a small corner of one of the articles sticking out of the top. *Thank you*, I said silently.

We headed back to our room and then took a bubble bath together in the large tub, soaking in the warm water, just enjoying the intimacy but mostly lost in our own thoughts. "Danae," Eden whispered. "It's unusual. I bet it's a Greek princess or something like that."

I kissed her shoulder. "Probably. You were right. All the Greek stuff…he was a Greek history teacher. God, my girl is smart." I smiled against her skin and rubbed my nose over it, trying to make her smile, to get out from under the emotional overload that had been pressing down on us since we'd left the library.

Eden let out a small breathy chuckle. "Do you think the police have a position open for me?"

"If they're smart, they do."

Eden rolled over in the water and brought her hands to my face and kissed me softly. After a few minutes, the water began to cool, and my blood began to heat. We got out of the bath and dried off, and I made love to her in the spacious hotel room bed.

We ordered room service after that, content to spend our last night there wrapped up in each other. Personally, I felt like I needed that after what we'd found out earlier in the day. I needed to find my emotional equilibrium again and there was no better way to do that than to block out the world and focus solely on Eden.

The next morning as I was drying off from the shower and throwing my stuff back in my bag, Eden sat at the small desk scrolling through the internet on her laptop. She turned to me. "What would you think about driving through the town Indiana University Southeast is in? The college Thomas Greer worked at?"

I paused. "Why?"

She cast her eyes to the side. "I don't know. I thought I might recognize something there...maybe the house where he kept me? I went out into the yard every now and again... What do you think?"

I went over to her and squatted down next to her chair and she turned toward me. "Eden, if you need that, I'll do it. But I don't want this to upset you. I don't want to risk your health in some way—"

"I'm stronger than that, Calder," she said. "And besides, knowledge, information, it has *always* made me feel more powerful, more in control. Plus, we're so close. I don't know if we'll be back this way, you know? Once life gets underway"—she put her hand on her stomach in an unconscious gesture—"we won't want to focus on any of this. We'll want it behind us in every sense. We'll want to look to the future, not stay stuck in the past."

"Yeah." I paused. "Okay, sure, we'll drive through the town and see if anything looks familiar to you, and then we'll head home."

"Okay." She tilted her head, obviously thinking. "Do you think...? Well, Hector tried to recruit my father as the first council member and he was basically local. You were among the first people who lived in Acadia. Do you think maybe you were local too? I mean, obviously he came back and forth between here and Acadia, and then he brought me here."

I shrugged. "Maybe, but he gathered the other people

267

who lived at Acadia from all over the place. I could be from anywhere. I'll probably never know." A strange feeling of loss wound through me, even though I had no idea who I was grieving for, if anyone at all. Or perhaps it was mostly because I knew no one was grieving for me.

CHAPTER SEVENTEEN
Calder

We drove in silence for a while, headed toward New Albany, Indiana. The radio played softly as we watched the beautiful fall scenery go by. I marveled at the vibrant colors of the trees. This was the first year since I'd lived in the Midwest that I had the heart to appreciate the beauty of nature and all the ways this part of the country was so different than the desert landscape I'd known all my life. There was beauty there too, but it was such a different kind. Looking through the windshield now at the reds, yellows, and golds of the trees passing by, something about it felt…familiar. I frowned distractedly out at the trees, uncertain about whether what I was feeling was recognition or not. Maybe it was just the painter in me, who'd always been attracted to the play between color and light. Maybe it wasn't recognition so much as…appreciation.

I looked over at Eden, my gaze moving over her profile for a moment. "What names do you like?" I asked.

"What?"

"For the baby."

She paused and then looked out the front windshield. "I think we should wait until we know everything is okay before we choose names."

I reached over and took her hand. "Hey, everything's gonna be okay."

She nodded. "Hopefully. I just—"

"You don't want to get attached yet," I said quietly. I understood that particular fear because deep inside, I felt the same way, even despite the fact that I had only found out about Eden's first pregnancy after it was already gone. I pictured that moment in Hector's jail, a spear of anger lancing down my spine and causing me sit up a little straighter in my seat.

"I'm already attached," Eden said. "I just think maybe I shouldn't get any *more* attached."

"I understand." I brought her hand to my lips and kissed her knuckle.

"I know you do."

When we pulled into the town of New Albany, we plugged the address of the university into the car GPS and then headed in that direction. We cruised slowly through the residential neighborhoods close to the college. We didn't have what had been Thomas Greer's address and so we just drove aimlessly. After about an hour, Eden huffed out a breath and said, "Nothing even looks vaguely familiar about this town. And all these houses are starting to look the same to me. I mean, even if he did bring me here, to this place, even if we drove right past the house I lived in, the yard might be completely different now. It's been fourteen years." She gave a heavy sigh. "Oh well, at least we tried. I'm sure the police will be able to get his address and they can show me a picture. Maybe I'll recognize it. Maybe it doesn't even matter."

"Why don't we stop by the university?" I suggested. "It's lunchtime. We could get some college cafeteria food and pretend like we're just two kids from suburbia who spotted each other across the bleachers at a football game and fell in love at first sight."

She smiled. "Okay. I like that plan."

As I thought about it, I realized that it would have been true. No matter where Eden and I had been placed together in this world, we would have fallen in love. Whether we'd been two college freshmen, two farmhands, two band members, two *anything*, the falling-in-love part of our story would have been the same. She would have pulled my heart from across a gymnasium or a cornfield or a soundstage.

We parked in the visitors' lot and held hands as we strolled through the campus. It was a strange feeling. On one hand, I loved just walking with Eden and blending in among the other people close to our age. It made it feel like we really *were* just two average college students and that we fit in here just like anyone else. For that moment, we didn't have a past that was much different than any other average American kid's. For that moment, we hadn't lived through heartbreak and struggle and trauma. But on the other hand, this was the place where Hector had worked... where he had taught students and perhaps where the idea of Acadia was born. A small chill went down my spine when I thought about the fact that right here, this was the place where the idea that would change my and Eden's life forever might have been conceptualized.

And yet.

This was also the place where the idea that would bring

271

Eden and I together came to be. It was hard to know how to feel about that. It was difficult to wish something away that had resulted in joy. Sometimes it seemed so much of the beauty in life resulted from the ugly. And how did you make sense of such things? How could you be thankful for an outcome that had sprung from suffering? Or maybe… maybe that the very thing that defined real beauty—light after darkness. A transformative miracle right here on earth.

It turned out there was no cafeteria on this campus, but there was a food truck parked nearby and so we made our way there. After waiting in line to purchase sandwiches, we sat at one of the tables and chatted and ate. I couldn't help but notice all the guys who kept stealing glances at Eden. I couldn't blame them. She was the prettiest girl at this school. She was the prettiest girl in Indiana, hell, the world as far as I was concerned. And she had *my* baby growing inside her. A fierce feeling of pride swept through me and I grinned.

"What's that look for?" Eden popped a chip in her mouth.

I took a bite of my turkey sandwich and tried not to smile as I chewed. When I'd swallowed, I said, "I just feel good, proud. I'm happy. Even in this place, even knowing why we came here."

Eden's eyes got soft and she reached across the table for my hand. "Me too."

An older man in a maintenance uniform was walking by, and when he caught my eye, his head jerked back and he looked momentarily stunned. His eyes hung on me until he passed our table and disappeared out of sight. *Well, that was odd.* "Ready to get going?" I asked Eden as I began gathering our trash.

She stood. "Should we see if there's anyone we can ask

about Thomas Greer? I mean, maybe someone knows why he left...or can give us some information about him?"

"It's been so long, Eden," I said as I tossed our wrappers in a garbage can. "But yeah, let's give it a shot."

She shot me a glance. "It's a long shot, but there are probably still some professors who worked with him, you know? He wasn't here that long ago."

"Come on. We'll walk through the building once. We'll find out where the history department is."

Eden smiled. "Okay." I couldn't help but chuckle. Who would have thought she could turn an information dig on Hector into some kind of adventure? I shook my head but pulled her toward me and kissed the top of her head. Maybe it wasn't the most pleasant of topics, but *we* were in charge here, not him—*never him, never again.* And I guessed Eden was right to pursue it because that part of it felt powerful.

We asked directions from a guy with an oversized backpack and a large coffee in his hand, and then made our way to the part of the building that housed the history department. The hallways were mostly deserted. Either the history classes were scheduled for earlier in the day on Fridays or they had been canceled for some reason. Either way, it seemed we were out of luck.

I heard footsteps behind us, and when I looked back, I spotted the same maintenance man who had been looking at me strangely a little earlier. "What is it?" Eden asked when I came to a stop.

Without answering her, I called out to the man, "Excuse me, sir?" I pulled Eden with me as I headed toward him. His eyes widened and it appeared as if he was considering whether to turn away, but evidently decided not to, as he waited for us to approach him.

When we got closer, I saw he was a little older than I had originally thought, with leathery and wrinkled skin and hair that was far more white than the blond I had thought it was. He was thin and wiry and stood hunched over slightly in what I guessed was his natural stance. As we stepped up to him, I noticed that one of his eyes was cloudy.

"Hi. My name is Calder Raynes. We were hoping you might be able to answer a couple questions about someone who used to work here."

He glanced over at Eden quickly and then back to me, his gaze lingering in a way that made me uncomfortable. "Well, I'll be," he said, his voice deep and raspy with a slight rattle behind it that told me he was probably a heavy smoker. The smell of tobacco smoke wafting off of him confirmed that guess. He didn't offer his name.

"Uh, hi," I glanced at Eden. "We just had a quick question we hoped you could help with. Did you work here when a man named Thomas Greer taught Greek history?"

The man stared, looking slightly confused, and then turned his head and coughed, a rattling, mucous-y sound. I almost flinched but held my expression steady until he'd turned back to us. "Yeah, I knew Tom," he said. "Or at least, knew *of* him, knew him in passing. We didn't associate much."

"Oh," Eden said. "Well, do you know why he left?"

He studied Eden for a minute. "Wife and daughter was murdered," he said. He gave his head a small shake. "Been a long time, but...sure was a sad case."

Eden nodded. "Yes, we...heard about his family. So that's why he left, then?"

The man coughed again and then said, "Nah, they fired him—years later, though. They kept it hush-hush. Let him resign. He had taken a bad turn after that crime that killed his family. Always spoutin' off in his classes, scaring the students, saying weird stuff about gods talking to him. He was constantly taking leaves of absence, and each time he came back, he was crazier than ever. Went out of his head from the tragedy is my guess. He left and I never heard anything about him again."

We both stood staring at him. "Right," I said quietly. "Well, thank you for your time. It's been very helpful."

"You look just like him, you know?" he said. We'd started to turn away and pivoted back around to see him staring at me.

"I'm sorry? Like who?"

"Your father. Worked here in maintenance with me. Up and quit a couple years before Thomas resigned."

My heart slammed to a stop and then resumed beating rapidly. "My...what?"

"You're darker in coloring, but you've definitely got his face. Never had any trouble getting ladies, that one." He chuckled, a choking, loose sound, but recovered quickly and stared at me with something that looked like regret on his face. "He told me your mama came and took you with her somewhere. That true?"

"What's his name?" I interrupted. "Do you know where we can find him?"

"Oh yeah, I do, but you better be quick about it. My sister works at the hospital. Hospice was called out to his place a while back. Don't figure he has much time left. He's been sick for years. His name is Morris Reed. Thought you were here looking for *him*, not Thomas."

My heart was still racing and my thoughts were all jumbled. This was the last thing I'd expected. *Morris Reed. Morris Reed. My father is Morris Reed?*

The man continued. "He's about a mile from here out on Abaddon Road." He spelled it and rattled off a street number; then he started to turn and walk away.

"Wait," I said. "Do you know if this man you think is my father—did he know Thomas?"

He shrugged. "Not as far as I knew, but Morris and I didn't associate outside of work." He paused, seeming as if he was considering his next words. He met my gaze, that rheumy eye unblinking. "I figure you shouldn't talk ill of the dead, but your father isn't dead quite yet so I'll tell you this—as far as I was concerned, it was best to stay far away from him. Face of some kind of angel, but the devil was in his eyes."

I gaped, the feeling that something cold and thick was dripping down my spine. Suddenly Eden was pulling me and I stumbled behind her, looking back at the man as we practically ran for the door and out into the bright sunshine of the outside world.

CHAPTER EIGHTEEN
Eden

My heart was pounding and my throat felt dry as I turned toward Calder and looked into his shell-shocked face. "What are you thinking?" I asked. "Are you okay?"

He shook his head slowly, his eyes looking absently at something, or nothing, behind me. "I don't know what to think. Maybe it's not even true."

"Do you want to find out?" I asked, lowering the volume of my voice almost to a whisper. "This is up to you."

Calder took in a deep breath and blew it out slowly before meeting my eyes. "Something tells me it's not a good idea."

I chewed at my lip. Something told me the same thing. But…we had to find out, didn't we? "It could be your only chance. The man inside said there's not much time." I paused. "He—Morris—could give you your name, Calder."

"My name. Yeah," he finally said, his gaze landing on my stomach momentarily.

"I'm with you," I told him, taking his hand in mine.

"I'm here. And someone very wise once told me that you never know when a little bit of knowledge is going to come in handy and maybe even change your life."

Calder's lips curved, even if very slightly, and he squeezed my hand.

Twenty minutes later, after making several wrong turns that Calder muttered were probably signs, we pulled onto a dirt road and then slowed in front of a tilted mailbox with the street number the maintenance man had given us.

I scanned the property as we pulled the car into the dirt driveway. It was a hoarder's dream: three broken-down vehicles stripped of most of the external parts were sitting on large blocks, a dilapidated brown couch sat next to the front steps of the tiny house, and there was unrecognizable junk and garbage strewn everywhere.

My gaze moved to the house itself—the roof was sagging, the paint was peeling, and one shutter was hanging sideways on the front window. Calder turned off the ignition and just sat there for a minute, unmoving as he stared at the wreckage before us. "I don't think either one of us is going to like where I came from, Eden."

I put my hand on his arm. "He's been sick for a long time," I said. "And he probably doesn't have a lot of money. That doesn't mean he's not a decent person. And even if he isn't, he deserves to know who took his son from him at the very least, don't you think?"

Calder ran a hand through his hair and nodded. We exited the vehicle and then met in front of the car, joining hands and maneuvering silently through the trash. I wanted to cover my nose at the smell lingering in the air, decay and…sulfur, but I forced myself not to. The last thing Calder needed was for me to make this worse by acting repelled by where he came from.

We got to the door and I had a brief flash of picking up that huge brass lion's head knocker on my mom's front door. This was that moment for Calder. "You can do this," I said.

He hesitated briefly, but then knocked, three loud raps. We both stood there, listening as someone came toward us on the other side. High overhead an eagle cried out, the sound piercing. I squinted up into the bright but overcast sky to see it circling above us.

The door swung open and a young woman in jeans and a green turtleneck sweater stood there, looking expectantly at us.

"Uh, hi," Calder said.

The woman blinked and tilted her head as she looked at Calder. "You must be a relative," she said.

"Yes," Calder said, spacing the letters out. "My name is Calder Raynes and this is my girlfriend, Eden Everson."

The woman smiled. "Please, come in. I'm Addy Dover." Her face took on a sympathetic expression. "You did know—"

"Yes," Calder said. "And you're from hospice?"

"Oh no, no." She leaned forward and lowered her voice. "Hospice employees won't come here. I'm from Our Lady of Mercy Church. I was a home health nurse though." Her lips flattened into a thin line for a second before she said, "No one should have to die completely alone." But despite her statement, her expression held doubt.

We started to take a step inside, but before we could, Addy looked backward and then turned toward us again. "You've, um…met him before, right?"

Calder shook his head.

"Oh, okay, well…he's…well, he's not the nicest person."

She raised a hand. "I don't say that to be disrespectful of your family, but, well…since you haven't met him before, I think it's good that you're prepared. It's very nice of you to come visit him for this last time. No one else has."

We both nodded and started to step inside once again, but again, Addy stopped. "Oh," she said, turning around and grabbing something off a narrow table on the wall next to the door. She handed us a small plastic container and pointed to under her nose. It was then I saw that there was a very light bluish tint on the skin right under her nostrils. "The smell," she explained simply, wrinkling her nose. "You'll want this."

My gaze darted to Calder, whose face had drained of color. He glanced at me, looking embarrassed, as if he wanted to run. I unscrewed the cap on the container and smeared some of the blue stuff under my nose and handed it to Calder, who haltingly did the same.

Despite the strong camphor-smelling gel under my nostrils, when we stepped fully inside, the smell of the place hit me like a ton of bricks and I almost stumbled back. I must not have hidden my reaction well because Addy nodded knowingly and said, "I know. You'll need to change clothes when you leave here too. It will…linger." I swallowed down the bile that wanted to come up my throat and tried not to breathe. Next to me, Calder was scanning the inside of the house, his eyes wide with what looked like shock mixed with an equal amount of disgust.

There were boxes, papers, *stuff* piled high everywhere, flies buzzed lazily through the air, and the few areas of wall you could see looked wet and coated in some kind of oil. Did a person actually live here?

Addy started walking through the small pathway in the middle of the junk. Surely this was dangerous and unhealthy?

As if to answer my question, Addy said, her voice low, "The state has ordered him to clean this up, but obviously he's in no condition to do that. They'll come in and remove him if he doesn't... Well, he can't live here for very much longer. I like to say everyone deserves to die at home, but in this case"—she looked around, not turning back to us—"I don't know."

We followed her down a small dingy hallway and through a door. Addy stood back as we entered the room tentatively. She gave me a small concerned smile as I passed. "I'll be in the front room if you need me," she said, then nodded as if to encourage us.

"Thank you," I muttered.

The bedroom we entered was dim, and unlike the rest of the house, this room was virtually empty except for a hospital bed all the way on the far wall. I squinted, my eyes trying to adjust to the even dimmer lighting back here. I could see a human shape in the bed but couldn't make out the details of the man. He was utterly still and I assumed he was sleeping.

Calder came up short, holding me back as I moved forward. "This can't be good for you," he whispered out of the side of his mouth. I wasn't sure if he was referring to the smell, the possible stress of the situation, or what, but I merely turned to him and said, "I'm fine."

His eyes darted around the room as though in search of a threat. I watched him as his gaze landed on a window that was raised a few inches. His shoulders seemed to relax slightly as he took in that slip of fresh air. Or was he considering it some kind of emergency exit? This house was disgusting, there was no getting around that fact, and the man in the bed in front of us may very well be extremely unpleasant. But I didn't imagine we'd have to make a run for it.

"Always wondered if you'd ever find me" came a deep, smooth voice from the bed.

Calder and I both startled. We glanced at each other and then moved forward.

"Dad?" Calder said haltingly, his voice cracking. "Do you know who I am?"

My heart thumped rapidly.

The man in the bed came into view, the small bedside lamp illuminating him just enough to make out his features as we got closer. I sucked in a rancid breath of air, nausea hitting me in the gut as I forced myself not to stumble back—away. He was bloated, his skin bruised and mottled, peeling in areas, with an underlying yellow tinge. He was clearly extremely ill if not halfway dead. In fact, I had a brief flash of the bodies I'd seen before escaping the flooded cellar at Acadia. But the part that made me gasp in horror was that underneath the distortion of the sickness, I could see *Calder*. Underneath the disease and the ugliness, there was…*beauty*. It made my stomach churn and I latched on to Calder's arm and forced my gaze away from the man and up into Calder's strong, healthy face. *The man is dying, Eden. He can't help the way he looks.*

"Well, come closer so I can get a look at you, Kieran," the man, Morris, said.

"Kieran?" Calder asked. I looked back at the bloated… person in the bed and we both took another step forward until we were standing near the end of the bed.

"Name I gave you. Kieran Reed."

"Kieran Reed," Calder repeated, a small note of wonder in his voice. My heart gave a hard thump. *Kieran Reed. His name. His real name.*

Morris suddenly laughed, and like his voice, the sound

was deep and melodious, in complete and utter contrast to the look of him. I unconsciously took another step closer at the sound of it, but Calder pulled me back. The man's swollen lips turned up into what I assumed was meant to be a smile.

"He wanted to name you something different. 'Fine by me,' I said. 'He's yours now.'" He stared at us and a shiver went down my spine as I attempted not to look away in disgust.

"He?" Calder whispered. "Hector?"

Morris looked surprised for a second. "No, Thomas."

"Thomas, yes," Calder said, his voice even but laced with confusion. "You knew he took me? I don't... You *let* him take me?"

"Take you?" Morris leered. "I sold you to him."

No one said a word for several horror-filled moments as we digested that information. The steady beep of some kind of machine to the right of Morris was the only sound filling the thick, stale air. Morris picked up an oxygen mask next to him and took several long inhales.

"Sold me?" Calder finally asked.

Morris leaned back on his pillow, contemplating Calder, his eyes bright with...*something*. "Said he needed you to balance out his nutty community." He let out another musical laugh. "Not that I cared...*much*. You were a little thorn in my side anyway—always following me around everywhere, wanting *something*."

"How old was I?" Calder croaked.

My body had begun shaking and I couldn't seem to get it to stop. *Oh, Calder.* I could practically feel the grief emanating off of him. A buzz of rage took up beneath my skin.

"Three."

"Gods above," Calder choked, letting go of my hand and grabbing the hair at his temples.

"How'd you know Thomas?" I asked, trying not to tear up. *Get information and get out, get out, get out.*

Morris's eyes swung toward me. "Look at you, pretty thing." His head jutted forward. "Used to have little girls like you between my legs all the time," he said, his eyes drooping slightly.

"Don't look at her!" Calder yelled, breaking the near quiet of the room and startling me. He took my arm and moved me halfway behind his body. "Keep your eyes on me, you sick, disgusting old man."

As I peeked out from behind Calder, Morris's eyes filled with amusement. He was enjoying this. Who *was* this person? The whole situation felt unreal—a grotesque nightmare— something you tried to describe to someone else later and couldn't find the words because there were none.

"Well now, this is good timing," Morris said, ignoring Calder's insult. "I'm glad I get to tell this story before I meet my maker." His face moved into that same leering semblance of a grin and I imagined exactly who this man's maker was. "It's a good one." His eyes narrowed on Calder and then moved between us for several tense moments as if he was making sure we were as interested as he wanted us to be.

"I knew Thomas from the university," he said, obviously judging our interest to be adequate. "I had to bring you along with me a couple times to get my paycheck when you wouldn't keep your trap shut. He saw you. Took an interest. Came out to see me one day and made me an offer I could hardly refuse." My scalp prickled and the hair on my arms stood up in alarm. I held tightly to Calder when I felt him sway slightly.

Morris sighed. "I always did like the drink and the gambling," he said. "You like the drink, Kieran? If you do, you get that from me." He winked, showing us his full swollen eyelid, and then laughed heartily as if he'd made some sort of joke.

"What'd you think he wanted me for?" Calder asked, ignoring his question, his voice sounding dead.

The man let out another smooth laugh and shrugged. "Figured he liked pretty kids. What he did with you was his business." He leaned forward very slightly. "I made him pay though. Every year, he paid me. Came in person to deliver me cash."

"Came in person?" Calder repeated. It sounded like he was in shock. I considered pulling him out of there, bolting out of this house of horror and disgust. But my legs wouldn't move. It felt like I was glued to the spot as my mind tried to grasp the evil of the story this man, *Calder's father*, was telling us. And for what? To relieve his own conscience? No, for his amusement. It was clear he was enjoying this.

"I cried for you," Calder said. "Holy gods, I cried for you." And now I could hear the anguish in his voice and everything in me screamed out to protect him. I pulled at him, but he resisted, staying rooted to the spot. "So much it damaged my throat."

Morris's expression took on a glittering interest. "Oh yeah? Yeah," he said as if realizing how much sense that made. "You liked me. 'Da' this and 'Da' that, even cleaned up after me when I was too drunk to move. That's why I made sure I got paid."

The room around me seemed to sway. This was too ghastly to be real. I gave my head a small shake in case this *was* all a terrifying nightmare I might wake from.

Calder sucked in a breath. His expression was calm, but there was a clear glaze of panic in his eyes. He reached out to wipe a tear from my cheek and it was only then that I realized I was silently crying. "Who was my mother?" he asked.

Morris seemed confused by the question. "Oh, *her*? Some little girl claimed I took advantage of her." He shrugged slowly and then huffed out a breath, as if the small raise of his shoulders was an effort. "I didn't even remember who she was when she showed up here, dropping you off on my doorstep and practically running away. I could see you were mine though. You had my good looks." He laughed, the deep melody ringing throughout the room, and again, my muscles tensed. "She was an Indian. You know, the feather kind." He brought one bloated hand slowly up to his lips and rapped it against his open mouth, making an *ow wow wow wow* sound.

I flinched as he laughed again, deep and hearty. *Disgusting pig.* We turned to leave.

"Don't you want to hear the *real* secret though?" Morris raised his voice.

We turned again in unison and stared at him, Morris wheezed in a couple sharp breaths and grabbed the oxygen mask again and brought it to his face, sucking in several gasping breaths before lowering it.

"Thomas came here several years back when you'd turned eighteen to make me the final payment." He put the mask to his face and sucked in a breath and then brought it away again. How was his voice so deep and clear if he could barely breathe?

"I had just gotten my diagnosis. Was already in this hospital bed. The docs told me I only had six months at the most and yet here I am. Anyway, at the time, I figured there wasn't any reason not to tell *him* the truth. You know, time to clear my conscience and all that." He paused as if for effect, his eyes moving between the two of us. "I killed his family. Broke into the rich professor's house. They weren't even supposed to be home." He looked toward the window and those bulbous lips tipped as if recalling a precious memory. "I thought he was going to drop dead right here before *I* got a chance to."

"You killed his family?" Calder asked. "You stabbed them. It was you. All those years, he paid you for me, the man who had murdered his family." His voice sounded cold and matter-of-fact, and the lack of emotion sent dread through my body. *That's why, oh God, that's why Hector came back from that pilgrimage disheveled and...crazed.* The truth slammed into me. It was the final thing that had irreparably broken him.

Morris eyed us with something that looked like disappointment on his sickly, bloated face. "Yup. That was the way of it. He just walked out of here. Didn't even try to kill me."

"That's because you're already dead," Calder said. He grabbed my hand and started walking out of the room and I followed on numb legs, glancing behind me once. Morris was in shadow again and it felt like spiders skittered over the back of my neck.

"That's it?" he called. "Kieran? Kieran? Get back here, boy! Your father's giving you an order. Get back here!"

Calder picked up his pace, practically dragging me through the narrow space as Morris's velvety, impossibly booming voice called after us. Addy stepped out of the front room next to the doorway, her expression confused as we flew by her. When we got to the door, Calder turned to her and said, "You should get out of here. He's a dangerous man—"

We all froze as we heard something overturn, the oxygen machine, I assumed, and then Morris calling out for help. Cajoling and then demanding it with slurs and epithets. Despite the hostility, I had the inexplicable instinct to move toward that smooth voice, to comply with the demands being shouted. I reached out a hand and made contact with a box next to me, holding it as though I'd be pulled back down that hall by some unseen force.

We all stood there, our eyes wide with fear and surprise as we looked from one to the other. None of us moved. Then the shrill sound of the heart machine that had been declaring the steady beat of his black heart suddenly flatlined. We still didn't move. Addy took a deep breath and turned back toward the front room. We watched as she sat back down on a small wooden stool next to an open window and picked up the book she'd been reading and flipped one of the pages. "You should go," she said without looking up.

Yes. Yes, we should. We pushed at the door, stumbled outside and sucked in big gulps of air. I followed Calder to the car and waited as he pulled clothes out of our suitcases. His movements were quick and jerky and he struggled several times with the easy task. "Calder—"

"Please, Eden, take those clothes off," he said, his voice cracking.

I nodded, struggling to hold back tears. We both stripped behind the car and pulled on the clean outfits and Calder kicked the ones we'd removed to the side, not bothering to pick them up. No one would notice a couple more pieces of trash on this lot anyway.

We got in the car, and Calder pulled out onto the road, his hands shaking on the wheel.

"Find a hotel," I whispered.

Calder gave no indication he heard me, but twenty minutes out of town, there was a sign for a hotel off one of the highway exits and Calder took it. We checked in to the hotel, not speaking a word to each other. Up in our room, Calder went quickly into the bathroom and shut the door behind him. I heard the shower turn on and sunk down in the chair by the window.

I was still shaking, trying to get ahold of my emotions, trying to calm my racing heart. Naturally, Calder was devastated by what he'd just learned, I was sure even more so than me. I prayed the shower would give him a little time to compose himself and figure out what he was feeling. I was so eager to comfort him but didn't really know how. Every minute spent waiting for him hurt, but I knew in my heart he needed to be by himself for now. How much more betrayal could this man take? *He was sold by his father.* For alcohol and gambling money. My mind still reeled. How could anyone do that to such a beautiful boy? I wanted to fall down on my knees and sob. But I wouldn't. I would hold myself together for Calder. I would be his strong Morning Glory.

Fifteen minutes later, Calder came out of the bathroom. His eyes were rimmed in red and I thought he'd been crying. I stood up to go to him but he held a hand up, halting me. "You should take a shower," he said, numbly. "Wash him, that smell, off you. I can't stand it."

I blinked but nodded. "Are you—"

"Please, Eden," he said, his expression miserable, his voice extra raspy.

We stared at each other for a few seconds and then I nodded again and he moved out of the way as I passed him. When I glanced down at his hands, I saw that they were still shaking. *Oh, Calder.* It felt like my heart was breaking, so I could barely imagine what his was doing.

I shut the bathroom door behind me and took a long hot shower, washing my hair three times and scrubbing my skin with a washcloth until it stung.

When I emerged, wearing only a towel, I looked around the empty room. Calder was gone.

CHAPTER NINETEEN
Eden

I lay awake on the hotel room bed, not moving a muscle, listening to the soft whir of the fan I had left on in the bathroom. Calder had taken the car and left. I knew he wouldn't desert me, pregnant and alone here in the middle of a state I'd never been to before. *He wouldn't.* We'd been through much worse than this, and Calder had always sought to protect me. I refused to believe this had broken him for good. Yes, the truth of where he'd come from and how he'd ended up in Acadia was horrifyingly awful, unthinkable, devastating, and sick on so many levels, I hadn't even tried to count. But we'd deal with the emotions of it together— we'd have to. What other choice was there?

I thought about texting Xander, but I couldn't bring myself to give him part of the story and then leave him hanging. And I couldn't bear to talk to him about Morris when I hadn't even talked to Calder about him yet.

I lay there, feeling anxious. I put my hand on my stomach and drew strength from the knowledge that inside of me, a tiny group of cells was miraculously forming into a human that I already loved. There was another heart beating in the depths of my body when I'd believed my womb would always remain empty. *Breathe in. Breathe out. Have faith.*

Hours later, I finally heard footsteps coming toward the door on the cement walkway outside. They sounded unsteady and off-balance and I stilled as I listened to his approach. The door clicked and I sat up as Calder pushed it open, swaying very slightly, a dark shadow in front of the pale light of the lit hallway behind him.

Calder stepped inside and kicked the door shut behind him as I clutched a pillow to my stomach. "Hi," he mumbled. His walk was unsteady as he approached me, his eyes unfocused. He'd obviously been drinking. He fell onto the edge of the bed and let out a soft groan. I remained quiet as I attempted to rein in my irritation and after a minute he squinted over at me. "Are you mad at me, Morning Glory?"

I huffed out a breath. "Did it help?" I asked. "Drinking alone at a bar? Did it help?"

Calder's brow lowered, and he kept squinting as though he was working out a puzzle. "I didn't know what else to do."

"You could have stayed here. You could have talked to me about your feelings."

He laughed, a brittle sound. "My feelings? Where do I even start? How can you not be disgusted by me? Did you see where I came from?" He started laughing a raspy laugh that died quickly and morphed into a grimace. "Holy *fuck*. Did you see what I have running through my veins, Eden? Did you *see*? What was that thing? Was it even human?"

"Calder…"

"That baby in your belly, that baby has the same blood

292

coursing through it as that *thing* in that house today. We both do. How does that make you feel? You've always been so pure, and I've always been so dirty. Hector was right. I *am* Satan's spawn. No fucking wonder."

I tossed the pillow to the side and walked on my knees to where he lay at the end of the bed. "You listen to me, Calder Raynes," I said, my lips tight. "You are nothing like the man we met today. I don't care whether his blood runs through your veins or not. I don't care that his DNA created you. *That does not define your heart.* And all that tells me is that even someone evil and disgusting and lewd can do something beautiful. That ghastly, horrifying human, *even him*, he did something wonderful for this world. He created you. And. You. Are. *Good.*"

Grief floated over his face. "No. No, you're wrong. I'm bad. I *am* evil. Everyone sees it. Hector saw it. My parents saw it—they tried to burn me, Eden." His voice choked on the last word. "Oh God, they tried to burn me."

I sucked back a sob, moving closer to him so quickly I didn't even make a conscious choice to do it. Suddenly my arms were around him and I was cradling him to me, his head between my breasts, my cheek resting on the top of his head. It was the first time he'd mentioned his parents. Even in that beautiful Bed of Healing, he hadn't been ready to go there, had skirted around the topic. Even after three years and despite the alcohol in his system, when he looked up at me, the devastation and heartbreak were clear in his deep brown eyes. He didn't shed a tear, but I did, remembering the horror and the helplessness as I waited to watch him die. I held him now because I couldn't then. I cried for him. I cried for the agony I knew lived in his heart because of the ultimate betrayal of that one moment in time, a moment that left him feeling scarred and unlovable. Thrown away, sacrificed in a way that still made him bleed inside.

"Sometimes," he whispered, "I feel like even though the fire didn't touch me, it burned me all the same. I feel like it melted my skin away and that the world is looking at my raw, charred insides. It feels that way, Eden. And now I know that it wasn't even the first time I was burned. I felt *raw* again today. That's how I felt, standing there before my *father* being told he sold me. He *sold* me when I was three years old."

I squeezed him with all my might, wishing I could open myself up and pour my love straight into his heart, that I could tear my own skin off and give it to him to wrap around his wounds.

"I see only goodness," I whispered. "I see only beauty."

"I thought I might just drive off tonight and never come back," he said, and I couldn't help tensing at his words. "Just so you would never be able to love me again. So you'd go on without me and forget I ever existed. You and that innocent baby."

I paused. "Obviously you didn't follow through with that plan." *He must know that losing him again is my greatest fear.*

"No," he said. "I'd never do that. Never. I'd wouldn't desert you and the baby." He shook his head against my chest as if the statement itself was ridiculous. And it was.

I sighed, relaxing. "Evil," I said.

"Are you making fun of me?"

"Kind of, yeah."

I leaned back and took his face in my hands, my eyes roaming over his beloved features. "You're not even a very mean drunk," I said. "I think you're failing epically if your master plan is to follow in your father's footsteps."

Calder let out a pained chuckle as he fell back to the bed. "This can't be funny," he said. "There's nothing funny about this. It's only tragic and awful."

I lay down next to him. "Sometimes tragic and awful can be funny too. Sometimes it has to be."

We stared up at the textured ceiling for a few minutes. Finally, Calder said, "It's not that it's my master plan to become like my father. But what if...what if I can't help turning into him?" He shuddered. "What if it's just my destiny?"

I thought about that for a moment. "Someone tried to tell me what my destiny was once. I knew in my heart it wasn't true. It felt wrong. I don't think other people get to tell us what our destiny is, Calder. Do you feel in your heart your destiny is to be an evil, disgusting monster?"

He sighed. "No."

"No," I confirmed. "Not possible. I've known you all my life. I know you through and through, Calder Raynes. Not possible."

He was quiet for a minute. "That's not even my real name."

"Kieran Reed," I said quietly. I frowned up at the ceiling, wondering if I could get used to calling him by another name.

"I'd never take that name."

"Then Calder it is."

"I guess so."

"Unless you want me to call you Storm."

He let out a short laugh. "No. Xander's right. It does sound like a stripper."

"Then Calder it is," I repeated. I heard his lips move into a smile.

We were quiet for a minute. "I'm not even really that drunk," he said. "I like the Coke more than I like the rum."

I snorted softly and reached down between us and took his hand in mine. We lay like that a little longer. I didn't look over at him, but I thought he'd probably fallen asleep so I was surprised when he spoke. "I do have to say that I'm epic at one thing at least."

"What's that?"

"Getting you knocked up."

I turned toward him with raised brows. He met my eyes and we both started laughing at the same time. "True enough." I laughed again.

Calder grinned, his eyes still slightly glazed and heavy-lidded. "I'm a badass when it comes to knocking you up," he said, looking overly pleased with himself. And then he promptly fell off the bed.

I rolled over and peered over the side to see him staring up at me with an expression of shock and I tilted my head back and laughed so hard I thought I'd pee my pants. I fell back on the bed gripping my waist and howling with laughter, part hilarity, part hysteria. And for some reason, it felt just as good as crying. It was a release, and one I needed.

Calder pounced on me and I laughed harder, and so did he, until we couldn't laugh anymore. We lay on our sides, face-to-face, getting ahold of our breathing and letting the laughter fade. "I love you so much," he said, pushing my hair out of my face.

"I love you too."

He brought his hand up, watching his finger as it trailed over my cheekbone and down to my jaw. "Hey, Eden," Calder murmured after a minute.

"Yeah?" I whispered.

He sucked his bottom lip into his mouth as a crease formed between his brows. "You remember how you said that at the end, in that cellar, there was love? And that maybe that's where God was?"

I nodded.

"Well," he continued, his gaze meeting mine. "When I was tied to that pole, when my father..." He sucked in a shaky breath.

"Yes?" I put my leg over his, wanting him to feel me all around him as he spoke of his greatest pain.

"I tried not to think about it for so long because it hurt so much. And I just wonder, in that moment, where was God then? Where was the love then?" His eyes searched mine, looking for...something. Hope? Insight that would make it better?

My gaze moved over his features, that strong jaw I loved so much, that beautifully expressive mouth, those deep brown eyes that could fill up with pain or with love in an instant. I allowed my mind to travel back to that moment even though I too had tried to avoid it over the past three years. I remembered the terror that had filled me—the unfathomable grief—and I thought about Calder's promise to meet me at a spring in Elysium. I reflected on how, in what he believed to be his final moments, he had thought only of me. He had sought to protect me in the one way he had left. *Don't watch this, Eden. Turn away.*

I studied the man lying next to me, the one I had fallen in love with because he'd gifted me with the knowledge he possessed despite the danger it posed. I'd fallen in love with him because he was decent and fair and *good*. I'd fallen in love with him because he had the strength and wisdom to listen to his heart and value truth over lies. I had fallen in love with him as he carried his best friend twenty miles to safety rather than leave him behind. I had fallen in love with him because he knew how to tease in a way that felt loving, because he laughed easily and loved deeply, and because he looked at me like I was precious. Love beat through my blood. "We were the love," I said. "In that moment, we were the love."

His eyes moved over my face, looking for the truth of that and seeming to find it. He smiled that same crooked, tentative smile I had loved the first time I saw it, the one that had calmed me when I was a terrified nine-year-old girl sitting in front of a temple full of strangers who expected something of me I didn't understand.

"Will my emotions always feel like one step forward, one step back? Will I always be this unbearable mess?" he asked.

"Probably," I answered.

He leaned back and let out a soft laugh.

I smiled. "And I'm okay with that," I said. "And we'll create a Bed of Healing, Version 2.0. It'll always be the place where we can be as messy as we need to be, in all sorts of ways." I gave him a cheeky wink.

He laughed and so did I, leaning into each other, sharing up close both the laughter and the tears. And I thought to myself, even though life could be horrifying and earth-shattering, terrible and tragic, it was also filled with moments of breathtaking beauty. And sometimes you just had to laugh.

It was true what I'd once said about the stars—some things are seen more clearly in light…and some things are seen more clearly in darkness. Because somewhere in the dark of the night, Calder pulled me close to him and we agreed in ways both spoken and unspoken that the world was ugly and broken, and love was ridiculously dangerous and absurdly unsafe...*and that we would love anyway.* We would keep our fierce and tender hearts open. It felt foolish and ridiculous and *right.* It felt like the bravest thing we'd ever do.

CHAPTER TWENTY
Eden

We got on the road bright and early the next morning. We were ready to leave Indiana behind. We were ready to go home. Our new life beckoned to us, and we finally had everything we needed to really begin building it.

As we drove, we held hands, silent in our own thoughts. Calder seemed more peaceful this morning, more himself. We stopped at Starbucks and got coffees and muffins and sat in the parking lot. I felt like the world was different today. Something had shifted. Maybe it was the fact that we finally had answers, or at least the answers we needed. I would tear down all those papers I had pinned to the back of my closet door—the project I'd taken up in an effort to *do something* with my pain and confusion. I didn't need it anymore.

"You know what I've been thinking about this morning, Morning Glory?" Calder asked.

"What?"

He stared out the front window, giving me the beauty of his profile. "Xander told me once that he believed there was a purpose to me surviving Acadia that day." He paused. "And a purpose for all the suffering."

I nodded. "Yes, I like to believe that too," I said. "For all of us."

He looked over at me. "Do you think we'll know it when we see it? Do you think we'll understand the reason for the pain someday?"

I thought about that as I sipped my decaf latté. "Maybe it's not so much about one reason or one purpose. Maybe it's like this." I considered my words, staring out the window at the seemingly endless cornfields stretched below a golden sky. "We all attach things to our hearts, kind of like how I pinned those articles up on the back of my closet door or the way you covered your studio with paintings of me. We attach the things we value, the things we need, the things that make us brave in the face of fear. But maybe…maybe it's only when our hearts are broken open that those things can fall inside. Maybe it's only then that those things truly become part of us in a transformative sense, and because of it, we're more able to understand and recognize pain in others. Perhaps that's where real mercy comes from. And mercy in a world lacking in it, is the purpose of pain. It's that light in the darkness."

Calder watched me, seeming to take in my words and turn them over in his mind. After a minute he said, "Mercy and strength. That's your light."

I breathed out on a smile. "Mercy and goodness. That's *your* light."

A look of hurt passed over Calder's face despite the small smile he gave me. "Sometimes I wish we didn't shine so brightly."

I let out a soft laugh and reached over and touched his

cheek. "Me neither. But we do. We earned it. So let's make the most of it. Let's go out and find some darkness, Calder Raynes. Let's light it up."

He grabbed my hand and kissed it and then leaned back in his seat as he took a sip of his coffee. "You know the weirdest thing? Hector tried to kill me." A shaky breath escaped his mouth. "But he saved my life too. Once upon a time, regardless of his motives, he ended up saving me from a sure life of hell with the monster who was my real father."

He paused and I waited for him to organize his thoughts and emotions. "I don't know what to do with that. I hate him to the depths of my soul for what he did to me, to you, to all those innocent people, and yet..." He shook his head and looked over at me, his whole heart in his eyes. "What fell into Hector's heart when it broke, Eden? What things did he have attached to him that became part of the fabric of who he was when he broke open?"

"Shame, grief, rage," I said. "It's hard to even imagine. He didn't just feel those things and find a way to let them go. He attached them. He became them. Add in some insanity and just a touch of charisma..." I took a deep breath. "We'll never know completely what was in his mind, and I have to think that's a good thing."

He nodded. "Yeah..."

"I think...I think, Calder, that we have to figure out how to forgive, not for the people who wronged us but for *us*. We can't keep bitterness attached to our hearts because eventually, it might become part of us—so deeply ingrained we can't work it back out. I believe with all my heart we have to focus on the beauty we've been given in this life and make *that* the thing that defines us. Because people defined by bitterness end up destroying themselves from the inside

302

out, and eventually they destroy everyone who tries to love them too. That's not going to be us."

Calder leaned over and gathered me in his arms. "You're so damn smart. You must have had a really good life teacher."

I laughed. "I did. And he was hot too. I wanted to do dirty things to him. I *did* do dirty things to him."

Calder smiled and nuzzled my neck. "Maybe you can describe that to me in more detail when we get back home."

I laughed again and pulled away, smiling and brushing my thumb over his full bottom lip. "I will. I love you, Butterscotch. You have the most beautiful heart of anyone I've ever met. And maybe you feel like a mess sometimes, and *life* is a mess sometimes, but the way I see it, you're the beauty that came from the mess."

Calder let out a breath and leaned his forehead on mine. "I love you, Morning Glory. It's always been your heart that kept me alive. Your love. Your sweetness. I painted you to keep you alive, and that's what kept me breathing too."

I looked into his tender expression, loving him so deeply I could hardly breathe, and then I kissed him softly on his lips.

We got back on the road and Calder made a phone call to the police. He asked for Detective Lowe and when he got on the phone, he took a deep breath and told him everything we'd discovered on our trip. I sat listening and squeezing his hand. Detective Lowe must have been stunned, and at least a little bit speechless, because there weren't many pauses on Calder's end. I heard Calder tell the detective we'd be home around three. A small white lie. One last statement—I knew we'd be okay—but it'd be nice to have a few more hours to prepare. Plus, we needed to fill Xander in before the police. He deserved that.

It was just after noon, the sun high in the overcast sky, when we pulled in to my mom's driveway. We got out of the car, and no cameras came toward us, no journalists came running. I breathed deeply. One lone car door opened and closed, and we looked back to a young man in jeans and a brown leather jacket jogging slowly toward us.

"Hey," he said. "Sorry to bother you guys." He gave a bashful smile and a small shrug as he came to a stop. "I know you get harassed all the time. It must suck."

Calder chuckled and draped his arm over my shoulder.

"I just, uh." He held out his hand. "My name is Ryan Scott and—"

"Daddy?" a little girl called, getting out of the back seat of the car and walking toward us.

"Kelsey, honey," Ryan called, "I'll be there in just a sec. Get back in the car, okay?" He turned toward us. "Sorry, I was just taking my little girl to the park when I saw you pull in. My news station had me camping out here for weeks." He stuck his hands in his jacket pockets. "I saw you and it seemed like fate or something."

The little girl, not having listened to her father, joined him and looked up at us shyly. Her blond hair was in braids, she wore a pink jacket, and she was holding a kite in her hands. She clearly had Down syndrome. When I looked at her sweet face, it brought tears to my eyes. She looked so much like Maya, and her trusting smile must have melted Calder's heart too. He went down to her level and looked her right in the eyes.

"Hey there," Calder said reaching out his hand to her. "I'm Calder. This is Eden." The little girl glanced up at me, her gaze innocent and direct, and then back at Calder. She took his hand and squeezed it a couple times and I watched as Calder's eyes widened.

She held up her kite with her other hand. "You like to fly, don't you?" she asked.

"Yeah," he said, his voice gravelly and filled with a note of wonder. He cleared his throat. "I do." She grinned as if she'd known what his answer would be.

Ryan smiled down at his daughter and said, "So we won't keep you, and I wasn't stalking you, I swear. I mean, I was stalking you for a while." He gave a short chuckle. "But I wasn't today. Anyway, I had to stop and ask if you'd be interested in doing an interview."

Calder stood and I glanced at him, something unspoken moving between us. Calder looked back at Ryan. "Yeah, I think we'd be okay with that. I don't know how much we'll be able to talk about. Some of it is still an ongoing investigation."

Ryan's eyes widened. "Right. Yeah, of course. I mean, thanks. People really just want to hear your story, you know?" He paused, his brow creasing. "I have to be honest with you though. We're a small station. You'll get better offers from the big ones. I wouldn't feel right if I didn't mention that. I know you're a young couple, just starting off." He ran a hand over his daughter's head. "My wife and I are in the same boat. And I'd totally understand if you needed to take a bigger deal, we—"

"We'd like to go with you," Calder said. "You're right. Something about this feels like fate." He smiled back down at Kelsey and then over at me.

"Yeah," I said. "I couldn't agree more."

—————

A few weeks later, Calder and I called my mom into her living room to tell her that we had rented a small house just ten minutes from her. She looked crestfallen, and truthfully, I was a little sad too, because the environment in her home had been a hundred times better since we'd returned from Indiana. And I finally felt like our relationship was moving forward. Molly had told me about her conversation with my mom about embracing Calder and Xander, and it seemed she had really taken it to heart. But it was time. And soon, we'd need at least a little extra space.

Calder stood up to retrieve something he'd been working on up in the guest room using supplies we'd gone out and purchased when we first got home.

When he returned, he handed my mom two wrapped paintings and glanced at me nervously before sitting down.

"What is this?" my mom asked, smiling as she opened the one on top.

Neither of us answered, just watched her as she tore the last of the brown paper off and brought her hand to her mouth, gazing at the painting of me when I was fourteen, a small, secret smile on my face and a morning glory in my hand. She stared at it, tears coursing down her cheeks. When she looked up at Calder, she opened her mouth to speak, but nothing came out. "Thank you," she mouthed, standing up and going toward where he sat. He stood up too, and hugged her as she cried. I wiped the tears from my eyes as well and laughed when she pulled away, fanning her face as if that would stop the tears.

"Open the other one," I said, nodding my head toward it.

"Another one? I don't know if I can handle another one." She laughed softly and stared at the one of me again, a small joyful smile on her face. But she tore the wrapping off the second painting and sat staring at it, confusion in her expression. It was her, holding a baby wrapped in a white blanket, his or her dark hair just barely peeking out.

"The first one was the past…that one's the future," Calder said and I heard the nervousness in his voice. And the hope.

My mom raised her head, eyes wide and going back and forth between the two of us. "I… You're…" she squeaked. "I'm going to be a grandma? You're going to have a baby?" she asked, more tears coursing down her cheeks.

I nodded. "We hope you'll help us, Mom," I said softly. "We're going to need lots of it."

My mom's face crumpled and she cried silently for a moment, but there was a smile on her face beneath the tears.

She stood up and rushed to me, bending down and taking me in her arms. "A baby," she kept saying. "You're having a baby!" She grabbed onto Calder's shirt and pulled him toward us and wrapped her arms around both of us. "Thank you," she whispered to Calder. "Thank you for all the gifts you've given me today." We all hugged and laughed and cried, my heart bursting with relief and happiness.

A month after that, we sat holding hands on a set in a very small studio where we told the world our story. We didn't provide every detail. Those were ours and ours alone. But we talked about growing up in Acadia and living with Hector. We talked about the religion we'd believed in and why we had started to doubt. We talked about the forbidden nature of our love story and what we'd risked to be together.

We also talked about the day of the flood, and that was the hardest. But we were together and that made it bearable. And there was healing in the fact that there were no more secrets, nothing more to hide.

We told the world about how we'd lived without the other for three long, grief-filled years. And how miracles sometimes happen to even those of us who feel the least deserving.

We made it clear it was the only interview we were interested in doing and, for the most part, the press left us alone after that day.

Now that the police and the press had a real name, they delved into Hector's past, into his possible motives, his mental state, and his history. Articles and books were written about him, and he was added to the list of cult leaders who had convinced large groups of intelligent people to believe in lies. Much speculation ensued about how Hector predicted the disaster that came to pass that terrible day, and his role in the tragedy. I was fascinated too, and spent more time than Calder would have liked reading case studies. He accepted it, though. Knowledge made me feel powerful and enlightened—it always had. He had given me that gift, so I knew he'd never take it away.

Some things, however, would never be answered, some things Hector—if he even knew—took to his watery grave.

Unbelievably, small groups the news dubbed "Hectorites" popped up around the country, people who tried to mimic the religion and society Hector had created. I was at a loss with that one. Humanity astounded me sometimes.

One wonderful thing resulted from our singular interview and that was a young woman who called in to the station while we were recording. We were given her name and number afterwards—a Kristi Paulson (formerly Smith) who lived in Florida with her husband and one-year-old daughter.

Calder, Xander, and I called her on Skype later that day, and we all cried and laughed. I stood up and turned to the side, smoothing my dress over my growing belly. She shrieked and put her hands over her mouth, and I laughed. She invited us to Florida to visit her for a "babymoon," and we said we'd try our very best. There are angels on Earth. And for us, she'd been one.

Life had gotten pretty busy since we'd returned from Indiana. We moved into the house we'd rented, a charming bungalow with a front porch that had a cushioned swing and a big bright room on the second floor that Calder set up as his studio.

We bought a king-size bed and spent too much money on bedding and officially christened it the Bed of Healing, Version 2.0. We spent lazy Sundays lounging there until noon and long nights snuggled in safe warmth and deep intimacy, whispering our secrets and talking about our fears and worries, our hopes and dreams, and, sometimes, the things that still haunted us. It was the place where we could dig down deep into the darkness of our own pain and curl into the love that always waited to soften the ache and where the most deeply soothing words always came from the other: *"I'm here. You're not alone."* And yes, there was healing.

Calder bought me romance novels and put them up on my bedside table in towering piles. I laughed, and eventually, I read each one of them. He said it was one of the best investments he'd ever made. And we did finally find out what became of Hendrix and Polly—and it was as satisfying as we both imagined it would be.

We browsed stores for things that felt special enough to fill our home with, I experimented with new recipes and learned how to bake, and Calder started painting again.

On a magical, snowy day in March, two months after Calder got his social security card in the name Calder Raynes, we went down to the courthouse and vowed forever to each other. It felt like a mere formality. It felt like a miracle. *It felt like destiny.*

Later that night as we snuggled in bed, Calder said sleepily, "I guess I became Calder twice in my life." I turned toward him and studied the planes and angles of his face in the moonlight streaming through our window. "Once when I was three," he said, "and now again at twenty-three."

I thought about it for a minute, how despite the trauma he'd been put through, and the betrayals he'd suffered—when he was a child and again when he was a man—he'd never stopped loving, never ceased being anything but loyal. "Yes," I said, "and you did it beautifully both times."

His deep eyes gazed at me in the dim light, seeming to speak a thousand words. He pulled me close and held me tightly in his arms.

When the springtime came, my mom helped me plant a container garden on the small deck off the back of our house and she pored over baby item catalogs with me, helping me put together a neutral nursery in creamy yellow and crisp white. I sat in there at night, rocking in the overstuffed glider and dreaming of our baby's deep brown eyes and gentle smile.

Just as I knew she would, my mother grew to love Calder with all her heart once she allowed herself to see him for who he was, and not as a competitor. And he loved her back, fully and completely. My heart felt full with the knowledge that we both got the mother we so desperately needed. Each Sunday night, she hosted dinner at her home where Calder and I, Xander and Nikki, and Molly and Bentley gathered. Her home was filled with laughter, love, and more children than she ever bargained for. She came alive. Molly told me she'd never seen Carolyn looking so content and carefree. It made my heart so very, very glad.

When the weather turned warm and the roses were in bloom, my mom and Marissa, together, threw me a baby shower that was ridiculously fancy and obscenely overdone. I loved every minute of it.

Calder had two gallery showings that summer, the first showcasing gorgeous canvases of birds and rainstorms and church windows—all sorts of things he'd never painted before. The second showing was my favorite, though, a series of people who had lived at Acadia: Mother Willa's ageless eyes; Myles sitting on his mother's lap in Temple, sucking his thumb; Maya's pure and joyful smile. It was a beautiful remembrance. Calder wasn't yet at the point where he could paint his parents or Hector. Maybe he never would be. And either way, it was okay. Both showings sold out in an hour.

We splurged on a baby grand piano for our front room and I taught lessons there on Mondays and Wednesdays. Sometimes, as the music floated from my fingers, I'd glance in the mirror on the wall in front of me, and catch sight of Calder staring silently, his hands in his pockets as he watched me play. And a strange melding of *then* and *now* would weave through the notes, somehow making the melody that much more beautiful.

We both talked about getting our GEDs and going back to school. We'd studied together once, and to do it again felt right. But that would wait until after the baby came.

My husband planted a small morning glory bush at the edge of our garden, and when it bloomed, he'd leave flowers for me in places I didn't expect. I always had one in water on my windowsill and it brought me joy.

And I slipped butterscotch candies into his pockets and under his pillow and smiled when I kissed him and tasted the buttery sweetness on his lips.

On a balmy day in early July, my water broke as Calder and I took an evening stroll around our neighborhood. He rushed me to the hospital and I delivered our son five hours later. We named him John Grant. Grant after Felix, who had saved my life once upon a time, and John, which means "God is merciful." And as our beautiful boy blinked up at us, the reflection of heaven just fading in his newborn eyes, we believed it with all our hearts.

As I woke up late that night, drowsy from sleep, I saw Calder in the corner, standing and swaying with our son in that universal baby sway. "Hey, Jack," Calder whispered, using the nickname we'd agreed we'd call him. "I'm your dad. I'm going to do my very best to be a really good one." He hummed some nameless tune for a minute until Jack was still again. "I'm sure I'll mess up now and again. I'll probably give you way too many sweets, because I like them too, and I'll probably make you roll your eyes because I'll kiss your mom in front of you a whole lot."

Jack let out a small dissatisfied squeak and I almost laughed, but I didn't want to disturb the moment so bit my lip instead.

"I know," Calder crooned, "it's going to be so gross." He swayed quietly for a few minutes. "I won't always be able to protect you from the world. But I'm going to do my very best. And when I can't, what I can promise you, is that I'll always be there to help you through it. And I'll always, always nurture your dreams. The rest…well, we'll figure out, all right?"

Jack was quiet, lulled into dreams filled with milk and warmth and love, nestled in the safety of his father's arms.

EPILOGUE
Calder

My eyes focused on the place where the mountains collided with the sky as we turned down the dirt road, dust filling the air outside the windows of our rented minivan.

"Is that it, Dad?" Jack asked from the back seat. I looked at him in the rearview mirror as he leaned forward, his dark blue eyes scanning the desert landscape.

I moved my eyes back to the window where the worker cabins were just appearing around the curve in the road. My heart pounded hard against my ribs. "Yes," I said, "that's it. That's Acadia."

I grabbed Eden's hand in the seat next to me, and she met my eyes and gave me a small encouraging smile. In the back seat, our two-year-old daughter, Maya, let out a small whine as she came awake. She'd slept most of the way from the airport.

We had found out a month ago that the land Acadia had been built on was being sold to a developer who was planning a luxury spa. The healing water of the double spring was going to be the draw. It was our last chance to see Acadia before the buildings were torn down. It'd been ten years since we'd been there, but both of us agreed that visiting it one last time would bring us that final piece of closure.

Five minutes later, we were pulling up in front of what had once been the Temple. Eden and I sat there for a minute, breathing, taking in the now old and neglected building in front of us, me picturing a small beautiful girl walking through the doors and into my heart. There were going to be ghosts everywhere here. I took a cleansing breath and pulled on the door handle.

"Mom! Dad!" Jack said excitedly, bouncing up and down in his seat, eager to get out and explore. To him, this was an adventure.

We all got out of the van, Eden taking Maya in her arms as Maya's thumb went to her mouth, and she laid her head down on her mother's shoulder, still tender from sleep. I leaned in and kissed her smooth, still babyish cheek and drew in her sweet scent. "How's my girl?" I asked. "Sleep good?"

She nodded and smiled sleepily around her thumb.

"Dad!" Jack exclaimed. I looked behind me to see him squatted down, a green lizard staring back at him from a rock. He reached out to touch it and it darted away. Jack stood up, looking disappointed.

I chuckled. "You gotta be real quick to catch a lizard," I said. "Ask your mom for some tips. She used to wrangle snakes when she lived here."

Jack's eyes got wide. "You did?" he asked her incredulously.

Eden laughed. "It's true," she said. "I did."

Eden put Maya down and we all strolled together, Maya toddling in a zigzag as we followed behind her and Jack checking out the things that were interesting to a six-year-old boy.

I took my wife's hand and squeezed it. "How do you feel?" I asked, taking in a big breath of the dry desert air.

"Sad, and kind of scared." Her gaze hung on our kids before she looked back at me. "But thankful. So thankful."

I nodded. That about summed it up for me too.

The heavy door squeaked as we entered the Temple. It was run-down, with glass on the floor and lots of leaves and debris littering the center aisle, but other than that, it still looked the same. Eden picked Maya up so she wouldn't walk over the glass.

"What happened in here?" Jack asked, looking around.

I squatted down in front of him and looked him right in the eye. "In here," I said, "a man told a lot of lies to people who were very vulnerable, people who were looking to belong, people who were *desperate* to belong."

"Why didn't they already belong somewhere?"

"Well, because life had been really hard on them. Life had taken everything they had, and the man, he promised to return it all and even more. And to those people, his lies sounded like the truth."

Jack's lips came together as he seemed to consider his next question. I smiled—the look on his face was all Eden. "Dad? If life is hard on me, how will I know if someone is lying?"

I tapped on his chest. "You listen to your heart, Jack. And you listen to the voice that comes to you when you close your eyes. You'll know it because it will be something between a feeling and a whisper. And that voice? Jack, if your heart is good, like I know yours is, that voice never, ever lies." I glanced over at Eden, who was listening to us as she swayed Maya in her arms. Her smile was somehow happy and sad at the same time.

Jack glanced at his mother and then back to me. "The voice, Dad, will it always tell me the easiest thing to do?"

I smiled. "No. But it will always tell you the *right* thing to do."

"You know what else happened in this building?" Eden asked as she came closer to us.

Jack shook his head.

"I first saw your dad in this place," she said, and her voice sounded like it did when she said prayers with our children at night. The locket at her chest glinted in the light coming through the open door—the piece of jewelry that had taken her to Felix, and to her mother, and ultimately brought her back to me. Inside was a photo of our children.

We walked back out into the bright sunlight and we all shielded our eyes. "Where did you live, Dad?" Jack asked.

"Come on, I'll show you."

We walked a little ways and got to the first worker cabin. Somehow they were even smaller than I remembered. "You lived in *all* these?" Jack asked.

I laughed. "No, just one. This way."

Jack frowned. "How could anyone live in just one of these? They aren't even as big as my room."

We got to the doorway of my cabin and I paused, taking a deep breath. Grief tightened my chest as I pushed the door open. Jack raced inside and through the two little rooms. "You lived *here*?"

"Yeah," I said quietly, my voice scratchy. I cleared my throat. Eden and Maya came in, and Eden put her arms around me from behind and hugged me tightly while the kids explored what little there was to look at.

I took Eden's hands in mine from the front and squeezed them. And as I looked around the cabin where I'd spent most of my young life, what came swift and fierce into my gut was that I forgave them. The ache would last forever, but the bitterness wouldn't. They had made their choices and I was making mine. I let out a breath, and in that breath…it was gone.

"I love you," Eden murmured, laying her cheek on my back.

"I love you too, Morning Glory."

Jack came walking back to us from the other room. "I'm glad life turned out better for you," he said, giving me a sympathetic look.

I let out a surprised laugh and ran my hand over his dark hair. "Yeah, me too, buddy."

We stepped out of the cabin. It was the very last time I ever would.

"Where did Uncle Xander live?" Jack asked.

I squinted behind us and pointed to another cabin. "Over there." Xander had built Jack a tree house in our backyard last year that was just about the same size as the cabin he grew up in. It was hard to believe. And now he owned a company that built large homes all over Cincinnati. My friend, my brother. I was ridiculously proud of him.

We all walked around the small cabin toward the trail. "A mama fwower," Maya said, pointing at the side of my old cabin. We all turned, and right there, growing up the side of the wood, were morning glories, vining their way right to the top. Maya had recognized them as the same ones Eden always kept in water on our kitchen windowsill.

"Cool," Jack said, picking one and handing it to Eden. She turned to me, her eyes wide with surprised wonder, and

I looked back over my shoulder toward the overgrown fields behind us.

When I shielded my eyes from the sun, I saw those deep blue flowers all throughout the weeds, leading right to the edge of the field. The seeds must have blown over to the cabins, and now they were growing up the outside of a few. "It took over," I murmured, pulling Eden into my side, picturing the small plant I had nurtured so long ago, taking care of it so I could make a princess smile with its gifts.

As pretty as a flower...as strong as a weed.

We turned to see our little girl toddling away, following a trail of the morning glories up the edge of the field toward the main lodge.

Jack ran to catch up to Maya and took her hand so she wouldn't fall. As we walked behind them, Jack bent down to pick morning glories here and there until he held a bouquet of them in his hand.

Our feet slowed as we walked past the area that had once been the cellar. It was filled in now, just a large area of new, compacted soil. But the morning glories grew there too. Eden took in a shaky breath and squeezed my hand. As the kids waited for us, throwing pebbles into a small puddle, we stood holding each other and letting the grief wash over us. This place was hallowed ground.

A very light rain started to fall, almost like tears trailing slowly down our cheeks and nourishing the morning glories sprinkled across the ground.

After a minute, we were ready to move on. I took my wife's hand as the sky cleared.

We all walked to the grove of trees that stood in front of the entrance to the path that led down to our spring. Eden and I had talked about whether we'd make the steep descent with the kids or not, especially because Maya was so young, but right then, without speaking about it, we both seemed to agree we needed it. We made our way down slowly, me picking Maya up in spots that were extra steep. In my mind I was a seventeen-year-old boy, racing down the path, excitement and anticipation of seeing a beautiful girl lighting up my heart.

When we finally arrived at the first spring below, Jack let out an excited yell and Maya laughed.

"You think this is pretty," I said to Jack, "just wait until you see the other one."

"Other one?" he asked excitedly.

I smiled and Eden pointed to the opening in the rocks. All the brush had been moved aside, the first indication that others had been here.

We walked through the open area between the springs, and when we ducked between the rocks again, Eden leading and me in the rear, we all stood and simply looked at the beauty surrounding us: the towering rocks, the crystal blue water with the trickling waterfall, and the flourishing plants. It was paradise. It was the place where our love had first blossomed. Emotion overwhelmed me. Eden turned to me with tears in her eyes and a smile on her face. "It's even more beautiful than I remembered," she whispered.

"It is," I choked, pulling her into me and kissing the top of her head, inhaling her sweet scent, apple blossoms and springtime.

"Mama's spwing," Maya said enthusiastically. I looked down at her and laughed with the realization that she recognized it from the paintings we had hanging in our home—the ones that reminded us where we'd fallen in love.

"That's right, baby," I said to Maya.

We looked around for things we might have left there, but there was no trace of anything. The kids played and splashed at the edge of the spring as Eden and I enjoyed simply watching their innocent joy. We sat against the same rock I had leaned against so long ago as I'd sketched. My arm was around Eden, her head on my shoulder. We squinted upward to see an eagle circling above us, the sky a soft, peaceful blue.

Here, I had fallen desperately in love with a girl and she had offered herself to me with her whole, beautifully tender heart. Here, we had shown each other how to be brave, what it was to truly be known. Here, we had learned how to *live*. Perhaps the land over the cellar was hallowed ground, but this place...this place was holy too. This was the place where I had first found Eden.

When we were ready, we gathered our kids and went back through the opening in the rock. As Eden was ducking through ahead of me, she glanced back at the spring and then up into my eyes, her gaze tender and full of love. My breath caught. She smiled a smile I had seen a thousand times at this spring and a thousand times since. I smiled back, realizing in that moment the depth of the heartache and love, the hurt and forgiveness we had experienced since the last time we were here. And my heart filled with gratitude for all of it, even the pain, because it had brought us here, to this very moment.

We ascended slowly and took the path to the main lodge. When we reached it, we stood looking up at what had once seemed like the grandest place on earth. We walked around to the far side, and Eden gasped softly. Morning glories vined up the wood, over the windows, and reached for the roof, filling in the cracks and covering the ugliness. The entire side of the structure was draped in deep blue beauty, each yellow center appearing like a light shining from the middle.

And as I stood there with my family, I realized, in the end, it was the beauty that had taken over. It was the beauty we looked upon. And when we walked away from Acadia that day, it was the beauty that we attached to our hearts.

Acknowledgments

It takes many people to complete a book and I am so blessed to have the very best on my team. Special, special thanks from the bottom of my heart to my storyline editors: Angela Smith, who not only talked story arrangement with me to the point of exhaustion but provided wine and emotional support often and tirelessly, and Larissa Kahle, who spends what little free time she has helping me to ramp up the emotions of my story and perfect the character development. Thank you to my developmental and line editor, Marion Archer. She is new to my process, but I'll never write a book without her again—*never*. Her expertise and enthusiasm— not to mention the little notes she wrote in the margin of my manuscript that made me laugh and swoon—not only taught me things but made my story richer and full of more depth. And to Karen Lawson, whose bionic eyes perfected my manuscript even further.

I am also lucky enough to have an incredible group of beta readers who provided invaluable feedback on Calder and Eden's story, and cheerleaded for me when I needed it most: Cat Bracht, Elena Eckmeyer, Michelle Finkle, Natasha Gentile, Karin Hoffpauir Klein, Nikki Larazo, and Kim Parr. And to my author beta, A.L. Jackson, who read the first draft of my manuscript when it was just three hundred pages of my ramblings and before I'd even spell-checked it. Her feedback and assurances gave me the courage to continue on.

Thank you as well to my wonderful sprinting partner, Jessica Prince. Many of these words would not have been written if not for her diligent 9 a.m. texts that generally included one word: *sprint?*

Big thanks to my amazing formatter, Elle Chardou, for saving my sanity and my carpal tunnel.

An updated thank you to Bloom Books for reintroducing this story, and assisting me in adding some finesse.

Love and gratitude to my husband for his patience through this process—and for being understanding when every date night for three months included plot talk. You make it all fun—and you make it all possible.

About the Author

Mia Sheridan is a *New York Times*, *USA Today*, and *Wall Street Journal* bestselling author. Her passion is weaving true love stories about people destined to be together. Mia lives in Cincinnati, Ohio, with her husband. They have four children here on earth and one in heaven.

Website: MiaSheridan.com
Twitter: @MSheridanAuthor
Instagram: @MiaSheridanAuthor
Facebook: MiaSheridanAuthor